61 BANG

MARK NADJA

The Afterhuman Press * 2007

61 Bang

ISBN: 978-0-6151-5582-1

Five Days in Early January

61 Bang

4

61 Bang

1.

It was snowing lightly, turning to rain, or the other way around. Case turned off the interstate looking for a convenience store. He found one within five minutes. He needed a Ho-Ho.

Not counting his own, there were only two cars in the parking lot when he pulled in. One of them, parked by the dumpster, some kind of SUV painted a ubiquitous gun-metal grey. Case stopped his engine next to a battered Toyota parked without handicapped tags, illegally, in a handicapped spot.

Case stepped out of the car, pocketed his keys, and looked around. A road—and around the road a lot of woods filled with wet black trees. Case stood there a while and felt the wet snow on his face, in his hair. He stood there for a while and then he went inside the convenience store.

The first thing Case looked for was the TV monitor: the image of himself coming into the convenience store and looking for himself.

It didn't take long to find himself on TV. The camera was mounted in the corner of the ceiling with a bird's-eye view of the store. The TV monitor hung from the ceiling in front of the check-

61 Bang

out counter right by the entrance. That's pretty much the way it always is, Case reflected.

Behind the counter, some kind of middle-eastern guy was working the cash drawer, even here in Alabama, Pakistani or Arab, what difference did it make? He had just turned back from fetching a carton of cigarettes for a huge hulking guy in a worn Army surplus jacket. Six-six, at least, the hulk, long, scorched hair draped over his shoulders like a cape and a sunburned bald spot in the middle. Case couldn't see his face but he'd seen a thousand men just like him. A whole country populated by that type of maniac. Back in the day. That accounted for the two cars in the lot. Unless there was a surprise in the toilet, it would be easy money. Pop and grab. Just like back in the day.

The hulking guy at the counter was buying a carton of Camels. That's what Case really wanted, that's what he really craved. Instead, he headed directly for the snack food aisle to look for the box of Ho-Hos.

Nutter Butter. Snackwells. Chips Ahoy. Oreo. Fig Newton. Pepperidge Farm Mini Milano. Keebler. Mrs. Field. Honeymaid Cinammon Sticks. Fifty kinds of Entenmann's cakes, donuts, and cookies.

There wasn't a goddamn box of Ho-Ho's in sight. Case suddenly wondered if they even made Ho-Ho's anymore. It seemed somehow inconceivable to him that they didn't. Maybe they'd been repackaged and were now sold under a different name?

Case picked up a box of generic low-fat cherry pop tarts. He read the list of ingredients on the bottom to waste time. Truth was, Case was waiting for the guy in the army surplus jacket buying the carton of Camels to leave. He figured that a store like this might realistically be worth three, four hundred dollars. No more than fifty dollars on the premises? The cashier doesn't have the combo to the safe. Well, that was a tune that often changed quickly enough once the gun came out. Memories sharpened. People were suddenly capable of small miracles. He'd have to shoot the cashier in the head, of course, fuck up the video somehow. Well, that's how he would do it back in the day. Just a habit of thinking, now, it was. Like working out a chess problem.

Ha.

He looked up from the cherry poptarts and saw the girl standing at the end of the aisle looking directly at him.

She looked no more than twelve or thirteen, thin, washed-out, waifish. She had a pale little face, stringy hair dyed trailer-trash blonde, and a mouth like a dead rosebud. She was dressed in soiled shorts and a denim jacket with arms long enough for a gorilla. Her skinny white legs were bare and so were her dirty feet inside cork-soled platform sandals.

What the hell was a hardly-dressed kid doing out at this hour, anyway?

Case figured she had to belong to the guy at the register buying the smokes. They were most likely traveling between somewhere and somewhere else. She'd probably been sleeping in the backseat until daddy's nicotine craving drove him off the road into this middle of nowhere. She'd woken up, thrown on the jacket and sandals, and joined daddy in the store. She'd wandered down the snack food aisle just like Case had in search of something artificially sweet.

The kid didn't say anything, just kept staring at Case with haunted eyes. They looked kind of smudged, those eyes, as if she'd been sleeping in her eye makeup. With her pale round face and ashen eyes, she reminded Case of the ghost of a child. She looked like she knew something bad was about to happen. She looked like she knew what Case was thinking. Case, like a lot of crooks, like a lot of people whose life depends on chance, like a lot of people, in other words, was a superstitious man.

He was about to say something, something like "beat it" or "scram" but the kid seemed to see it coming. She put a finger to her lips. It was a thin, filthy finger with a short, broken nail that was painted the color of a blueberry.

At the same time she reached her other hand into the pocket of the jean jacket. When she pulled her hand back out, there was a piece of paper between her dirty fingers. The paper was folded so many times it was about the size of a matchbook. She put the folded paper carefully down on the rack at the end of the aisle where Case was standing. She put it down nestled in the folds of a shiny foil bag of cheese puffs.

Where you got to, girl!

The voice made Case flinch, too. The kid said nothing, but looked paler for a moment or two, like she might fade from visibility altogether. Then the hulking guy rounded the corner of the aisle and stood there towering over the kid. He laid his big paws on her shoulders and you could see the shudder pass through that tiny body from thirty feet away.

Case was right: he'd seen a thousand guys just like this one in his life. And that was a thousand too many. The small shit-colored eyes stared coldly and appraisingly at Case above high wind-burned cheekbones. The rest of the face was covered with a thick John Brown beard threaded through with silver hair that looked like soldering wire.

Those raw-boned hands on her shoulders, that imprimatur of ownership—it was unmistakable. The man didn't take his two turd-pellet eyes off Case for half-a-second. He had one of the Camels in his mouth already and he lit it with a green disposable lighter. He lit up among all the "No Smoking" signs and squinted through his exhalation at Case.

What I tell you about wandering off on your own, bitch? Lot's of crazy dangerous assholes in the world looking to snatch a sweet young piece like you. You want that to happen?

No daddy. I'm sorry, daddy.

Daddy seemed pleased by the answer, more satisfied than one might have expected. His manner softened, but not by much.

That's better honey. Now you go and git yourself back to the vehicle

Yes daddy.

And off she went.

The man stood there at the head of the aisle staring at Case long and steady. Smoking. Case still had the box of cherry pop tarts in his hand. Felt like an idiot, too. He had the gun in his pocket and he felt like taking it out and shooting the big fat motherfucker in the

61 Bang

middle of his big fat motherfucking face, shoot him right there at the end of the snack food aisle.

Sorry if the little one was bothering you mister. It's late. She's a little groggy. She knows I don't like her talking to strangers. It's not safe, you know?

Case knew that the man wasn't really apologizing for anything. What was there to apologize for, anyway? He slowly put the cherry pop tart box back on the shelf and slipped both hands casually into the pockets of his black poplin jacket.

No problem. She didn't say boo to me. Just stood there, looking.

The big man watched Case, looked him up, looked him back down, taking his measure. He took another couple of slow drags on the Camel. A little tic of satisfaction. As if to say, not much to look at, is there? Why? Because Case had glanced away? Because...? He nodded towards the window. You couldn't see anything out of it but the inside of the store reflected back at you. Another scene just like this one.

Okay then. We understand each other. Best me and the girl get back on the road. You take care of yourself.

2.

He seemed to leave an oily groove in the atmosphere, a sucking black hallway that drew Case, like a sleepwalker, halfway down the aisle, as if he were going to follow the bastard right out to the parking lot and settle it all right then and there. Instead, Case stopped at the head of the aisle, hesitated, and noticed the folded piece of paper the girl had left propped on the foil bag of cheese puffs.

He picked it up and continued around the front of the store. He stood behind a sales display of Diet Canada Dry ginger ale boxes and looked out the window at the wet parking lot.

The kid was standing obediently by the locked door of the SUV waiting for her father. She tottered there by the dumpster in her ridiculous platform sandals. The big man jerked open the passenger door. The kid clambered inside. He slammed the door behind her. Then he walked around to the other side of the SUV and climbed behind the wheel. He pulled away without putting his lights on until he'd turned out onto the road. It didn't make a lot of difference about the lights, though. Case hadn't been able to pick out the license plate number in the gloomy shadows of the dumpster either. That was because the SUV didn't have any license plates.

That left only the cashier's battered Toyota. Well, assuming it was the cashier's. He still hadn't seen anyone else in the store, no other customers but the girl and the bearded guy. It was still possible that there was another employee in the back, or a customer in the toilet, but Case would have gambled there wasn't. That it was just him and the cashier now. But it didn't matter. Even if he considered it fifteen minutes ago, it was out of the question now. The hillbilly with the kid had looked long and hard at Case. The kid, too. They'd remember if it came to that. So Case's mind worked, just out of habit.

Hitting convenience stores was behind him now, or below him, not beyond him, but definitely behind him. That's what Case told himself, anyway.

It was like he was trying to remember me for later. Or as if I were somehow just as familiar to him as he was to me.

As if he'd seen a thousand guys like me, too...

A fellow alumni, maybe? Case shook the idea from his head. Paranoia—that's what it was and that was something he didn't need at the moment. Well, not in any excess quantity, anyway. In general, it was a fair hypothesis that what had kept Case alive up to now was paranoia. Case could easily believe it when the shrink told him he suffered from a persecution complex. Of course, Schonemann hadn't actually called it a "persecution complex," not in so many words, but that's what it amounted to when you took away all the fancy, tactful, $200-an-hour gobbledygook. Case had participated in the program because they told him the parole board would consider shaving time off the back-end of his sentence if he did. Good behavior, rehabilitation. So Case emoted, revealed, remembered, let his "emotional armor" down—or pretended, too, anyway. Because like any good sociopath, he knew that what people wanted to hear was what they expected to hear, with just enough of an original twist to keep it "real." Inside, though, where it counted, he remained armed and dangerous.

And very afraid.

Easy for that loafer-wearing egghead to say that Case had a persecution complex as he sat there theorizing about "the criminal mind" for his latest bestseller, backed by his Ivy League credentials, his homes in Manhattan and Montana, his relationship with the Dalai Lama, and his jet-setting private practice as a "spiritual counselor" to movie stars and celebrity criminals. Easy for him to say with his connections, with his wealth, with the police paid to protect him and his property. But Case, and people like him, lived in a different world—a world where someone really was out to get you, where they'd take everything from you in a heartbeat, including your heartbeat, and there wasn't a damn person anywhere you could complain to about it.

It was the world that most people only saw dramatized on TV. Or in books. Or in movies. Or in the newspapers. But it was the world we all lived in at one remove or another.

The world where the owl swoops down and carries off the mouse just because.

Where the spider catches what can't fly through the net.

Where the weak don't matter because the weak don't count.

Not for long, anyway.

That girl, for instance. There was something about that girl that didn't count. Whether Case realized it or not, she was the reason he'd gone to the window. It wasn't the bastard who'd eye-fucked him in the aisle. She was the reason. The reason why he was still standing at the window watching the hanging exhaust of the minivan twist and vanish into the night. Something about the way the girl stood there in her ill-fitting clothes, watching him from the end of the snack food aisle, like a memory that wouldn't fade away.

She was still there.

Haunting him.

On the verge of saying something she would never say. That she was waiting for him to guess, maybe. What?

Case remembered the folded paper he'd picked up. The note she'd left for him propped on the shiny bag of cheese puffs. She must have written it before she'd even entered the convenience store. She must have had it ready. Just in case she got the chance to give it to someone.

Anyone.

And that anyone happened to be him.

Case unfolded the tight, grimy triangle of paper. It was the torn corner of a page: thin, yellow, printed with cheap black ink. The Yellow Pages. The creases were black with gunk and lint and in danger of tearing. It looked as if the message had been carried for a long time, held in a small sweaty palm, folded and re-folded to make certain the message was just right.

That it got the point across.

So that maybe someone would get it. Someone might answer…

Case didn't really want to see what was written on the paper. Somehow he knew it wasn't going to be good. He had the feeling that whatever was written on the paper was an invitation to a whole lot of hurt. A long detour of troubled road to a place he didn't want to visit.

He looked anyway. It was like the fortune in the fortune cookie. How could you not look?

There were only four words written on the page. The words were smudged and looked like they were written with charcoal. Only later did it occur to Case what the kid had really used to write them: eyeliner pencil.

The message was big and simple and easy enough to read.

HELP US GOD PLEASE

3.

Paradise, that's what some joker named this dump. You couldn't say much for his sense of humor.

A bed. A table. A desk. A mirror. Lots of fake wood. A soupy seascape over the bed. Or maybe it was a wheatfield. Christ, it might have been a pastel-colored puke. Frame it in brushed aluminum, it really didn't matter.

A motel, in other words, just like a thousand others. A place to lie down, hide, pass safely into a temporary, all too temporary, oblivion.

The desk clerk was appropriately disinterested. Barely gave Case a glance. You couldn't ask for more. He'd seen a thousand just like Case. Didn't need to look up and trouble himself to see one more. Besides, the camera was watching for him. Cameras here, too, even in Paradise. Cameras all over, recording everything; there wasn't a place you could go, a thing you could do anymore, that wasn't on film somewhere waiting for someone to care enough to watch it. Most of the time, no one did.

A thousand rooms for a thousand guys like Case. Hard to believe, but true.

Truly horrifying.

Case shook his head. Sadly? No, not quite. He unscrewed the bottle of Jim Beam. He took a pull while ripping off the cellophane on a plastic cup he found on the formica desk/shelf outside the bathroom. Poured himself a proper cocktail. He was sure he could

61 Bang

scare up a local bar or two but tonight wasn't a night for social drinking. He walked back to the bed. Sat on the side of it.

Hmm.

Enriched wheat flour, corn syrup, dextrose, TBHQ for freshness, xanthum gum, red #40, blue #1, all of it coming in at two hundred. That was a cherry pop tart, for you. Case ate it while sitting there on the edge of the bed, the wrapper on the floor by his feet. When he finished it, he opened up another. Four hundred calories. Sipped the Jim Beam. Fine dining on the road.

Ha ha.

One cheek full, chewing, he yanked open the drawer of the bedside table, more or less just for something to do, to have something new to look at. To confirm something. Sure enough, there it was, tucked in the corner of the empty drawer, just like always. The Holy Bible. Was it a law? A joke that they put it there? Some kind of hotel tradition that no one meant literally, like saying break a leg in the theater? Ah, the little verities. When there weren't any big ones, you had to appreciate the smaller.

Case refilled his plastic cup. Glug-a-lug. He opened the Bible up on his lap, thumbed pages to Ecclesiastes, brushed away some pop tart crumbs. A living dog is better than a dead lion. That was wisdom, that was the real stuff. Case had seen plenty of dead lions in his time. He was better than all of them, right this moment, believe it or not, eating his cherry pop tart in a dank motel room in the middle of nowhere. What dead man wouldn't envy him, even this? Cause even if you're remembered, Case considered, chewing, a dead lion lives on only in the memory of dogs.

Enough philosophy.

Case brushed the rest of the crumbs off his lap, returned the Bible to its corner of the drawer where it would probably sit for another twenty-five years unnoticed, and took off his shoes and socks. Swung his legs up on the bed. These kinds of rooms were the same everywhere, so nearly identical you'd almost think you were somewhere like home; it was just the superficial resemblance, of course, but the surface was enough. You didn't put down roots in a life lived in rooms like these, but it felt familiar, comforting, as much as anything can be. Case propped himself up on a couple of cold flat pillows and reached for the remote. The TV came on with an electrical snap. Satisfying, that snap of connection.

The weather across America, none of it looking especially good. Blizzards here, nor-easters there, cyclones somewhere else. Cold fronts, coastal floodings, icy conditions, trials and tribulations everywhere, signs and significations, it was good, all in all, Case thought, lighting up, his third and last of the day, to be in Paradise.

Thumbing the remote, changing realities. This far out, deep in the belly of the red states, it didn't make the news, probably would be just a nostalgic reminder of the good ole days, even if it did. Maybe it would earn a non-commital shake of the head, from the more enlightened of the yokels, the local Erasmus, just for show, if that. Lip-service aside, everyone knew the score. Everyone could feel that black tide rising. One less no-good nigger, that would be the unspoken truth, the underlying reality of the situation.

61 shots.

Trigger-happy cops. Not evil. Not a racist hit-squad like the minister is shouting, hoarse, in rhyme and unreason, for the cameras, that pompous, pampered, be-pompadoured asshole. Probably scared shitless is more like it. Who wouldn't be? You pull over a throbbing car with blacked-out windows in the dead of night, the plates of some badass wanted multiple-times for armed robbery, drug-related arrests, assault going back to when he was nine-years-old. Sealed records. Half the bad shit this dude done no one would ever know about. Born in poverty, raised in violence, six-foot-five, 320 pounds, a street nick something like Bloodbeast or Maniacman, a gangbanger from the darkest corner of the darkhood from way back when, and meanwhile you grew up shooting basketballs in the driveway of a split-level house somewhere out in Lilysville. Worst thing you ever did was break some windows out of the school gymnasium, lifted a couple of six-packs of beer from the local minimart, got stopped on a DUI joyriding in the Lexus of some friend's mom. Out of your element, scared? You're A-fucking right you are. You'd be a fool not to be. You weren't trained for the kind of animal you'd meet on those streets. No one could be trained for that.

61 Bang

But 61 shots? Did they really need that many to kill off one goddamn nigger?

Christ, 61 shots would have made a martyr out of anyone. Genghis Khan, probably. Frankenstein.

Case listened to farm reports, livestock reports, stories about fairs and craft shows, more weather reports, all of the news tied into the weather somehow. Out here, the weather was far more important than anywhere else. Out here, the sky still mattered. Case ran through the channels, the whole spectrum of realities being broadcast. He thumbed the mute button and watched the heads talking in silence. It was more interesting that way, making up the dialogue coming out of their mouths. Well, Jim, it may be raining in Kansas but I'd really like a hot wet seven inches up the poop chute right about now. Okay, Diane, but first, let me finish masturbating to this story about the starving millions in Chad. The commercials were best, no sophomoric commentary was needed. All the wild gesticulations and exaggerated expressions to sell a bar of soap or a hemorrhoid cream were surreal enough.

Case would leave the Paradise in the morning. Get back on the road. Keep moving. But first he needed a good night's sleep. How long had it been since he'd had one of those? Two weeks? Three? He didn't sleep much anymore as it was, didn't need much sleep, viewed it with suspicion, like you would a woman you didn't quite trust, but that you still somehow couldn't do completely without, so you laid down beside her with one eye open. Case was human, after all, in a manner of speaking, of course.

He turned off the TV and heaved himself off the bed. Grabbed his overnight bag and carried it into the bathroom. He brushed his teeth at the sink. Stared at himself in the mirror without curiosity but without belief. Swallowed two Remerol tablets. Pissed in the toilet. Turned off the light.

The bedroom was lit by the pinkish glare of the motel's neon sign. Case had requested a first-floor room. Around the back. His car parked right outside the door.

He stripped off his clothes down to his underwear and laid back on the bed. Oblivion was always a relief. Case, such as he was, didn't have to worry about dreams. He never dreamt. He was aware of the theory that all men dreamt and those that claimed they didn't simply didn't remember their dreams. But Case knew differently. He didn't dream. Period. If he did, he would have remembered. And if he remembered, he would have found life unbearable.

He laid there in the darkness, waiting.

Even emptied out as he was, sleep was as elusive as ever, demanded to be seduced. Case waited for the drug to take effect the way you'd wait for a mugger. When it came it clobbered his consciousness into submission.

4.

Case woke feeling as if a shovelful of dirt had been thrown in his face. Cold and gritty. The room was cast in a preternatural twilight. With the heavy curtains drawn, it would always be twilight in a room like this. Another reason you had to like it. Case lay there a long time, staring ceiling-ward, seeing old movies full of snow. In other words, the past. If he looked hard enough he could see things, so he didn't look too hard. A past like Case's being what it was. Outside, water was dripping off the roof.

Rain? Snow?

Case sat up, rubbed his unshaved jaw, as if he were feeling around to discover if it were still there. Rub some life into the old rubber death-mask.

Christ.

He sat up on the edge of the bed, damn, damn, damn, head bowed to the mold-scented rug between the clawed bare feet. When he looked up, slowly, the room was just a little lopsided, but no more than usual. A deep dull thud on the right side of his head. Again, again, again, etc. Some tenderness at the back of the mouth. The coppery taste of blood mixed in stale saliva.

January 6th, in other words.

Well, time to stand up, Case thought, resignedly.

Not too bad, he had to admit, once he was erect. All considered.

He clutched the bottle of Jim Beam by the throat and limped on over to the window. Pulled back the curtain. Nothing surprising there. A grey view: the Mustang, the parking lot, some nude trees, the empty highway. He let the curtain fall back into place.

A shower was in order. A shave. A face to meet the faces that you meet, as T.S. Eliot said in one poem or other. Case retaining a few bits and pieces of his education, such as that was. A man, after all, didn't set out to become what Case had become. Whatever it was that he'd become. For so little, it was still goddamn hard to define.

Sitting on the toilet, he took a couple of pulls of the Jim Beam. First a shorter one, then a longer. The first one, tinged pink, he leaned over and spit out into the sink. The morning mouthwash. The second, he swallowed. Underwear shackled around his ankles, bottle in his lap, sitting on the can, forty-five years old, Case considered his destiny. How it all had added up. Well, it wasn't over yet, but you didn't have to be Archimedes to see where the equation was going.

He flushed and stood up.

The shower, the shave, the drive into the center of what they called town in this third-rate Hicksville. A diner. Hardly any point even seeing it, let alone describing it, he'd read so many descriptions of one's just like this in books he'd read, seen so many of them in movies he'd watched, so have you. He could have made the place up in his imagination right down to the rice in the catsup-smeared salt shaker if he weren't actually sitting in the place. A booth along the wall beneath a fly-specked puzzle of the Leaning Tower of Pisa mounted on cardboard. Three pieces missing. The waitress, too, he could have invented. A woman who you might say had seen better days, except you know she hadn't. She'd seen only days like this one, one after another, for as long as she could remember. She'd see a lot more of them, too, before stopped seeing anything at all. Death, in short, would happen; that's the only novelty this woman could reasonably expect.

Coffee?

Please.

She turned over the cup ten thousand lips had touched, sloshed the black stuff in, and stepped back. She left the choking scent of drugstore perfume in his face. She loomed over him with a pad and pencil she didn't end up needing.

61 Bang

Know what you want?

Eggs. Scrambled. Well-done. Hash browns. Toast. Rye. And sausage.

Links or patties?

Links. No. Patties.

Off she goes, and Case is done, thank God, making decisions, at least for ten minutes or so. He sips the coffee and stares out the window. Eight a.m. He barely managed to sleep four hours after all. A few pick-ups on the street outside. Three or four hunched figures at the counter. Regulars. An old man or two thrown in for good measure. The usual yak about the weather, the war, the Hawks or Saints or whatever. Someone was losing their back acres. Someone else was selling a chain-saw. Someone else had a kid arrested for drunken assault. Blah, blah, blah, the usual bullshit with a country flair. Case sipped his coffee, buttered his toast, cut his sausage, ate his eggs. She brought the links, after all.

The local law ambled in.

Howdy Chief.

Shoot anyone this morning?

A pair of calloused hands fly up. I didn't do it whatever it was.

Ha ha ha. Jokes all around, the general bonhomie.

This was America. For the most part, anyway. You forgot how it really was, living in L.A. or New York. On the little concrete islands of sanity, so called. In between, though, all those states with cows, miles and miles of Piggly Wigglys, and tractors. Not that he was passing judgment. Just a different flavor of stupidity as far as Case was concerned.

On it went, up at the counter.

Howsit hanging fellas?

Low and heavy sheriff.

It's a crime, I swear.

Old age, Chief. Arrest the bastard.

I hear ya, boys. I hear you. Don't think I wouldnta already if I could've. Look what the bastard done to me. Out of my jurisdiction, though. Tragic to say.

Har Har Har.

61 Bang

Straight out of Mayberry, these yokels, Case thought, Mayberry via Deliverance, maybe by way of David Lynch You got the feeling they were all playing a part, but for who? Him?

Case sipped a third cup of coffee, the plate of breakfast ruins slid away from under his chin. That cheap perfume again, back like a peristaltic wave. He considered the Law at the counter.

Big guy, just like you'd expect, a body good for pulling drunk hillbillies off other drunk hillbillies, or intimidating out-of-state motorists, all creeping for the South Pole, a frozen landslide of hard flab. Red face. Thin white hair laid over his scalp like a tattered flag on a shiny coffin. Piggy blue eyes, with that pig's look of sadistic humor; they hadn't strayed too far from Case no matter what good ole boy nonsense was coming out of his wide, flat, down-turned mouth.

Checking me out, Case sighed to himself, pretending, pointlessly, not to notice being noticed. Square peg in a round hole. What doesn't fit in this diner? Well, there's no altogether avoiding that, now is there, he thought philosophically.

While we're at it: Why do we live? Why do we die?

Case continued to stare out the window. A view that never changed. If it wasn't raining, it sure looked like it was.

Assault on a police officer, such as it was. More like grappling with one to keep from getting shot for no good reason. That's what they shelved him away for last time. A routine traffic stop. Case couldn't believe what for. He'd stopped at the stop sign. Blinked at that turn. Yeilded when instructed. Merged when required. He was inspected, licensed, registered, and insured. What more could they want from him, for crissakes? You run out to get a bunch of goddamn bananas and you get hassled. Some punk with a gun and a piece of metal stapled on her chest, yes, her chest, do you really think it makes a difference, man or woman, assholes are assholes, and there she is standing there examining his IDs and registrations and asks him where he's going, where he's coming from.

This is America, mind you, still, at least in theory, and what she's stopped him for, what she's writing the ticket for is because the dealer that affixed the self-promoting frame around his license plate

61 Bang

covered up the state motto. Case can't believe it, he asks for clarification. You stopped me because you can't read the fucking state motto on my license plate? That's right sir, and the ticket book comes slapping out. Upon such petty-mindedness an entire world of bullshit pivots. The fucking state motto—which in this case being Live Free or Die, a healthy sentiment if there ever was one, translated in this day and age to the briefer and unambiguous Die. No or about it anymore. The choice taken out of it.

Case, a free man for a few minutes more, is practically beside himself. In fact, that's pretty much what his lawyer argues at trial. Case was beside himself, it wasn't him, but some temporarily insane doppelganger who leapt out of the car in an 'aggressive and threatening manner' instead of stepping out with hands raise when ordered and who proceeded to grapple with the officer when reason failed and there was an unfortunate misinterpretations of certain verbal and physical manifestations of Case's uncontained rage. The State contained it, thought. For three years. Try not to feel paranoid after that. Try to ever enjoy a fucking banana again. Go ahead. Just try.

When he looked down, there was the check on the table. He hadn't noticed it coming. Didn't remember answering the question, Anything else? But he might have, he probably did. He must have answered that question at least a thousand times in his life. Always the same answer, by the way.

He fished out a couple of singles, put them under the salt shaker, and took the check to the counter with a twenty.

At the cash register, he waited for the waitress to come back from somewhere or other. From the looks of it she's doing everything but the cooking this morning. Maybe she always does. That awkward moment when human interaction seems unavoidable. Just to keep things from getting any more unbearable than they already are without them. So a nod to the Law who's looking him over without any pretence of doing anything else. Up and down. Down and up. Then right back in the face, like reading a text in a bad translation. Not liking what it sees, not liking it at all.

Enjoy your breakfast?

61 Bang

Yes, pretty good.

Best in town.

Only in town. One of the local comedians offers.

The Law, dead-pan, his eyes not leaving Chase's for a moment. Like I said. Best in town.

Yeah. The waitress finally arrives, along with her pal, the stench of a black garden. He holds up the local rag. And a newspaper, please. Case does something with the change the waitress hands him from the twenty. Something not strictly necessary, you understand, just some misdirection, like a sleight-of-hand artist. The trick is, to get out of here without any further inquiry.

Where you from?

New York.

Long way from Broadway aren't you?

Case organizing the bills in his wallet.

Right. Guess that's one way to look at it.

A little tic over the Law's left brow. As if a fly had landed there.

Where you heading? Can't be here.

L.A.

Swimming pools, movie stars. That the idea?

Drugs, he was thinking. Case could see it when he looked up into the Law's blood-rimmed eyes.

He shrugged. Something like that. Winters up north, you know?

When you heading out. This said without a trace of a question mark.

Tomorrow morning. At the latest.

Well then. A smile that thins that thin mouth even thinner. Enjoy the sights. Such as they are.

Thanks. Nod. Wallet in back pocket, fold newspaper in half, turn and head for the exit. Message received. Case with his hand on the door. No looking back. Behind him, nothing but an uncomfortable silence.

5.

Dry goods, a feed store, a barber shop. That's Main Street he's walking down. Engine repairs. A liquor store. A laundromat. Jimmy's BBQ Sandwiches. Case walked clear to the end of the street to a small lake. Trees all around, inky, denuded. He sat down on a damp bench. Stared out at the unmoving water. Could have been an abandoned parking lot. Some dirty-looking ducks sitting on a surface flat and dull as the bottom of an iron. A couple of hundred yards in either direction, above the surrounding woods, and they could be blown out of the sky for someone's lunch. Maybe the ducks thought they'd flown far enough away from the coming winter. Maybe this had been far enough once upon a time. Instinct not correcting itself for the increasingly erratic weather patterns. Or maybe they'd just grown tired and decided to give up here.

Once Case had seen a movie about penguins. The little bastards traveled back and forth across hundreds and hundreds of miles of snow. Through blizzards. Frozen oceans. Ice storms. An entire continent of misery. They starved. They fought. They got lost. They were eaten by sharks and polar bears and wolves. They got carried off by birds-of-prey. And the point—the point of it all—was to lay an egg to make another penguin to go through the same thing all over again.

It was the stupidest goddamn thing that Case had ever seen.

61 Bang

Life, that's what it was. The meaning of it, in fact. When all was said and done.

When we finally curled up our toes and croaked, who had we left behind to carry that egg, to keep it traveling into the future? To keep human beings in the world. Or penguins. Or antelope. Or whatever.

Case considered not reproducing to be the most moral thing he'd ever done. Not that he spent a lot of time thinking about it one way or another.

He opened the paper in his lap. Nothing on the front page. Nothing on the second. Nothing all the way through. Just the usual robberies, auto accidents, assaults, and reports of missing children. Front page news back home, but a shooting in Manhattan just didn't cause a ripple here in Paradise, Case mused.

He stood up, threw the paper away in a trashcan, and walked back through the center of town. Back to his car. He grabbed the duffel stuffed behind the driver's seat and then went on to the laundromat.

Warm inside. The thump-thump of a few dryers spinning their loads. A couple of taciturn trailer-park wives. A farmer in his last clean pair of jeans and shorts staring at a little porthole full of suds. A TV up in the corner with more weather news. Behind the corner, the attendant: a fat little Mexican woman with a wall-eye. She was eating an egg sandwich out of tinfoil.

Feeding a dollar bill into the change machine. Another. Then another. Scooping out the quarters. Then to the vending machine that dispensed little packages of detergent. Case overturned the duffel into a washer by the window, fed in the quarters, the detergent, and threw in the empty duffel for good measure. He sat there watching his clothes spinning around, just like everyone else. His clothes without him in them. Whatever the hell that meant. But it seemed to mean something. Almost meditative somehow. The thump-thump of the dryers, the warmth, the wall-eyed Mexican woman turning the pages of her magazine as she ate, the weather in Seattle and Provo and countless other places where you weren't.

Not to get metaphysical about it, Case thought. But still—

61 Bang

He hadn't forgotten. He knew he wouldn't. One of his big problems is that he couldn't forget, not without a lot of effort, and not even then. He reached into the pocket of his coat. His fingers went right to it. He unfolded it, held it in front of him, stared at the filthy piece of scrap paper. The smudged words.

HELP US GOD PLEASE

He was here for a reason, but this wasn't it. That's what Case told himself. That's what he told himself from the moment that kid left him the folded note in the snack food aisle where he picked up the box of cherry pop tarts. He was here, traveling through this lower bowel of the country for a purpose that had nothing to do with whatever this note in his hand meant. Not to mention his life, whatever inconceivable reason he was living that for, it certainly had nothing to do with this. These were the things Case told himself. The things he knew to be true. The path and the way through temptation. He also knew that it made no difference.

He moved the sodden lump of his clothing from the washer to a dryer, fed in more quarters, slammed the door shut. The wall-eyed Mexican woman flipped another page of her gossip magazine. On TV: the weather in St. Paul. Thump-thump. A farmer blinked.

Forty minutes.

He take a drive down to the convenience store. He had some time to kill. Forty minutes out of a life that was, all in all, a waste of time. Yeah, he had a few minutes to spare.

Case was in luck for a change, and how often could you say that, goddammit. On the drive to the convenience store, he'd convinced himself that he'd never find the same guy behind the cash register, it was an exercise in futility, as just about all exercise was, but there he was, counting out change to some hillbilly buying a fistful of lottery tickets and a carton of Marlboro Lites. He must have had the midnight to eight a.m. shift. If Case had woken up an hour later this morning, he probably would have missed the bastard altogether and that would have been that. He'd have been on his way. Never given the matter another thought.

Yeah, it was his lucky day.

Case passed yesterday's hot dogs, a case of shriveled donuts. He headed down an aisle, picked up a box of zip-loc bags. That breakfast had sure made him thirsty, more salt in it than the Sinai. Up another aisle on the way back to the front of the store. He grabbed a six-pack of Fresca. At the register the hillbilly was heading for the door. Off to smoke his Marlboros and wait for the next lottery drawing. Good luck, sucker.

Case laid the box of zip-loc bags and the Fresca on the counter. The Pakistani ran them over the scanner.

There was a guy in here last night.

Seven-fifty-nine.

You remember him?

He takes the ten dollar bill Case hands him. Who?

The guy last night. Big guy. Long hair. You couldn't miss him. Had a little half-naked girl with him.

Amazing that look. Utter incomprehension. Case might have been talking a cow.

I was in here at the same time. Must have been after two, maybe going on three a.m. I bought a box of cherry pop tarts.

Lot of people come in and out of here. Lot of people passing through. Like you.

I thought he might have been a regular.

He hands Case back his change. Why?

Because of his ride. A beat-up SUV. It had no plates.

So?

Wouldn't have been able to drive anywhere but locally without plates.

The Pakistani shrugged. Like it was an answer.

Do you need a bag?

No.

Case let his eyes drift upward. To the TV over the register. He saw himself, this whole scene. In black and white. Just like that, he tried to think over the whole situation. Objectively.

61 Bang

I just thought, if he were local. If you saw him again.

What? What difference does it make?

That you could give him something. Something he dropped.

Oh.

Suspicion? Disbelief? Case was probably reading too much into it. That blank expression. Apathy, that was more likely.

Yeah. A key to something. Must have fallen out of his pocket. Off his key-ring. Who knows?

Uh.

A Sphinx, that's what this guy was. Selling Slurpees and packaged coffee cakes in the middle of nowhere. Who'd have thought it?

That kind of thing, it can be a real bitch. You come to something locked, one day, you've got no key to open it. You know what I mean?

Mm.

Case took a Bic from a display of pens by the register. Jotted his name and cell phone number on the back of one of the losing lottery tickets the hillbilly had left on the counter. He slid it over to the mute Pakistani. Scratching at something on the side of his head. Looking at whatever it was beneath his fingernail.

If he happens back. You can tell him I've got his key. Whatever it's a key to. Got it?

The Pakistani looks up. No calculation in his eyes. No malice. Nothing. Just nothing. A guy that doesn't care.

Yeah.

Case picked up the box of zip-loc bags and the six-pack of Fresca. He'd done what he could do in this scene and headed for the door. His clothes should be dry by now, he figured.

Back to the laundromat.

6.

In Paradise again, waiting for dark. Clothes folded. Rain tip-tapping the window. TV back on, muted. This was as good a place to bury it as anywhere else, Case figured. Middle of no place. Lots of woods all around. Who ever comes here? Just a dot left off of a lot of maps. What was the name of the place anyway? Damned if he even knew.

Carbonated water, citric acid, potassium citrate, aspartame acesulfame, glycerol ester of wood resin, vegetable oil, carob bean gum. And all of it, amazingly, zero calories. That was a can of Fresca, which Case thumbed open, drank half of, without stopping.

He sat at the edge of the bed.

Nothing left to do. Just wait. Sit. Stare.

For lunch he ate two more pop tarts. Got up and took a piss. Then he stretched out on the bed, propped up on the pillows. Sipped at the bottle of Jim Beam. Had another Fresca.

The rain kept tapping.

On the TV buildings exploding, dead soldiers, floods, couples yelling at each other, kids throwing rocks at tanks, charred bodies, Dick Van Dyke dressed up like a doctor. Is he still alive?

The desk clerk—a different one this time—had taken his cash without comment. One more night. No room service. Understand? A nod of the head, eyes averted. An open magazine hurriedly, but not quite covered: a sneering black woman looking back at the camera, spreading the cheeks of her enormous buttocks between red vulture talons. The rubbery purple ring of her asshole.

Taking the metal cash box out of the trunk on the way back to the room. At the bottom of the concealed wheel well where the spare

61 Bang

tire goes. Wrapped in oily rags. It sat on the night table now, waiting, just like Case.

What's this all about?

It's better you don't know.

The hell it is.

You need to make it disappear, that's all you need to know.

Who'd it kill?

No one.

No one? I don't understand.

Don't try. Let's keep it simple. You deliver it to the right people, you don't have to worry about having to flip burgers at Mickey D's when you're sixty-five. You don't have to worry about anything.

If the wrong people get it?

Then you have a lot to worry about.

How much Case might have to worry about became graphically clear four days later. He'd come to get the initial payment. Knocked on the door for five minutes, waited another fifteen, no answer on Eddie's home or cell phone. Music playing. Not so loud that anyone would complain, but loud enough. Then he realized the door wasn't locked. He felt as if his soul had dropped down a few dozen floors.

Tried to ignore it. Failed. Told himself that Eddie was expecting him, had left the door open in anticipation. Wasn't convincing himself. Turn around and leave. Get the hell out of here. That's what common sense was advising. He ignored it.

It was too late the moment he set foot in the apartment. Everything was a mess. Chaos. Like some hurricane had gotten loose in there. Like some Leviathan had devoured the place and vomited it all back out. The walls stripped. Couch cushions slashed. Glass crunched underfoot. Drawers overturned. Furniture turned on its side. Even the refrigerator emptied out. The stench of thawing food. It was like the Apocalypse had come to a fourth floor walk-up on Rivington.

On the stereo's CD-player, set to repeat for eternity if it came to that, Leonard Cohen.

I've seen the future, brother. It is murder.

61 Bang

Eddie was in the bathtub. Not taking a bath. Naked, sort of crouched on all-fours like a raw turkey, his head brutally twisted round. It made you wince just to see it. To imagine what that must have felt like.

Well, Ed. I guess this must be what you were talking about.

Crouched there, in a cold marinade of his own fluids—blood, urine, watery feces. No dignity in death. Can't hold anything back at that point. Like a revelation it was and Case stood transfixed before it. Only later he realized how dumb that had been. How fucking fatally stupid. They could have been waiting for someone to show up. For him. They could have cut his throat as he stood there. He would have bled to death right there on the white tiles, without a murmur of protest, like a sacrificial lamb.

The initial payment Case had come to get, it was there in plain sight, a big thick roll of bills, twenty-five thousand in cash, rolled up and stuffed deep into Eddie's ruptured asshole. How bad do you want it? That's what you have to ask yourself, Case asked himself. Eddie's face, hollowed out and ghostly, just resembling Eddie enough not to mistake him for anyone else, was staring, goggle-eyed at whatever death looked like when it had come. But Eddie would never be able to describe it, even if he were still alive, because his mouth, from which all the teeth that should have been visible were missing, was lacking a tongue. It was hardly anything that could be called a mouth anymore. Just a hole, a pit, from which the demons that had once inhabited Eddie had escaped in an eruption of blood and vomit.

The tongue, that flap of meat that got us into so much trouble in this life, it was floating harmless and forever quiet in the toilet. It was floating there among cigarette butts and a couple of prodigious yellow turds.

The mark of the squealer.

This was the end of Eddie's road. This was his destination, after all that planning, all that dreaming, all that conniving. And Eddie was a cop. Who could have seen that coming?

The room was filling up with shadows. Case sat up, stood up, put the Jim Beam on the night table beside the metal cash box. He carried the cash box over to the dresser beneath the mirror. Opened

61 Bang

it. Inside, wrapped in a powder blue Martha Stewart hand towel, the semi-automatic handgun. Never fired. Case put it, still wrapped in the powder blue Martha Stewart hand towel, in one of the zip-lock bags he bought at the convenience store. Then he put that zip-lock bag into another and that in another. Then he returned the package to the metal cash box and put the metal cash box into a fourth zip-lock bag. That, he figured, should do the trick.

He walked to the window, the rain, maybe by now it was ice, still quietly tip-tapping.

Case pulled back the heavy curtain.

The parking lot. The highway. The neon Paradise sign.

Ah, it's dark.

7.

The cards never lie, but they do mislead. That was Leonard Tournier philosophizing to himself as he watched Maynard staring at his two and four of clubs. The four of them sitting around the table in the cramped dining room of Bradley's ramshackle house on Pike Drive. The Widowers Club, that's what they called it. Each of them having lost a wife or two to something or other over the years, divorce or cancer. Leonard had lost three. He still wasn't sure which he preferred to lose them to, if lose them he must. A picnic no one would compare either to.

You seem a little preoccupied tonight Len.

A little Maynard. A little.

What's on your mind? If you don't mind me asking in the middle of a pot, that is.

No never mind. I can have something on my mind and still win the pants off the likes of you Maynard.

Hmm…are those bluffing words, I hear?

Could be May. Could be.

Leonard watched Maynard playing with the corner of that card at the end of hand. Should he, shouldn't he?

Jimmy coming back from the kitchen with a fresh beer. He's a multitasker. That's what he's trying to tell us.

Bill finally wiped away the orange powder from a handful of Cheese Doodles he ate ten minutes ago. You mean masturbator, don't you.

Let him who is without sin.

Sin? At my age? It's a miracle, father.

61 Bang

Arch laid down his cards. The local pastor, he was younger than any of them, but not much. His prostate still functioned unaided, that's how you could tell. I'm out. He reached into the snapped pocket of his cowboy-style work shirt and pulled out a pack of Lucky Strikes.

So what's got your shorts in a bunch Sheriff?

Ran into a non-local at Rudy's over the morning ham and eggs. Upset my digestion a little, I have to admit.

Lowering his beer can, relief registering in his eyes like a man letting loose a long withheld piss, Jimmy burped and said, He seemed like an alright sort to me.

I'll see you ten, Maynard. And…and I'll raise you twenty-five. Sliding the chips into the center of the table, notching, but not lingering, on the quicksilver movement in Maynard's eyes. Now, you see, that's the difference between a professional lawman and a layman, Jimmy.

Oh yeah? How so chief?

Well, where you see but a man sipping his coffee and minding his own business, I see portents and presentiments.

Hear that reverend? We got a prophet in our midst.

Arch took a Tostito from the chip bowl and scooped some salsa from the salsa jar.

A prophet hath no honor in his hometown. That's the Bible, Jim.

You boys can laugh. But the Law, of which I am the sole full-time representative in these environs, doesn't have the luxury of the idle guffaw.

Maynard, still flicking the corner of his card, was trying to find something in Leonard's face. Good luck, Maynard, good luck with that old boy, Leonard was thinking.

Bill had pulled off his shoe and was rubbing his stocking foot. Probably wasn't even aware that's what he'd done. A fungus, the man itches. So what. This guy got some kind of record or something? Was he acting strange?

Nothing quite like that Bill.

61 Bang

Jimmy was staring at the center of the table, the last and biggest pot of the night, maybe seventy-five bucks. He'd never once, in the seven-plus years they'd been playing, won one of those big pots. You could see his eyeballs salivating. What was that? Three hundred and sixty-something games? Could your luck get any worse?

He was driving from New York, but he was from Virginia. That's what the plates on his car said. How bad could he be?

That boy was not from Virginia.

Now what makes you say that Len?

Just one of those things you know, Arch. Like the existence of God, for a pastor. Call it faith. You see, that man this morning. It's not where he comes from or where he doesn't that matters. It's not what he said or he didn't. It's not that he stands out like a sore thumb, that he doesn't fit in this crappy little town of ours. Who does, really? Present company of misfits excluded, naturally. No, it's more basic. That man doesn't fit in anywhere. That man is uncomfortable in this world. There are men like that, I know, I seen them. I recognize them. When you seen a few you never forget what they look like. They aren't just passing through this town, they're passing through this world. They're passing through life itself. They're heading for death without setting down any roots.

Okay you bastard.

Across the table Maynard had stopped flicking his card. He'd read something, finally, in Leonard's inscrutable face. He'd come to a decision. He pushed his chips into the pot. I'll pay to see you regret your bluff. Now what you got?

Maynard thought he'd finally deciphered something in Leonard's face because he thought what he saw in Leonard's face was a blankness hiding something devilishly clever and indescribably complex. He thought that blank mask concealed mysteries. His mistake was to try to figure out what he thought was behind that mask because what was there was really nothing at all.

Leonard flipped up his concealed cards.

Queen. Ace.

How the fuck…you son-of-a-bitch.

Easy Maynard. Don't blow out that ventricle again.

61 Bang

Fuck you Jimmy.

Leonard smiled thinly.

Arch guffawed. Bill snorted Cheese Doodle dust.

Hoodwinked you again. When are you gonna learn not to draw down on the Sheriff, Maynard? He wins every goddamn time he has half a mind to.

Maynard, his face still full of blood, but willing himself back to conviviality. He squinted one eye, as if looking through a microscope at something that could not possibly be there.

If I didn't have absolute confidence in your honor Leonard, I'd swear you were cheating. Dammit, I'd still swear it, but I can't figure out how you could be doing it. I thought I had you dead-to-rights that time.

Why thank you Maynard. I'll take that as a compliment. Since I'm obliged to take it at all.

Well, you ain't natural, that's all there is to it. You're playing with the devil at your elbow. Either that, or you're just plain fucking evil incarnated and that's all there is to it.

Now you aren't telling me anything my second wife didn't tell me. Or was that the first. Hell, I guess all three of them told me that or similar at one time or another. Leonard reached across the table and shepherded the pot towards him. A lesson learned, Maynard, long long ago. He winked. Probably the main reason why there isn't a fourth Mrs. Tournier. Why there probably won't ever be.

Bill munching, lips flecked with orange foam. What say you, Pastor? You're the expert here. Is our pal Leonard the Prince of Darkness or what?

Arch drew on his Lucky Strike. He looked like he was giving the matter some serious theological consideration. He exhaled. Peering through a cloud of smoke. Could be. Could be. The Dark One does come in all disguises. Or so they say.

Jimmy slumped in his chair, that last beer doing the job. So care to come clean Leonard? Care to share your secret?

No secret at all boys. That's the secret if there is one. Which, as I said, there isn't. It's just a feeling. You either have it or you don't. You either recognize the signs or you don't. Like a sixth sense, you know, but not really. Like that guy at the diner. Just something not right about him, something that doesn't fit. You sense it in your bones.

You getting all woo-woo on us now Len old buddy? All mystic-like. You like a guru or something?

No Maynard, not at all. Least I don't think so. Counting the bills as he organized them into a little pile, like the pack of cards he'd won them with. Eight-six dollars. Taking out his wallet, stuffing them inside. In any event, I guess it's just not a thing you can talk about. Not without sounding like an idiot. So a man don't, generally speaking. He stood up. And with that said, Gentlemen, I bid you adieu until next week.

You going already Chief? Win and run?

Got a date with an angel. You know how it is, fellas. Even the devil can't keep a lady waiting.

Jimmy, sloppily. Hell hath no fury.

Bill, muttering, though no one could remember him with a woman it had been that long. Ain't that the gospel, brother. Ain't that the gospel.

Leonard standing, stuffing the wallet into his back pocket, surveying the casualties around the table. Wagging a jocular paternal finger. Now you boys be sure to enjoy Bradley's fine hospitality until you sober up. I don't want to have to peel any of your ugly mugs off a fencepost at three a.m.

Who knew you cared so much? I'm touched.

Not that Bill, not that at all. I just don't want to have to get out of bed. Deadpan. He winked. It didn't make him less so. Bill shot him the finger. Happy trails, boys. Jimmy was snoring. Maynard had left the room. From down the hall, a toilet flushed. Bradley, presumably. He'd slipped out. He re-entered the room, still doing up his pants.

What'd I miss?

8.

Well, it was true, Leonard reflected, staring out the windshield, wrist resting on the top of the steering wheel. The night separating quickly in front of him, sliding passed the sides of his car, grasping ghosts. There was something not quite right about that guy, some fox-like look about him. The look of a man not just hunted, but used to being hunted. Like being hunted was a condition written into his genes. Not that it was any of Leonard's business, so long as the man kept moving, so long as he didn't make it any of Leonard's business. Keep it moving, let the lightning fall somewhere else, that was Leonard's theory of the Law. Bad things happened, make sure they happen somewhere else.

What he didn't tell them back at Bradley's was that he'd gotten a call from a detective he knew up in Asheville. A double-homicide. Two out-of-towners found murdered in a motel room. Each tied to a chair. Tortured for hours from the looks of them, which were none too good, according to those who'd been there to see it. A local shot three times in the head and found stuffed in the back of his Ford Bronco on the road leaving town. His wife, currently missing. The surrounding woods currently being searched.

All this way up in North Carolina, no logical connection, none at all. No way to explain it either. Only sound insane if you tried. Talk yourself into circles. How many violent deaths had occurred in the last five days? What were the odds that any of them were connected to a guy who'd done nothing more suspicious than sit in a diner and eat his breakfast in silence? In the periphery of his headlights Tournier saw the body, thrown to the edge of the road, the long and graceful white throat, the bared teeth, the single glassy eye. He'd seen it this morning, belly ruptured, intestines exploded from its anus like a bouquet of meaty flowers. Goddamn that road crew; bunch of freaks and deadbeats and backwoods rednecks as it was. Practically criminals their own selves. He'd have to call it in again in the morning. Give Buck Hartwell a reaming himself if the town manager wasn't up to it. True, the world might be going to Hell in a hand-basket, but still. This was the main access to town, goddammit.

Most people in these parts still left their doors unlocked. Like the idiots they were. What could they be thinking? This wasn't the Garden of Eden, for crissakes. Or the 1950s. They were living under a false impression. Not Mei, though. She locked it up nice and tight, Tournier reflected, taking out his key. Maybe that was the result of living in the middle of a genocidal war, although he didn't suppose they had any locks on that thatched hut she grew up in anyway. Mustn't have helped either to be living all those years with Elwood Boozer who brought her home from that war decades before. A tiny terrified thing she was. Looked less like a woman than a malnourished ten-year-old boy. Raped a dozen or so times by half a platoon of the U.S. Army infantry's finest, according to Elwood who should know, who told them, one drunken night at the Evergreen, cause he was there. He was her hero, in a manner of speaking, which wasn't hard to be, given the circumstances of her life.

For thirty years you didn't see much of her in town, which meant you didn't see much of her anywhere. Once every week or two, at the grocery, you'd catch a glimpse of her, shopping for Elwood's meals. Elwood preferred it that way, preferred she stay put in the neat little house he'd built at the end of Blackberry Lane, and you could see why, since he didn't want to chance her finding anything better and it wasn't hard to find better than Elwood Boozer, all you had to do was close your eyes on Broad Street and open them at the first person you bumped into. But, truth to tell, she seemed to prefer it that way herself, a meek skittish little mouse of a woman, wearing a fresh black-and-blue every time you saw her, never said a word to anyone, and how could she, hardly speaking English as far as anyone could tell.

61 Bang

Never found it much of an advantage speaking English to a woman anyway. Thus Luther, that moron, had opined on one occasion down at the Evergreen. And Elwood, he agreed, recounting some recent conjugal episode involving anal sex and, what he called, gobbledygook. Hilarity ensued. Tournier had smiled politely, nodded, tipped his beer toward Elwood and wondered what he'd look like with a bullet in his chest.

Then came the day, predictably enough, but still an unpredictably long time coming , that Tournier had to interrupt himself from the enjoyment of the usual ham-and-swiss to answer a report of a naked woman covered in blood running south along 57. Called in by some horrified motorist on a cell phone. Speeding, by the way, right on passed. Didn't take a soothsayer to tell Leonard who it was before he got there. The bastard had nearly cut her left nipple clean off. That's what the doctors told him, after they cleaned her up at Mercy General.

Well, fact was, you couldn't help but sympathize with Elwood, up to a point. They forbid him to see his woman after that, and then, on top of it all, they kick him out of his own house. The house he built with his own hands, his own nails, his own sweat. Don't go within two hundred yards of the place they tell him or we throw your ass in jail. That's not easy for a man like Elwood to swallow. That a man don't really own anything in this world, not even what he bought and paid for; that don't seem like justice to a man like Elwood. But that's the Law. Sometimes it's on your side, sometimes it aint. It changes. It doesn't seem like it should, but it does. Even if men like Elwood don't.

So Tournier had to go out there on any number of occasions to explain it to him. But these explanations don't make anything much clearer to Elwood, except how he's getting screwed at every turn. Tournier keeps trying. At the filling station. At the Evergreen. At Town Hall.

In court.

In the street.

Elwood just doesn't get it. Because now people are starting to talk, like they always will. Whether there's anything to talk about or not, they'll talk. Except that in this case there is. It's not hard to end up Mei's new hero, as it turns out, given her old one.

Can't say I blame you none. Those chink gals sure hold up over the years. Like Toyotas.

This at the Evergreen again, over a couple of beers. Maynard putting his two cents in.

She ain't Japanese, you ignorant hayseed.

Huh?

Toyotas are a Japanese car.

There a difference? Point is, you get a good mileage on slash like that. Go Jap, you never go back. Right? Har. Har. Har.

He didn't hit him more than half-serious, just enough to knock him back off his stool. He looked up from the floor, his shirt soaked, the palm of Tournier's right hand imprinted red on his big forehead.

Christ, Leonard. What the fuck. But Maynard had the good sense to stay there on the floor. Read the expression on Tournier's face right for once. Didn't call him, or raise the stakes. Cracked a joke instead. You seem to have knocked over my beer.

Get off the floor and have a drink up here at the bar like a member of society and I'll buy you another.

They canceled the poker game that week. But everything went back to normal the week after. How's Mei doing? Just fine boys just fine. I'll be sure to tell her you asked, was the full extent of the conversation if she were ever brought up again.

You late.

She spoke English better than anyone knew. Better than she let on. Taught it herself, mainly, watching reruns of *Law and Order* and *Jeopardy* on TV. She was dressed in a pink satin slip, a little bit of lace across the top. Sitting up against the pillows. Not much in the tit department he had to admit it himself, but goddammit Maynard was right. Fifty-two, at the very least, and she still could pass for nineteen in the candlelight.

Sorry. Took longer to beat the pants off those yokels tonight. He slipped the wallet from his back pocket. Removed the eighty-six dollars. Laid the neat stack of bills on the dresser among the little jars of potions and perfumes and ointments.

61 Bang

What that for?

Buy yourself something.

What?

How do I know? Go to the beauty shop. Get your nails done. Whatever women do.

She'd taken him on like you'd buy a used car when the old one conked out on you. Sizing him up. Figuring, he'd do. Get her where she needed to go. Like in the Old West or something like that, Tournier thought. When it wasn't love that brought people together, but a need to survive on some wild frontier. Man provided protection and in return a woman provided what she provided. Back when he was a romantic, that kind of thing would have bothered Tournier. But like the Law, love had changed too. Changed with age. So had he. He was a man of the times. You either kept up or you got put under. And who says love don't come after? After you helped someone else survive and they helped you. Who says it couldn't be gratitude? Survival is what it's all about, aint it? Where would we be without it?

Mei patted the bed. You come lie down. Don't just stand staring me.

Tournier had seen her strangling chickens for dinner. She talked the same way. With harsh economy. Not a word not strictly necessary. Even when she was being tender. Especially then. It took some getting used to. Even then Tournier had never gotten used to it. He undid his gunbelt. Hung it over a chair. Slid off his pants.

It all went nice and easy. He still had the juice and the ladder to get to the little bit of Heaven a man was entitled to on earth. And when he didn't, he figured he'd try those drugs that helped you get there. No shame in that. You did what you had to. Mei had quit some time ago, couldn't bear the stench of it in the house anymore. So he rolled out of bed, pulled his pants on, and headed to the back porch for a smoke.

Standing there under the stars, he lit up. Stared into the dark yard. Back at the spot where he'd called Elwood out of the woods that night. He'd been watching the windows, the son-of-a-bitch. Had a big old buck knife on him, too. He always did, it's true, but still.

61 Bang

Words were exchanged, you can imagine. A summer night, not like this one. Sultry. Tournier in his skivvies, not much left to the imagination. Revolver in hand. A wail from the tree line, like it come from a wounded animal. That's my wife, goddammit. The cold reply, No more she isn't. For a long time afterward there was a lot of talk in town about whether what happened next was necessary, not that Tournier heard much of it. Usually the conversation changed when he came around. Only two people knew the answer and only one of them was left and Tournier wasn't telling.

He smoked the last of the cigarette, crushed it against the wood railing, and put the butt into the pocket of his thermal vest. Mei gave him hell if she saw them thrown in the yard, in the bushes, the flowerbeds and whatnot. He stared long and hard at that dark place in the woods. Exhaled. Over the years he must have imagined it a thousand times. What Elwood Boozer would look like with a bullet in his chest. When it happened for real, it looked a lot different.

9.

Up into the darkness, Case climbed. Struggling and stumbling over the wet sticks and slippery stones. Mud sucking off his shoes. The earth giving way, shifting under his feet in all directions at once. Branches cutting and clawing across his face no matter how careful he was. Taking a beating, he was. Leaning into the shovel-handle, using it as a walking stick. The shovel he bought at a hardware store back in Asheville. Along with the metal cash-box. Scattering the clues behind him, like the pieces of a jigsaw puzzle.

Every so often a torrent surged downhill through the mini-ravines. Gushed over his shoe-tops and rose around his ankles. The freezing water shockingly refreshing for three or four seconds, then miserable. By now his socks were sodden, his toes numb. The grit seemed to be wearing the flesh away to the bone.

He stopped, reached into his pocket, and broke another plastic light-stick. Held it up to the surrounding woods. Everything glowed blue. Wet and sickly. Like the insides of something the insides of which you weren't meant to see.

What was he looking for?

The last place on earth, that's what.

Case laughed.

A curiously lunatic sound here in the last place on earth. But you had to laugh in the end. What else was there to do? The worse the joke the louder the laugh. That was comedy's law of survival.

He was looking for the last place on earth anyone would think of looking for a metal cash box containing a semi-automatic pistol that had only been fired once but that had already gotten at least half-a-dozen people killed, including his old connection, Eddie. A pistol that someone was willing to pay a lot of cash to have delivered to some unnamed people clear across the country. A pistol that Case had been contracted to deliver by said Eddie, now horrifically deceased.

The light stick in his grimy fist began to fade.

And Case climbed on.

He'd already fallen a few times. Kept tripping and slipping no matter how cautiously he proceeded. He could feel the large soaked patch extending from his right hip all the way down to his knee. Thanks to his most recent tumble. It felt like he was hauling a hundred pounds of mud in his pockets. Like he was turning to mud himself, starting with his right leg.

He'd found this place on a road atlas—a great big area of nothing, between one nowhere and another. A great big empty area of map green with no dots, no names, no symbols, no nothing, and all of it shaped like a lopsided egg. As good a place as any. Which meant not good enough, but it'd have to do.

Because it should be obvious by now to everyone that he wasn't delivering the gun to anyone. Not yet. Maybe not ever. Not until he'd figured out a few things for himself. Like who wanted it. Like why. Like were they ever going to leave him alone. The way Case figured, that gun was as close to an insurance policy that he'd ever have. His one bargaining chip against the kind of abrupt and undignified exit that Eddie had been shown, poor bastard, and a cop no less.

Christ, it was cold. Cold and dank. You felt it *inside* your bones. No coat ever made to keep that kind of weather out. How far had he walked? It felt like miles and miles, but progress was tortured, probably it was far less than he imagined. He dug the shovel blade into the earth. The sound of meat. Hauled himself up. Swung the shovel. Sound of meat. Hauled. Swung the shovel. Clang. The blade slid off a stone and Case caught himself halfway down the handle. That's the way it went on for as long as it went on. Case looking for that spot, that perfect spot of nowhere he'd never be able to describe. That precious bit of real estate he'd never be able to lead anyone back to even if his life depended on it. Because it might. Taped to a chair in a cold room somewhere, his pants down, facing a forceps, a blow-torch, a hacksaw. He didn't want to be able to betray himself, like he knew he would, like we all do in the end. Yeah, even the toughest, even the smartest, the most noble, of which Case was not. The body isn't made to keep secrets. The mind, if you know how to hurt it, even less. Forget the movies. There's only so much pain a human body can withstand before the animal takes over. The animal that wants to keep living. The animal wants the pain to stop no matter what. My God why hast Thou forsaken me? Happens to us all. The only way not to falter in the end is not to know anything. To be innocent. Imagine that. Listen to me, getting mystical in my old age. Case swung the shovel. Hauled. Reached into his pocket, broke another light stick. Sickly blue glow. Repeat of everything he'd seen before. Vista of dripping black trees, rotten logs, mud, stone. An inky wasteland.

Here.

He dug.

The rain fell sporadically. But it fell. When didn't it? He'd gotten used to the sound of it hitting the carpet of last year's dead leaves. The sound of someone coming. But no one was. He'd been fooled enough times already to convince himself. Sort of.

He dug, not deep enough to be thinking of digging his own grave, but to imagine he was digging a grave for his heart, or his soul, one of those small valuable and vulnerable things that had died in him a long time ago. His conscience, maybe? Don't make me laugh. He didn't. He was too winded. Too spooked. He wanted to get the hell out of these woods, off this blasted hill, out of this dopey town. He wanted to get back on the road, going somewhere else, anywhere else, that was imperative.

No bigger than the grave for a small childhood pet—a guinea pig, maybe. A cat. That's all that was necessary in the end. Case knelt in the mud, laid the metal cash box inside. Hoped to see it again only under better circumstances. Whatever those might be.

He stood up. He shoveled the sodden earth back into the hole. Each shovelful, a thousand pounds. But he didn't stop until he'd finished. If he did, he might never. He leaned against the shovel handle, took a deep shuddering breath, and heard the cry.

Some kind of animal. In terrible pain. Something getting rent unseen in the night. What was it? What difference did it make? In enough pain, we were all the same kind of animal.

The cry, again. Louder this time.

Law of the Jungle, beneath all the others. Don't let anyone fool you. And of all the many, many variations, the original was still the fairest. The most honest. The most understandable. No matter what anyone said.

Case stood there in the darkness, leaning against the shovel handle. Listening. Why? For what?

The tip-tap of rain. Silence.

A series of wracked sobs.

Maybe all animals had their own variation of it when the pain let up enough to allow, but he didn't know enough about zoology to say. He sort of doubted it though. He figured only man had the capacity to beg. For mercy, among other things. Could an animal mimic a sound like that?

Case stood there and listened. That animal, a pretty young one from the sound of it, was moaning. But its moans seemed to have taken on the form of a very simple but highly expressive language. Still in pain, but now able to articulate a request. A plea. A prayer. Who knew if anyone was listening? If anyone could grant it. If anyone would have any mercy even if they could.

Please. No, no no. Please, no. Please daddy please. Please. No.

Case stood and listened to that cry in the dripping woods for a while. Hard to say how long. Hard to say if it weren't possibly just a figment of his overwrought imagination. It died away after a little while. How long had it been going on, unheard, while he worked? No matter. It was gone now. What a relief. Gone like it had never been there to begin with. He didn't dare break another light-stick. He didn't really want to see anything. Didn't need to. He'd seen more than enough to know where he was. The last place on earth. And, dammit, if it still wasn't quite far enough. He peered into the darkness. He walked back down the hill.

10.

Because he didn't dream, Case knew it was no dream, that grim pounding on the door, that battering on the outskirts of his oblivion. He recognized it as the sound of someone who wanted an answer. Even worse. Someone who wasn't going away until he got it. Shit. Shit. Shit. He threw an arm over his eyes. Ground his teeth. Felt his heart flubbering around in his chest like a wet bag of worms. His temples ached with a dark pressure. Like he were being lifted off the bed by a set of pincers. His vision filled with blood. Shit.

Who is it.

He fumbled under the bed for his .38.

Who's there.

He tried to find his voice a third time because he didn't like the sound of it the first two times. The third time was no better.

What do you want.

Open up. It's the Law.

Shit. Already?

Okay. Just a minute.

For a few seconds there, blinded and palpitating, Case thought he just might drop dead of a stroke, solving all his many problems all at once. But no such luck. He looked up at the motel room door. Down at the worn rug. He couldn't find his pants.

More rapping on the door. Let's shake a leg in there son. Don't worry about your make-up. No need to look pretty for me.

Case found a bath towel on the floor. Damp. Wrapped it around his waist and walked to the window with the .38. Nudged the curtain back with the knuckle of his middle finger. Big. The way a big

61 Bang

guy is when age makes him a little smaller. White-haired. Red-faced. One of those dramatic Smokey-the-Bear-style hats on his head. Underneath, those small blue eyes that look like they know your darkest secret. Staring right at the crack Case had opened between the curtains. In other words, the Law, just as announced. Or, even worse, what passed for it in this part of the universe.

Case let the curtain fall back. Bent down and slid the .38 behind the desk. Under the heating vent beneath the window. Stood up. Readjusted the towel tied around his waist. Walked to the door. Wondered just what kind of car wreck his face must look like.

Good morning, Mr. Case. Hope you don't mind if I come in and set a spell. He said this while coming in like he owned the place. Here you go. Light on the cream and sweet. But I have some extra packets of sugar if you want it.

Case took the paper cup of coffee the chief handed him. Turned and watched as the man settled himself into the desk chair. Removed his Smokey-the-Bear-style hat, set it down on the desk, and prepared the lid of his coffee. He blew inside the cup, took a sip. Mmm. Best coffee in town. Smiled. Without humor. Please. Have a seat.

Case pushed the door closed. Sighed. Wondered what kind of game he'd gotten himself into now. He was too tired, too hung over. It was too early. He couldn't locate his pants. He sat down on the edge of the bed across from Tournier, fixed the lid on his own cup, careful not to spill scalding coffee on his lap. Covered only by the bath-towel. Uncomfortably conscious of his bare legs. The Law smiled that thin knowing smile again. What did it know? Did it know anything? Was it only bluffing?

Coffee okay?

Fine. Thanks. You always roll out the welcome wagon like this?

Not always.

So. Why now.

As you might imagine, we don't get many distinguished visitors in our little corner of the world.

I don't follow.

61 Bang

VIPs don't often stop here. We're not on the map so to speak. We don't hang out a shingle. Welcome visitors. We're no more than a pit stop on the way to someplace else. You're on the highway, you blink, and we're in the rearview mirror. To be honest, I, for one, like it that way. But then, you know, I'm older. Set in my ways. Don't much like all the excitement. Maybe I'm xenophobic.

Xenophobic?

Don't like strangers.

I know what it means. Look, I'm just a guy passing through. Nothing more.

Oh now don't be modest. Maybe you're traveling incognito, but you can't fool me Mister John Case from Virginia. The chief took a sip from his cup. That is you, isn't it? John Case from Virginia. He regarded Case sitting on the bed. Eyes now like two ice-blue dice. Without dots.

You came out here to tell me my name?

It all checks out. Car. License. Registration. Residency information. All of it.

Any law against that?

None.

What's the problem then?

I don't believe any of it. Not for one of them proverbial cotton-picking seconds.

It's early, sheriff.

No, its really not.

If there's something...

Someone went through a lot of trouble to arrange for all those papers. To get all those records in order. Dotted a lot of Is. Crossed a lot of Ts to make it seem as if you are who you say you are.

I really don't know what you're talking about.

How'd I guess you'd say something exactly like that? There are some folks around here that say I'm psychic. Never put much stock in it, being nothing but the backwoods country redneck that I am, but I wonder if it's true, after all? Now I personally have never given much credence to shit like that, but still. Has to be something to explain how I know what I know. These feelings I get. Like you ain't no one named John Case from Virginia.

Case needed a shower. A shave. He needed to go back to sleep for another ten thousand years. He needed to get up and take a piss. He needed his pants.

You really look like hell, Mr. Case. What happened to your face and arms? Looks like you lost a wrestling match with a couple of angry blackberry bushes.

I took a walk. In the woods. He shrugged. Got a little scratched up. Just a city boy, I guess.

Whatever this game is, I can't play it now, Case thought, sitting there in a towel at the edge of the bed. I don't know the rules. I'm going to make a mistake, if I haven't made one already. This bastard is playing the bumpkin from Mayberry, but he's nine miles of bad road. Anyone can see that. I need a slug or two of Jim Beam. I need to put on my socks. Case sipped his coffee. They both did. Time hung there between them like a flayed carcass in a meat locker Tournier with his legs spread, his gut stretching the fabric of his uniform shirt. His florid face with the expression of a wise old bull that had outlasted a thousand roundups. Put out to pasture. But still dangerous as hell.

I want you out of my town.

I was planning to leave.

Before dark.

I'm going. No problem.

Don't fuck with me, Mr. John Case.

I'm not.

I don't like mysteries, Mr. Case. I don't like things that don't have their exact place in the scheme of things. This town, it may not look like much, but it's twenty-seven square miles of order. In light of the state of the rest of the world, that's saying something. That's an achievement I take some pride in. I won't suffer some stranger coming in and throwing everything into discord and despair. The Law is a delicate balance, Mr. Case, and that's all. I keep that balance.

I hear you.

61 Bang

Tournier regarded the man on the bed. Took a sip of coffee. I sure hope you do. Move on. That's my word to the wise. And you look like a smart man to me, Mr. John Case. Maybe not wise, but smart. Smart enough, anyway. Please don't get up.

The sheriff was in the process of doing so; Case hadn't moved. Had no intention to. Felt like he might pitch over onto his face if he tried. I'm sorry to have troubled you so early in the morning. Sorry to have troubled either of us. Seems like it wasn't necessary after all. He smiled, even more unpleasantly. You leaving by nightfall as you are. I'll let myself out. Then he carefully set his big Smokey-the-Bear hat on his head and did just that.

11.

A waste of time, that's what it was, but you had to try, you had to take your shot. That was Tournier, eyeballing the Coors Silver Bullet can at the end of his gun barrel. It sat on a plank of wood which was resting on three bales of hay, the center-piece of his otherwise barren lot. His allotted parcel of earth. Sodden. Grey. Not much time for gardening in the life of Leonard Tournier. Well, plenty of time, to be perfectly accurate, but a complete lack of whatever else was necessary. A waste of time. But you had to do it anyway. Maybe you get lucky and save yourself some trouble, a shot in a thousand, one of these days you've got to hit something, right?

He wasn't going anywhere. Tournier, of course. But that guy in the Paradise Motel, too. He would have staked the pot on it.

He was getting too old for this shit. Standing in the cold drizzle holding a gun on an empty beer can. Getting? Too old for this was a picture in an old scrap book by now. His gums were bleeding, his ulcer was bleeding, lately his asshole had begun bleeding—dammit, if he scratched the back of his neck too hard without thinking he found blood under his fingernails. That's what happened to you after a while. You wore out in all the vulnerable places. One of these fine days the dam holding back all that blood would break and that would be that. He'd explode in one giant hemorrhage. Just so long as it were quick, he wouldn't complain. No way he'd want to go out the way Carrie did, the cancer reaching up from her gut, slow-strangling the life out of her. Bitch that she'd been in the years before the diagnosis, no one deserved to die like that. It woulda made a stone weep. Christ, what a life it was when that's the best you could pray for: an instantaneous death.

Turns out they found another body in West Virginia, also tortured. Tournier had been doing a little web-work. A wonderful thing the internet. You could see the insanity everywhere in the world without leaving your living room. Without changing your undershirt. A retired cop, NYPD, this one. Murdered a few days before the three in Asheville. Connect the dots and you could see where this was heading. You could see that you were standing on the next dot. Nothing logical about it. Just a hunch. Tournier squinted over the sight at the end of the dripping gun barrel.

There was a time when he could've read you the list of ingredients off the side of that Silver Bullet can at fifty paces. And another time when he could recite them from memory. No fucking fooling. How long ago was that? Hard to say, the way you lost it, one millimeter at a time. The world getting harder and harder to see. Harder to remember, too. Maybe that wasn't such a bad thing, after all. Now he'd need a pair of reading glasses to read that same can. The extra-strength ones. Now the only thing he saw clearly was the tremor of the gun-sight. No. Be honest. The tremor of his hand. The tremor of his soul.

He should have retired from this job ten years ago. Fifteen, to be perfectly honest. Should have packed it in and quit this jerkwater town for good. Bought a mobile home. Driven it down to the Everglades. Spent the butt-end of his life fishing and shooting alligators. He should have. But, of course, that wasn't an option.

A lot of things weren't. Options, that is.

Life was like a game of poker. You got dealt some cards at the start. A whole lot of options cut out right there. No fault of your own. You had to play what cards you had. Make choices. More options lost. Go for this, abandon that. Hope. Gamble. Bluff. Someone else got the cards you wanted. Maybe the guy right next to you. Luck—what was it? Blind chance? Destiny? Suddenly, most of the cards have been played. You have to calculate. You've already made most of the choices possible. What's left? What can you

61 Bang

reasonably expect? Do you even want to be reasonable? You're scared shitless, but you try not to show it. How do you keep yourself from sweating? That's the hardest lesson of all. How do you keep your poker-face? At worst, you find yourself praying. You shoot for a full house and you end up with a pair of fives. That's life. Just like a game of poker, but there's only one hand. You win or lose. One pot. There are no second chances.

Sometimes your life was already over at sixteen. Because of a choice you made. No matter how you play the rest of your hand. Doesn't seem fair. But that's why they call it gambling. That's the thrill of it, when all's said and done.

Take a deep breath. Let it out. Squeeze the shot. Nice and easy, like exhaling a drag on a menthol cigarette. The second drag, not the first, desperate one. Savor it. He needed a haircut. Getting a little shaggy. Funny the things you thought about at times like this.

Something was coming. Tournier could sense it in the marrow of his bones. The older he got the easier it was to feel. The harder it was to do anything about. A change in the atmosphere of everything. A storm was on its way, and that guy in the Paradise Motel, whoever he might be, was the harbinger of all the bad things that were to come. Because the bad things were coming. You didn't need to be a psychic to see that. They were coming and not even the Law could stop them. You could put them off for thirty or forty years, hold a gun on them, so to speak, but they were coming all the same. Life, you might say, was nothing more than putting off, as long as humanly possible, the bad thing at the end.

The can wobbled, but didn't fall. The shot had missed, up and to the right. The blast echoed back from the leafless hills. It was a very lonely sound. Maybe the loneliest in the world. He could have taken another shot but that would have been cheating. And Leonard Tournier was an honest man. Never more so than when he was alone. Only when he was alone. To be perfectly honest. A startled crow flew up into the colorless sky.

12.

Ethanol, sorbital, 1, 010 milligrams of sodium, 30 grams of fat, azodicarbonide, 80 milligrams of cholesterol, polysorbate 80, propylene glycol alginate, 100 % onions, 560 calories. That was the Big Mac that Case had just taken a bite out of, sitting in a McDonald's at a rest stop off the interstate. His elbows on one of the crayon-colored formica tables by the window. He stared passed the parking lot, across a brown highway, at a strip mall soaking in the rain. Stared straight through a garish window painting of a Ronald McDonald offering passing motorists shakes and chicken nuggets. Was it just Case, or did representations of this clown keep getting creepier and more aggressive-looking as the years went by?

Well, to be sure, things change. Maybe he was just getting old. The kids seemed to like him all the same. But they might be getting creepier and more aggressive, too.

Case sat there and munched through another 570 calories of sodium acid pyrophosphate, natural flavor (beef, wheat, and dairy sources), dextrose, partially hydrogenated vegetable oils, and another thirty grams of fat. In other words, an order of French fries. If the Paradise Motel were America's bedroom, then McDonald's was its kitchen. Bright. Colorful. Shiny. Like living inside a cartoon or a graffiti-covered wall. Moms and chattering children. A dad here and there, looking dazed and overwhelmed. All of it as familiar as a sitcom. Case felt right at home.

He was heading west, no particular destination, but in the general direction of where he was supposed to be going: Los Angeles. He needed some time to think. To let whatever storm was gathering behind him take shape. He had to know what he was dealing with before he could figure out how to deal with it. That business with the police chief bothered him. He would have liked to get into and out of town without attracting any attention. Too late for that, obviously. As it was, Case didn't like leaving the metal cash box behind in a place where he'd been noticed. Where anyone would remember him. But with the Law watching him, going back up into the woods and unearthing it would have been impossible.

Case tried to tell himself there was no way the box could be found. No way that cop could know of its existence even if he did know that Case had been in the woods. What had Case been doing in the woods? Could have been anything. Fact was, even he would have been hard-pressed to find the exact spot where he'd buried the metal cash box. That had been the point of burying it in the place he buried it in the first place.

It looked like a circus in this place. Maybe that was the point. Case watched the families eating their happy meals and Quarter Pounders, their cellulose gum and FD&C Yellow #6, their Vanilla Shakes and autolyzed yeast. It would be wrong to say that he felt a part of it all, but it would be just as wrong to say that he didn't. He'd had it all once, the wife and family, even guys like Chase didn't climb out from under a rock, but he lost it. Had it again, lost it again. He wouldn't have it anymore. He'd had his chances. He wasn't sad about it, but he wasn't singing any hymns or hallelujahs either.

They say that in India the custom was that a man would establish himself in business, marry, raise a family. Become a respected and responsible member of society. Then, at fifty or so, his obligations met, his duties discharged, he was allowed to retire into the mountains. Live in a cave. To follow the inner-path. To cultivate his soul. Find Buddha, or whoever. Except for all the obligations unfulfilled, the duties abandoned, Case considered his life on a similar trajectory. One way or another, this was going to be his last job. His ride off into the sunset. He was retiring, not just from business, such as it was, but from the entire human race. He'd been running a long time and he wasn't getting any faster, that's for sure. He was only

61 Bang

getting tired, sore, winded. He was in the middle of the pack somewhere, losing ground. He'd had enough.

He'd told as much to Eddie and Eddie said he understood, but Eddie really didn't. Eddie was still in the race, still thought he could win. Hard not to picture the last time he'd seen Eddie. In that bathtub. Chump change from the winner's purse shoved up his rectum. All Case had to do was deliver the gun across the country to the representatives of some big-name guy who couldn't be named. Wink. You know how it is. That was it. All of it on the up-and-up, more or less. Nothing illegal, not really. Oh yeah sure. Well, don't tell me anymore. Get one last big pay-off then disappear to wherever he wanted. South of France? Tuscany? They say Shanghai has it all. You can even buy yourself a set of those foreign language tapes to listen to on the drive. Ha. Ha. Nothing is as simple as that.

Case should have known.

Case did know.

What he never told Eddie was that he'd already decided to just dump the gun and disappear without the cash if things got too hot. To hell with all of them. To hell with the money. You can't spend money in the joint. You aren't living the high life in a ditch with a hole in the back of your head no matter how much cash you got stashed away somewhere. Aint nothing more valuable than the breath in your lungs. Try getting by without it for three fucking minutes. That's the kind of guy Case was. A survivor, in other words. He did what he had to, didn't let a self-destructive attachment to idealism or dreams handicap him. The graves were filled with fools who had.

Also filled with fools who hadn't. Filled. Period.

Case figured he could probably make St. Louis, somewhere like that, by morning. Middle of the country. The muddy Mississippi, the great concrete Arch, home of Mark Twain, all that shit. Sit a spell there, anonymous in a big city, and take things from there. Hang out at the local Starbucks. They had those in St. Louis, didn't they?

He wiped his mouth, gathered up his tray, dumped it into a brightly-colored trash bin. Passed up on that free refill of Sprite. Held the door open for a family of fellow travelers. An All-American family who days on the interstate had given the edgy air of post-apocalyptic cannibals. Something about a life on the road, it gave you a different angle on things. You forgot all about it when you got wherever it was you were going. If you weren't going anywhere, though. Then what?

Across the parking lot, sticky and wet, to his car. Key in the lock and slide inside. All this damp weather making his herniated discs ache. Have to be careful tying his shoes. Sneezing. Bend over to pick up a fallen dime without thinking and he could be laid up for a week with sciatica. Jesus. Case started the car, let it warm up. The heater had two settings: too hot, not hot enough. Put on the wipers, the headlights. Slip it into gear. His cell phone rings. Take the car out of gear, sit there. Stare through the windshield. The wipers squealing. Is it even raining anymore?

Take the cell phone out of his jacket pocket. Look at the LCD display.

Unknown number.

That's no surprise. He knows so few, so few know him, and not many who do would call, and vice versa. Can't be good news, not likely, not the way things are going. He doesn't want to hear it, has enough bad news he can't handle, but it's better to know than not. That's the theory. If you're heading for a cliff, maybe there's still time to hit the brakes.

He thumbs the button.

Yeah.

I hear you got a key belongs to me.

Stare through the windshield. It's raining, alright.

13.

Keep it simple, stupid. That's the first rule. For everything. Everything without a single exception. The more complicated things get, the more things can go wrong. The more you guarantee things will go wrong. He knew the rules. Knew them by heart. So why was he breaking the very first one? Why did he turn the car around two hours out of town? Why was he now heading back to that mudhole in the middle of nowhere? Why was he making things complicated? Why was he making such a huge mistake?

On the phone the guy had sounded exactly as you'd expect him to sound. The same challenge in his voice that Case had seen in his eyes in the snack food aisle of the convenience store.

No, not really challenge. It was more than that. It was the contempt of someone who considered himself beyond challenge. Who was daring you to say a word he might take the wrong way. Even an innocuous one. Take it the wrong way just for the hell of it. Because it was Tuesday and he felt like taking it the wrong way. For the sheer joy of releasing the tornadoes and earthquakes pent-up inside him. Like God, in other words. He thought he was God.

Not that there were any shortage of those in the world. Gods, that is. Case had come across his share. Who didn't? In the joint, especially, on both sides of the bars. He'd never discovered so many gods as he had during those three years upstate. It was a fucking pantheon of gods, a regular house of worship. You couldn't cough without breaking a commandment. Foxholes? There were no atheists in the joint either. Oh no. Everyone was a believer on the inside. Every man needed God to survive. And Case was no different than every other man. He was no tough guy; he was no God. He'd gotten down on his knees just like the rest of them. He'd prayed, he'd worshipped, he'd spoken in tongues. And his God had kept His promise. He'd protected him, let him pass through the valley of the shadow of death. He'd walked out of that unholy place after four years still alive. Still intact. For the most part. The judge who'd sentenced Case had said that prison would be good for him and of course Case thought that was bullshit at the time but thirty-six months and four days later Case realized that judge had been right. Case found his faith behind those walls, got religion. He discovered the wisdom of Ecclesiastes. How many times had Case recited to himself those verses of Solomon's wisdom? Doubled over his cot, for instance, while his God descended upon him with His Lightning Bolt in hand?

Case watched the interstate slap passed his windows. Black and wet. Wet and black. The exact same interstate he'd traveled only two hours ago in the opposite direction. The direction he should still be going right now. Forward. Fast-forwarding is what he should be doing. Instead. He was rewinding the film. There was something we missed back there. Something important. It's a pain the ass, but we won't understand the ending if we don't go back. That's how it seemed to Case, that's the best he could explain it. That wasn't very good as explanations went, he'd be the first to admit it, but that would have to be good enough.

How about we meet at the Evergreen. I'm sure you know it.

No good.

Why not.

Just ain't.

Economy of words. Like the guy were speaking in haiku. Like he didn't expect to need to talk at all. He expected you to intuit his desires out of thin air. To hear his voice in your head. Case wanted to tell him to forget it then, to fuck off. He didn't need the trouble. He was the one doing the favor, returning the man's lost key and all. Of course, he wasn't doing anyone any favor, but this guy didn't know it. He wasn't supposed to know it anyway. He didn't have to know it.

61 Bang

He wouldn't have considered anything a favor. You don't do God any favors.

There's a gas station south out of town. Only one. That's the one. I'll be there at ten.

No more to it than that. Case folded the cell phone, slipped it back into his pocket, and sat in the rest stop parking lot for a long time. He watched the twilight descend like ashes over everything. He watched the rain start and stop. Then he watched it do something in between. He still had the grimy note. Folded now and tucked in his wallet behind his license and registration. No reason why. No reason why not. He'd kept it, that was all. That's what he told himself and he didn't go any further into it than that. Now he was going back. Now he was breaking the rules. He was making a mistake. Help us God please. Who was that kid talking to anyway? Did she think she was talking to Case? That he was God? Was that why he was going back? To prove her wrong? To prove himself right?

No that was too complicated.

Keep it simple, stupid.

That was the first rule.

There was something in the film he'd missed. That was all. It happened in the convenience store. It had something to do with that note the kid passed him in the snack food aisle when Case was looking for that package of Ho-Hos he never found. Do they even make Ho-Hos anymore? It had something to do with her father. Something he'd missed. Something he hadn't missed, not really, but something he wished he had. Case had to go back. If he didn't, he'd never understand the end.

That was the best explanation.

It was just as simple as that.

14.

She sat on the other side of his vast and polished desk. One fine-looking sister. Or half-sister. That exotic mix of races scribed like a delicate calligraphy into her flesh and bone. Into her genetic blueprint. No matter. None of us is 100% pure. We've all had a little bit of the devil raped into us over the centuries. Living in their cellars. Cleaning their bedrooms. Scrubbing their toilets. One day the wrong would be made right. Evil cast in chains and thrown into the bottomless pit. That day came ever closer every day; he had the faith. The meek would inherit the earth. He sincerely believed that. But not until they were armed to the teeth. Not until they climbed the mountain and wrested control by any means necessary. A tiny diamond in her left nostril. Four black tears tattooed in the cocoa-colored flesh under her right eye. Not his taste, this new generation and its self-mutilating fashions, but she made it work somehow; in her case, he could live with it. He smiled, steepled his immaculately manicured fingers in front of his face.

You know what this is about.

I know what it is about.

You understand how important it is.

I heard nothing about a gun.

And we want to keep it that way.

A conservative cream-colored suit, white silk blouse, all of it exquisitely tailored to a slim, athletic body. Five-ten, maybe five-eleven. Hard to say. Tall women always looked taller than they really were. Undressed, they all seemed a little smaller. Modest heels, he'd

61 Bang

seen them when she walked into the office. Tits not large, not even medium. But enough, oh yes, Lord, quite enough. Like pomegranates. Put him in mind of the Song of Songs, it did. She could have been a businesswoman, a marketing director, or even an assistant D.A., someone in the media. But not really. What was it about beautiful women? That palpable power they carried, that wisdom in their eyes—that allure that drove presidents and kings and, yes, even prophets, to their ruin. Gifts of God is what they were. But like any gift from the Almighty, they were dangerous. You had to handle them with extreme care. Like lightning. Like the burning bush, ha ha. Wield them with respect and skill and you had an invincible weapon. Handle them foolishly, and they exploded in your face. You ended up blasted and ruined.

Do you mind. She asked this after she'd already lifted a long, thin cigarette from a silver filigreed case. After she'd already placed it between her pearly lips, a lighter poised at the tip, her perfect thumbnail on the flint. She asked this like a woman who never hears the word "no." No more than once, in any event.

He spread his large, soft hands. A gesture of beneficence and infinite largesse. A practiced gesture, beloved by millions. As if he personally wielded the power to forgive your sins, even the ones you didn't confess. Did he not?

Please. Be my guest.

The little lick of flame. The inhale. The head tilted slightly back as she exhaled. The hand held, wrist up. The long elegant fingers holding the slender cigarette with exquisite familiarity. He'd seen these things before, many times, but not quite like this. He felt something shifting inside him, like great basalt blocks, his very foundations, no doubt. Underneath it, the pit. God was tempting him in His great wisdom. She was a dangerous weapon, alright, a woman, maybe the most dangerous. He had to be very careful.

She fixed her eyes on him again. Almond-shaped. Like a snake's, but with passion and fire. Black like the forest primeval. With something glittering deep inside. A diamond beyond price.? The meaning of life? Immortality? Damnation?

61 Bang

If the media learns about the gun, it changes everything. You understand, don't you?

Yes. Of course.

Right now, we have a martyr. With a gun, we have nothing. Just another ho-chasin', rap-lovin' cop-hatin niggah-thug who deserved what he got.

I understand.

Another drag on the cigarette. She stares up at the ceiling. No, not *at* the ceiling. *Through* the ceiling. Into the stars. Into heaven. Good lord, was it possible to sit across from her and not think in cheesy pick-up lines? Who on earth could have been this girl's father? Who? There he goes again. More pertinent, who on earth could be currently bedding her? He'd need do nothing more than sit there and watch her smoke a cigarette. Honest. It would be enough.

So you understand how important it is to have it in our possession. Whoever holds that gun, holds the future in their hands. Whoever has the gun, calls the shots. As usual.

And the police lost it? How?

We had a devil inside the devil's system. A man of greed and sin with access to the evidence room. We paid him to make sure the weapon didn't stay in the hands of those who would have used it against us.

And then?

He died. Like a pig.

I see.

But before he did, he was able to pass the gun into the hands of a courier. We trust this messenger is on his way to us right now.

So? Why am I doing here?

This messenger is going to need some help delivering his message. I won't lie to you. There are a lot of people being killed to stop him. There will probably be a lot more. They want to find him and get that gun back. They can't go to the media without it. Right now, the media is on our side. They won't be if that gun is found. Our enemies will do anything and everything to get it back.

Where is this messenger?

We don't know.

61 Bang

You don't know.

He's slipped out of view. Still somewhere in the southeast, we're assuming. Maybe laying low. Maybe in trouble.

Meaning he might already be dead. The gun may have already been recovered.

It's possible. But we don't think that's happened. Not yet.

Does he know what he's delivering?

He wasn't told. It's certainly possible he's figured it out.

Is he trustworthy?

The man who entrusted him with the gun believed him to be.

Was that man trustworthy?

He died believing it.

Any moron can die. Does our messenger know who he's working for?

He has a contact to whom he is to deliver the gun. But that's all he's been told. But again, we can't presume he's an idiot. At some point, he may figure it out for himself.

So you don't really trust him.

No. I suppose not.

What's his name?

John Case.

15.

You're late.

He was standing in the shadows around the side of the gas station, near the restroom. Towards the back by a cyclone fence that had sifted decades of trash from the wind passing through. Back by a large metal tank shaped like an ancient submarine set in a concrete base surrounded by tall dead weeds. He was filling the propane canisters lining the bed of a pick-up so beat-to-hell it looked like the ghost of a pick-up. He had only two canisters left to fill. He stood up from the one he was filling when Case walked up. The truck was running, its headlights, set on high-beam, staring unblinkingly at the rusted door of the station's toilet. Like there were a group of paparazzi waiting for George Clooney to emerge in a tuxedo on Oscar night. The door bearing the dents of countless frustrated feet and fists.

I know. I was still a ways off when you called. The weather, too. Slowed things down.

Just as big as before. Memory hadn't embellished the intimidating bulk of the guy. He was wearing a shapeless black work-jacket. Too small, as if they probably didn't make a size big enough. The rain falling unheeded on his bare head. The lank hair hanging in oily strands around his broad face. High cheekbones. Those round eyes, too bright, like a bird's. Beard a grizzled shovel blade. The light above the tank revealing all this. Half-revealing it, yellow and dying, at the top of its tall pole. The rain visible in its sickly corona, a mere mist, like atomized tears.

61 Bang

This vehicle had a license plate. Case made it a point to look. But the plate was from Louisiana. Hanging to the rear bumper by a twisted coat hanger. Like some kind of an afterthought. He tried to commit the number to memory, as if it might be significant.

So.

The man had caught Case's darting glances towards the truck. How could he not? There was nothing else in the vicinity of interest to him at the moment except for Case. Case had his undivided attention. The man watched him like an exotic insect on a stick. Advantage hillbilly.

He averted his head. Spit. Eyes never leaving Case. You had a key. A hint of mockery in his tone. He doesn't believe it, doesn't believe it for a moment.

Right. Case reaching into his coat, into the front pocket of his shirt. Something flickering across the hillbilly's face for a moment. A tightness. Then disappearing almost as quickly having seen an absence of something in Case's. The hose still in his left hand, dangling, hissing propane into the air. Case pointed at it. Shouldn't you shut that off?

Don't worry about it.

The girl wasn't in the truck. Not that Case could see anyway. She might be crouched down in the back of the cab. It was one of those large-bodied, heavy-duty pickups. V-8. Extra half-cab. She could be back there, sneaking peeks from one of the filthy windows. Waiting to see what miracle God could perform. But Case didn't think so. Didn't have a reason why he didn't think so. Just didn't.

You got my key or what.

The hillbilly thought this was about something else and he was right. So he was surprised to see the key between Case's fingers, held out towards him in the halogen glare. Case, stepping forward with it. It was a large gold key that he had slipped off his key-ring back in the parking lot of the rest stop. Case had long forgotten what lock it opened, what that lock protected. Whatever it was, it wasn't important to him anymore. Something he didn't need to protect. Something he was never going back for. There was a lot of that he'd left behind.

61 Bang

Taking a step forward, towering over Case, his tiny eyes fixed on the key. An amused look on his face. As if he were imagining what Case would look like with a broken neck. The hillbilly plucked the key from Case's fingers, held it aloft, turned it over in the light, one way, then the other.

His gun was back in the car, in the trunk, packed into a pocket carved out in the protective styrofoam of an empty George Foreman Grill box. He didn't think it would be necessary to carry it. He didn't even want to think of it as an option if things got dicey. Why should things get dicey, anyway? He was only here as a Good Samaritan. He wasn't here to cause any trouble. He had to get back on the road. He had a job to do. The very last thing he wanted to do right now, under any circumstances, was shoot someone.

That whole line of reasoning, Case now realized, was a mistake. He should have taken the gun with him.

You said you found this where? Squinting an amused eye down at Case, like it were a trick question.

At the convenience store. Near the counter. On the floor. Right after you left. I thought maybe it might have fallen out of your pocket when you reached for your change of something.

You usually go through all this trouble to return a key? You usually such a helpful son-of-a-bitch?

Case shrugged, hiding the cold in him. His voice sounded dead to his own ears. One thing led to another. It didn't start out seeming like it would be any trouble.

Things are like that sometimes, aint they? Start out one way, end another.

The hillbilly grinning. Never heard of flossing. Water pics not big sellers around here.

I guess so.

You guess so?

Yeah.

You seem pretty nervous.

Maybe it's that propane hose. I really think you should shut off the valve. If either of us light a cigarette, we're both going to the moon.

61 Bang

That's funny. You're a funny guy. Why do you keep looking at the truck?

What?

You heard me.

I heard you. I just don't know what you mean.

Yes you do. You looking for the girl?

Yes, Case thought, I wish I had the gun. The gun might be necessary after all. Sometimes you have to shoot people whether it's convenient or not. That's the tragedy of it. To say, 'what girl?' would sound stupid. To say anything else was trouble. Case said what was left. She your daughter?

What business is that of yours?

None.

Right.

Look, you got your key. That's all I came back for. I got to be on my way.

It ain't my key. I told you. I never seen it before. What she say to you. In the store. My daughter.

Nothing. She didn't say anything to me.

I told her a thousand times not to talk to strangers. Aint safe. Perverts all over the place. I gave her a good whippin' for talking to you. You might as well tell me what she said.

I told you. She didn't say anything.

Grinning through the thorns of his beard. This close up Case could even see bits of that day's meals between his teeth. Or the day's before. Did he know about the note? Had he beaten it out of the girl already? Was he going to try to beat it out of Case? He wished he had the gun. What the hell good was a gun if you didn't have it to hand? He thought he could smell the propane. Or did he just think so, because of the hissing?

Hope you don't mind if I keep the key. Already in the pocket of his greasy denim jacket. Never know. I might find something in this town it opens.

The grin again, if it ever really left. He doesn't move, standing his ground, planted like a bear, the leaking propane hose, the glittering eyes. No one around. If Case had the gun, would he have shot him on the spot? Spared that kid whatever grief she still had coming. Would he have made that awful mistake? Would it have been a mistake?

Case taking two steps back. A third. Trying to look casual. Don't run. Don't challenge. Don't turn your back, but don't stare directly into the eyes. The law of the jungle.

Suit yourself.

Turning his back, he had to eventually, couldn't walk backwards all the way to the Mustang. He wouldn't have been surprised if the hillbilly bum-rushed him. He could hear his footsteps on the wet macadam, feel his rough hands on the collar of his coat, jerking him back. What would Case be able to do about it, anyway? If he had the gun…

Back in the car, Case turned the key in the ignition. His hands were trembling. Glanced out the window. The hillbilly hadn't moved an inch. Just stood there, staring at Case, not grinning anymore. Just standing there, staring. Buried in his own thoughts regarding Case. What to do about him, if it came to that. Case put the car into gear and pulled out of the lot wondering if was going to come to that. He figured it probably was.

16.

The next morning she was standing in line at the security check at LAX. Boarding the first available flight to Atlanta. She was dressed for travel. Light-weight cable-knit sweater. Camouflage-patterned sweatpants. Avia sneakers. Pale blue bandana wrapped around her head. Big sunglasses. All very fashionable. One of thousands. She shuffled forward, emptied the contents of her handbag, submitted her carry-on to x-ray, collected her things on the other end of the conveyor belt. Removed her sneakers upon request. Stood there, like a scarecrow, like Christ, arms spread, as a security agent passed the magic wand over her.

Ms. Sassoon.

She turns her head. A second agent, a clipboard with a computer print-out in his hand.

Yes.

Can you please come with me?

What's this about.

Just routine. Please come with me.

Persha Sassoon. Perhsadonna Sassoon, if you were looking at her birth certificate, her passport, her driver's license. If you were looking at her criminal record, sealed, so you shouldn't be, since all of those crimes took place while she was still a minor. Not that terribly long ago either, if you were looking at things in the conventional sense, except there was nothing conventional about Pershadonna Sassoon, except that you might reasonably say that she was never really a minor.

Are you having a good time?

61 Bang

There were two of them in the little room. One of them a woman, heavy-set, with a look that said trouble if you didn't know what to look for. Persha, however, did. A woman, just to give the appearance that everything was on the up-and-up. She was manipulating Persha's breasts in a way that had nothing to do with looking for weapons of mass destruction.

Sorry ma'am. We're just doing our jobs. Homeland Security, you know. We're at level orange. Can you please remove your shoes?

I did that out there.

Yes, ma'am. We understand that. Can you please remove your shoes? Your socks, too.

It had taken Persha a long time to figure out what her mother had been thinking. Giving her a name like Pershadonna. Even with the explanation it didn't make any sense. Only some time later did Persha figure it out. Taking shelter in the Camden Public Library, pretending to be a student, fooling no one, but they took pity, let her be. She spent long hours sleeping over an open book at one of the reading carrels. One day she woke up drooling on a Who's Who in mythology and found the answer to the mystery. Her mother had named her, misnamed her, really, after Persephone. A Greek girl who'd been carried off by the King of the Underworld. Demeter, her grief-stricken mother, refused to allow Spring to come unless her daughter was returned. A deal was struck and Persephone was allowed back from the grave every six months. Did her mother even know about this myth, how beautiful it was, or was Persephone just a word she heard somewhere and thought sounded pretty? Unique. Special enough for the daughter she love, yet all but abandoned. Crack-addict that she was. Whore that she was. Her mother, who died when Persha was twelve. Died, at twenty-five. Who knows how exactly, or why, who cared but Persha, anyway?

Runaway. Crack-baby. Whore-spawn. She knew what she was on the food-chain. What the predators saw.

Anyone who pities the helplessness of the child doesn't know the resourcefulness possible in a twelve-year-old girl. Sugar and spice when necessary, but also everything not-so-nice. Persha worked all the circles of society south of its heart, the entire alimentary canal. It was surprising what you found down there; in fact, it seemed everything passed through at one point or another. Cops, celebrities, businessmen, politicians, everything and everyone, in the end, without exception, turned to shit. No one better than anyone else. With an upbringing like Persha's, that was the most important lesson of all.

She survived, doing what she had to. It might seem like a man's world, but it's not. It's really a woman's world. We just let them take it out and play with it. Her mother used to tell her that, and Persha confirmed it for herself over and over again.

Child's play, once you got the hang of it.

Hands *caressing* her vulva, the woman between her legs doing a very thorough job of it.

She killed her first man at twelve-and-a-half. At that age, you take things as they come. No big deal. You hardly think anything of it. What do you know about what's normal or not. Outside of the world you live in, that is. Her second and third before she was thirteen. Men were dangerous, but only like dogs were dangerous, if you didn't know how to take the upper hand. Keep the upper hand. If you didn't keep your wits about you. Cause they could turn. Turn at the first sign of weakness. Pack animals that they were, always seeking their master. They paid you to grovel at your feet, paid you to smack them around, paid you to expose themselves to you.

As for the Sassoon, well, that one was easy. The shampoo. Her mother thought it was such an elegant name. Persha had created a mythology of her own to explain her father, that mystery man not even her mother had known. For a long time she liked to imagine he was Michael Jordan. No real reason for that. Persha had no idea who Michael Jordan was at the time. Just that he was rich, famous, a legend of some sort. It could have been anyone similar. It was, after that. A series of black film stars, musicians, and sports legends. Whoever was the most popular at the moment. *That* was her father. Later, Persha developed a more realistic myth, almost as unreasonable, and far less glamorous. That she was engendered from the best qualities of the various men her mother had fucked. A kind of super-sperm. A distillation of the strongest qualities of the African race. Which left a lot of things unexplained, her cappuccino-colored skin, the exotic, vaguely Arabic features that were no doubt partly responsible for the special attention she routinely received. Sometimes unwanted, like now. At airports. The hands now running themselves over her toned ass. Not that she played down her look. Her radical chic. Ever. She was Persha to the maxxx. Persha 24/7/365 and 1 extra on the leap year. Rebel. Rock'n'roll nigger. Her diamond piercings. Her tattoos. Most people thought they were tears, black tears earned in prison, or in memory of some inconsolable heartbreak. Persha, who'd never been to prison. Persha, who never cried for nothing or noone. She didn't bother to correct them. Didn't bother to tell them they were yods. Symbols of the life-force. God's energy in the universe. His fire. His Word. She didn't bother, period.

Taken in at fifteen by a man in the neighborhood. Not exactly a pimp. Not exactly a drug dealer. But you couldn't say he wasn't those things either. A capitalist, you might say. Such as that neighborhood could produce. He'd taken note of Persha's aptitudes. Aptitudes, that's how he put it. She did some jobs for KO. This and that. And by the time she was sixteen, she'd killed nine men total. She didn't think much of it. It was something she was good at, that's all. Something she could make money doing at the same time. Not a bad deal. In the end she killed KO, too, rounding it off at ten, and used the money she made on the contract to pull up stakes. Leave Camden. Relocate in California. Start a business of her own.

Okay Ms. Sassoon. You can put your shoes and socks back on. You're good to go. Enjoy your trip to Atlanta.

What. No cavity search? Maybe I have a surface-to-air missile stashed in my rectum.

We're sorry for any inconvenience, Ms. Sassoon. Regulations. We have to be careful.

This from the male agent. The female, stripping off her rubber gloves, saying nothing. Like she's thinking about that cavity-search. Filing away images of it for later.

Right. I'm sure you do. Pulling on her socks, her shoes. Looking up at the female guard. No humor in either pair of eyes. Something far less humorous in Persha's.

61 Bang

You got off easy this time. I usually expect dinner and a movie before a groping like that.

Again, we're very sorry for the inconvenience. The male agent again, looking uncomfortable. Just wanting to get on with his life. No law suits or formal complains, etc.

Straightening her sweater. Retrieving her handbag. Her carry-on. Then on to the gate. On to the plane. First-class. Reclining seat. No more problems. Lift-off. Clouds.

A scotch after a few hundred miles. No one in the seat beside her.

More clouds.

Between them, all that cold clear frozen emptiness. One giant blue ice cube. Reminded her of a poem she once read in the library as a little girl. A woman falls out of an airplane and drops helplessly through the sky. Losing bits of clothing as she goes. shoes, dress, bra, panties…a free-fall striptease to earth. A girl falls out of an airplane and the poet turns it into a goddamn sex act. A wet dream. Some guy named Dickey wrote it. Dick, all right. Beautiful, romantic, complete nonsense. It figured. Just like a man.

17.

Another couple of days at the Paradise were in order. Case paid for them. In cash. The desk clerk making the smallest possible noise of surprise at seeing Case again. Probably didn't see very many of the same faces twice in his line of work. Lucky, for him, if you considered the faces he was likely to confront. He even permitted himself a small joke to mark the occasion.

The usual?

Yeah. The presidential suite wasn't it?

Case pocketed the card key. Left the same instructions as last time. No disturbances, no visitors, etc. Bought a Hershey's Krackel bar from the vending machine against the wall. A Biloxi Sun Herald from another next to it. Then he went to his room.

There it was again. Home Sweet Home, for the time being.

Desk. Mirror. Chair. Bed. Painting on the wall. Blah, blah, blah. All the same as before. A state all too often undervalued, in Case's worldly opinion.

He sat on the side of the bed. Unwrapped the Hershey Krackel bar.

Took a bite.

Chewed.

11 milligrams of cholesterol. 53 grams of sugar. 27 grams of fat. 512 calories.

Stared at the folds in the curtain hanging over the window.

Took another bite.

Chewed.

61 Bang

Okay, so here you are wiseguy. I told you not to come back, but here you are anyway. Now what?

Case listened hard, but there was no answer forthcoming. Not from anywhere. When was there ever?

What exactly had he hoped to accomplish by confronting that hillbilly again? Prove that his first and lingering impression of the man had been wrong? That whatever the note that ragamuffin kid slipped him in the snack food aisle of the convenience store hadn't really meant what Case feared it meant? Probably, but it didn't turn out that way. It seemed to Case that very seldom in his life was he ever right about anything, but when he was, Christ Almighty, was he sorry.

Case finished the candy bar. Crumpled the wrapper and threw it in the small wicker basket under the night table. Ecclesiastes and his bleak wisdom tucked away in a corner of the drawer. Case knew it all by heart.

He sat there, stared.

Now what? Not in the big sense, but in the next ten minutes.

A shower. Shave.

Case undressed in the bathroom. His clothes fresh that morning, limp already, secreting a perfume of soured sweat. Fear. Exhaustion. Eau de Failure. Not just regarding the present situation, but of an entire life. Poor nutrition. Sleeplessness. Age. The aroma of a sick animal, that's what it was, sick in its den, in its own skin. No deodorant in the world could cover that up. No soap scrub it away.

Case stood in the pile of his discarded clothes, lying at his feet like a discarded shell. Looked at himself in the mirror as the shower heated up. Surveyed the wreckage. Man, it was grim, this visual update. The accretions of fat in improbable places. The loss of tone and form. The skin like an elastic without any snap. Even the color was off—a white that reminded him of something poisonous, some kind of wet mushroom in the woods, maybe. The pouches under his eyes, the softening of the jawline, the sling of flesh under his chin. The steam from the shower mercifully obliterating the rest of it because otherwise Case might not have been able to look away, like a

61 Bang

deer in the headlights of a future racing towards him like the biggest tractor-trailer ever.

Into the shower then. Soaping himself. Feeling around, but none too carefully, for lumps where lumps shouldn't be. Pain, etc. Washing his hair, then rinsing away the hair that was left in his hands. The rotting of the body, right in front of your very eyes. Like a horror movie, but without any happy ending. Not even a chance of one.

What he wanted was enough money to finish rotting in comfort. In style, if you will. But mainly in comfort. In peace. He didn't want to have to fight to survive any more because he didn't have a lot of fight left in him. He wanted to retire. To see out his last twenty, twenty-five years without having to worry about how he was going to buy his next hamburger. Otherwise it really wouldn't be worth it. If it were too much trouble, it would be better to get it all over with it sooner rather than later.

Case, the Stoic.

Out of the shower, drying hair and feet, underarms, crotch. Wrapping himself in a towel and back to the bed and his homosexual relationship with Mr. Jim Beam. Remote. Click. TV. Yakking heads. Laugh tracks. Everything brighter and bigger and more real than it ever really is. Darling, the end of the world is coming and I haven't got anything to serve for dinner. Ha ha ha. People biting into cheese sticks and the expressions on their faces are like a kid's on Christmas morning. Gargling with mouthwash is orgasmic. Those new trash bags make you young again. He flicked through the channels looking for the news from anywhere north of nowhere. Went through about six hundred of them. Unscrewed the Jim Beam and took it straight from the bottle. Watched a commercial for something. Christ, he couldn't even tell what it was they were selling. But everyone happy, deliriously happy goddammit, to have it, whatever the hell it was. Spread open the Biloxi Sun Herald. An inch-and-a-half about a murder in North Carolina that was worth another pull of the Jim Beam. Then another. No suspects. No motive. No shit.

They were on the trail, but that was no surprise. Ever since he'd found Eddie the way he did, Case knew the chase had begun. There

61 Bang

was always a chance that the whole thing could have gone off without a hitch, the gun delivered, the deposit made, and off to sipping Mai Tai's in Tahiti or wherever they served them. There's always a chance that you'll wake up tomorrow to the announcement that they've found the cure for death. There's a chance but, admittedly, not much of one.

Case found the remote under one of his damp buttocks and waved it at the TV. Flicked through the next six hundred channels. Found CNN sandwiched between some guy hawking a real-estate buying course and a woman dicing onions in a food processor. You could make millions buying the foreclosed properties of befuddled widows and a mock Coq de Vin for dinner. It was all here, the secrets to everything, at the press of a thumb.

Case lifted the bottle. Stared at it for a moment.

Hi there Jim.

It's a big world, lots of wars and famines and genocides to cover, but a major U.S. city on the edge of a full-scale race riot can still be squeezed in for a minute or two. Case watched a lot of angry black faces behind a barricade. Police in masks and shields like something out of Star Wars. Night scenes of crowds throwing rocks and bottles. Blackened cars, fire licking out of their windows. Teenagers being led off in handcuffs. An overturned police cruiser. Citizens with bloodied clothes tied around their heads. They still had a lid on it, but it was trembling, steam leaking out the sides. A nervous-looking mayor addressing a press conference. Across town, his counterpart, an exultant pompadour-wearing character in a snake-oil salesman suit addressing a mob. Signs. Banners. Chants. Stop Police Brutality. Cop=Killer. End Racism. Etc. Cut to the latest explosion in Iraq. The latest pile of bodies in Somalia. A smoking tank pointed at something or other. Half a building. Case turned the TV off. Sat there. Stared at the milky green-black of the screen.

You didn't have to be a genius to figure out what Eddie had given him to deliver. Or why. You just had to be an idiot to agree to do it. Not that Case knew right off. Not that he really had any choice when he figured it out. Which was right about the time that he found Eddie taking that empty bath. Once Case knew, he was already fucked. Of all the people still alive who knew that kid had a gun when the cops stopped him, that he arguably had at least some of those sixty-one shots coming to him, Case was probably the one they'd trust the least. And yet, he was the one who had the truth. The gun. That ought to be good for something. A deal, of some sort. Shouldn't it?

He was sitting there in the dark, not awake, not sleeping. Just sitting there in the nothingness. He didn't even realize it until the headlights swept across the wall. A car, outside the window, idling. Another guest of Paradise?

Case sat there. The car did, too.

He heard what sounded like the squawk of a voice through a radio. Broken by static. Tried to hear what was being said. Impossible. Like a foreign language. More crackles and snippets of talk. Then dead silence. Lifted the bottle, forgotten at his side. Lowered it, unsipped. Now what? Waiting. Tick-tock tick-tock. For what? Tick-tock tick-tock. For nothing, apparently, nothing was happening, thank god. The squeal of tires in reverse, the light withdrawing, swinging wildly across the walls, exploding in the mirror. Pause. One last glance back, perhaps? Then the crunch and squeal of tires again. Darkness. Blessed darkness. You never guess how much you'll miss it until it's gone, until you're forced to see things in the light. Case relaxed, such as that word applied. Back against the pillows, into the darkness. Only the buzz, if you listened very closely, of the neon sign.

Case listened very closely.

Nothing.

Alone in Paradise. For now.

18.

Another day. Already. Case slits his eyes to confirm it. Like a lizard's, crusty with the desert sand. Yup. Another morning, alright. That makes what now? Sixteen thousand of them? Jesus Christ. He shuts his eyes. Back to sleep, dreamless as a rock. He wakes up again in the afternoon. The light a little better this time, a little more to his liking, less cheery for one thing, less of it for another. This time he gets all the way up. In stages. Like unfolding a complicated beach chair left out all winter. Off to the bathroom, where he shaves, after a fashion. Studies the grimace. Then, not remembering for sure, another shower. Soaping himself up, thinking, well, even if I took one last night, it's not like I'm going to smell too good if I take another one this morning. Okay, this afternoon, then.

He spends the day asking questions. Barber, grocer, filling station attendant, hardware store guy, waitress. No one has ever seen the hillbilly. No one knows who he's talking about. The same blank look. The same automatic response. Who? The guy looks like Bigfoot and no one has ever taken any notice of him passing through a town of maybe four hundred people? Case has spent less than forty-eight hours in this shithole and most of those alone in his motel room passed out cold and he's bumped into the bastard twice already. True. One of those times he asked for it. But still. The convenience store clerk again. Nope. He doesn't know who Case is talking about either. Doesn't fit any descriptions.

I left my cell phone number with you. In case he lost the key that I found here. Remember? Well, he called me for that key. Who did you give the number to?

61 Bang

Didn't give it to nobody.

This guy from Pakistan or Afghanistan. Wherever. But he's got the local vernacular down pat. The talking points.

Tacked it to the community board over there. He points to a corkboard covered with torn pieces of paper. Oil-stained. Smudged. Scrawled with handwritten messages. Mostly selling crap. Used backhoes. Car parts. Puppies. Guess someone must have taken it from there.

Yeah. Guess so.

Anything else?

No. Just the coffee. And a pack of Camels.

Breakfast, Case thinks, ten minutes later, lighting up by the dismal little pond. Lunch, too, for that matter. Maybe even an early dinner. Better make it another then. He lights a fresh cigarette. To hell with saving his lungs. He punches a hole in the coffee lid, takes a sip, stares at the flat grey surface of the pond. Take another sip. How deep is that thing? When was the last time I lay with a woman? A woman I loved? What have I done with my life? Etc. The usual monologue, in other words.

It was well passed dark when he went down to the Evergreen. Took a wobbly little table in the back. To which he added a beer and a dish of salted nuts. Sipped and stared. The typical rat box but with local accoutrements. A big old dusty boar's head sneering from the wall overhead. Ugly as the devil's ass. Yellowed newspaper articles of now irrelevant events. Hardly legible. So old even the glass hadn't protected them. The Stars and Bars. Some memorabilia from the Atlanta Olympics. A comically defaced portrait of William Tecumseh Sherman. That kind of thing. Cowboy crooning on the sound system, such as it was.

Not much in the way of a Thursday night crowd. A few old-timers at the bar, nursing beers. What conversation there was consisting largely of sentence fragments. Telegraphic. Filled with in-jokes. Just a few words necessary to reconstitute the full effect. A football game on the TV mounted above them, sound turned down. Once in a while someone looks up, points, makes a comment.

Case munching oily nuts.

61 Bang

Another beer. Yeah.

Waiting. For what he's not sure.

A taciturn farmer. A table of good-ole boys sharing a pitcher. A pool table with blighted green felt squeezed in by the one bathroom. Two guys in flannel shirts going through a rack of balls like they were trying their best to miss the pockets. The bartender couldn't say. Never seen any guy like Case was describing. Didn't do his drinking at the Evergreen, in any event. Can't say why he wouldn't, eh boys? The geezers at the end of the bar guffawing on cue.

Thanks.

Don't mention it.

Nothing happens. Three more beers worth of nothing happening. Case gets up to take a piss. Comes back and takes his seat. Sips, chews peanuts. Listens to the cowboy crooning, the truncated jokes, the bony clack of ineptly struck billiard balls. Then at eleven Tournier comes ambling in. He sits at the bar, nods his hellos to the geezers, the bartender, the assembled usuals, gets his beer lickety-split, and turns to look at Case sitting at his wobbly table as if he were expecting him.

You can see something in the Law's face, even though he quickly replaces it with something else. Case wouldn't venture to guess what it was he'd seen, but what replaced it wasn't good either, even if it was dressed up with a smile, especially dressed up with a smile such as the Law was wearing now. There was something a little boiled-eyed about it.

Tournier and that smile were coming towards him now, a beer in each hand, a fake country-howdy in his mouth.

Well, if it isn't our very own town V.I.P. sitting back here in the shadows. I'd recognize you anywhere, Mr. John Case. And wish I had recognized you anywhere but here. Just couldn't stay away from our lovely little burg, could you? The sheriff took the seat across the table, settled his bulk into it. He set one of the beers in front of Case.

Can't say as I blame you. It's the best-kept secret in the South. Could never get away from it myself. Enjoying the hospitality of the Evergreen? A fine establishment, no? Nods at the beer in front of

61 Bang

Case. Compliments of the sheriff's department. Taps it with his own, sips, grins. Drink up.

Thanks, but I think I might be at my limit. Don't want to leave here and have you pull me over. Can't afford a DWI. Got to move on, you know.

Oh I know. But experience tells me you're already over the limit. Just by the look of you.

Sip of beer. Eyes fixed on Case like a panther's. Ready to pounce.

What you say, I drop you off at the Paradise my own self when you're done? You can pick up your car tomorrow. It ain't but a fair hike. Otherwise, you're right. You just might get that DWI after all. Got to do my duty, after all. You might say it's kind of an obsession with me. No sense letting a good beer go to waste, is there? Or the fine southern hospitality.

That smile, Case thought, he'd be wearing it if he had a piece of my intestine in a pliers.

No sense in it at all.

Case shrugged, sipped the beer. You know, sheriff, maybe you can help me out with something else.

Oh? The Law lifts an eyebrow. Takes a sip of beer. Now maybe I can at that. Being a public servant and all.

There's a guy in this town. Big. Hairy. Drives a double-wide pick-up with Louisiana plates. An SUV stripped to its primer without any tags at a;;. Must be close to seven-feet tall, three hundred plus. Quite a fucking sight, and no one's ever seen him. In a town this size. That seems kind of odd to me.

Oh. How so?

Perfectly deadpan, the Law delivers this line. Time to raise the ante.

Had a little girl with him, too. The first time I ran into him. She didn't look well-cared for either, if you know what I mean.

Not exactly. Sip of beer. Maybe you can be clearer.

She didn't look like she belonged with him.

That so? You been here all of two days and you can tell who belongs with who? That's something. I must admit myself amazed.

61 Bang

Are you with Child Services, Mr. Case? Pause a beat for the answer that isn't necessary. I didn't think so. What is it that you want with this town, Mr. Case?

I told you straight at the start. I'm just passing through.

So why don't you pass? You see, I hear you say that you're passing through but then I ask myself if it's so, why do I see you still sitting here in front of me?

This guy, he hung me up, that's all. Something seems a little off about him.

And that's business of yours?

The kid, I guess. It's the kid.

Something's off about a lot of folks. Specially around here. Something frankly off about you, too, Mr. Case. If you don't mind me saying. Could be this man comes from someplace back in the hills. Pretty sparse and unpopulated country back there. Rough and isolated. Not much in the way of social conditioning. People like that take to doing things their own damn way. And we ought to let'em if they aren't hurting anyone else. They don't come to town much anyway, just to pick up essentials and such, and when they do they don't tend to do much interacting with the locals. Could be it was someone like that you seen and nothing more than that. No big mystery. No big conspiracy. Just country, Mr. Case. Country style.

Case didn't buy it. Not the explanation, not the corn-pone delivery. The Law put his big hands on the table. Not red and rawboned as you might expect, but pale and long, almost elegant, like the hands of harpist. A harpist! Now have I discharged my duties as a public servant to your satisfaction, Mr. Case?

Case shrugged. Sipped his beer. You've done your best. And he meant it.

Good, that's all we can in this vale of tears and ashes. In that case I'll leave you to enjoy your complimentary beer and a last night at our very own Mobile guide rated two-star roadside motel and then I trust you'll do what you came here to do first thing come morning. How did you put it? Pass through. Now you be sure to let me know when you're ready for that ride back to the Paradise, you hear?

61 Bang

And with that the Law rose and lumbered back to the bar with his beer. Took his place among the geezers. Case studied the vanishing the archipelagoes of foam on his beer. The clock ticked on. Things happened and didn't happen. Nothing was any clearer.

19.

Time to go, it was always that time, eventually, wherever you were, and this time it was long-past that time and that was the plain truth. Time it was for Case to move on to somewhere else and wait for it to be time to go there, too. Planting his palms on the table, none too steady itself, he was now reminded, Case stood up. Surveyed the situation. Took stock of himself. Until you've stood up, you never really know how much you've had, and when Case felt the floor steady under his feet after a couple of wooly seconds of wild uncertainty and fuzzy logic, he figured that he hadn't had nearly as much as he feared.

No Tournier.

The sheriff was nowhere in sight. Maybe he'd gone no further than the toilet in the corner. No matter. Case wasn't hanging around to find out. He had no intention, anyway, of accepting the sheriff's invitation of a ride back to the Paradise. He was gambling that the sheriff wasn't waiting outside, planning on pulling him over twenty yards out of the parking lot, and issuing him a DWI summons. Bullshit, all of it. Case hadn't been able to figure out what Tournier's game was, but he hoped to avoid playing it.

Across the floor to the exit. Uneven, the wood beneath his shoes. Rough-hewn boards. Like a choppy wooden lake. So Case worked on looking natural. Walking on water, like some kind of goddamn miracle. Case shaking his head. What the hell was he going on about?

61 Bang

No last second reappearance of the sheriff. Door. Opening as he reaches for it. A guy coming in as Case is going out. Mr. Bib Overalls and Mr. Lean Jeans.

After you.

After you.

No one moves. A comedy of courtesy. No, not really. A parody of it was more like it. A battle of wills in a doorway. Everything a fucking struggle. Even exiting a bar.

Okay. Thanks.

Case stepping passed the man holding the door. Is it still raining? It seems not, not really. He finds his car not too far from where he thinks he left it, doesn't take too long to figure out which key opens the thing, how to insert it in the door lock, all that. There are times, no exaggeration, that those things can take upwards of fifteen, twenty minutes. Safely ensconced behind the wheel. VA-ROOOM! The car starts right up. Damn, this is a fine piece of machinery, Case thinks, suddenly and unaccountably nostalgic. Maybe when this is all over I'll have it restored—paint job, chrome fitting, interiors, the works. Lights. Wipers, just in case. Check the mirrors. Put it into gear and back up. Slowly.

Out on the road. Dark and winding. Like he's riding up someone's small intestine. High-beams. Don't want to hit a fucking deer. Saw one on this very road on the drive into town. Exploded from the inside out, like someone had rigged a bomb inside it. Shit, the high-beams are already on. Driving with exaggerated care, like a sixteen-year-old testing for his license. Watching his speed. Tapping his brakes. Accelerating out of the curves. Hands at the ten and two o'clock positions. Ridiculous. Best way to get into an accident was to be too careful. To think too much. Damn, the road ahead. Black and shiny. Like a ribbon of oil. You'd think it had been laid down especially to throw him off it.

Behind him, headlights. Where'd they come from, anyway?

Where does anything come from? Death, for instance. One day, it's just there. For that matter. Where does anything go? Life, for example. One day, it's just gone. Christ almighty, a philosopher to the end, that's what I am. In the mirrors, Case watched the lights grow brighter, like in one of those movies about alien abductions. No, it was true, he'd driven a lot more fucked-up than this, which didn't really prove anything, except maybe just how relative everything was. The entire inside of the car was lit up now. What the hell did they have that thing equipped with anyway? Searchlights? Maybe Tournier had decided to pull him over for that DWI after all. Jesus Christ. Visions of horrific capture, Texas Chainsaw-style, in a tiny cell in this jerkwater town. Case waited for the explosion of cherry-red lights, the siren, all that commotion. The spiteful bastard. Just to fuck around with him a little more. The world was full of guys like that. That's what made the world what it was. Part of it, anyway.

Grip the wheel tighter. Set his jaw. Don't be suckered into going any faster, breaking any fucking laws. Don't give him any excuse. Any justification. What was this, a time-warp, Mississippi circa 1964, for crissakes? Bastard couldn't get any closer to him now if he were sitting in the passenger seat shining a flashlight in his face. What the hell did he think he was doing? Perfectly sober now. All he had to do was touch his fender, it could send Case careening for the ditch. No use looking in the rearview now—it was like looking through a mail slot into the fucking sun.

Imagine riding along like that for three miles because that's what they did, Case checked the odometer. And then the Hummer, because that's what it was, swung out into the narrow breakdown lane, sped up, held even for a few moments, and then sped up again and effortlessly passed the Mustang on the right. Case braked, had been breaking the moment the white Hummer pulled alongside of him, watching the tinted windows, waiting for the emergence of a gun barrel. At the side of the road himself now, idling in the breakdown lane, wipers wiping, headlights reaching out into the misty void. Trembling, all of him, with fear. Rage.

Assholes, that's all they'd been. Just a bunch of joyriding backwoods assholes. Could have gotten someone killed for no reason.

He got the car back onto the road. Arrived without further incident at the Paradise Motel. Pulled into his usual spot. Turned off the engine. Sat there. He was still shaking, dammit. He'd need to get

61 Bang

drunk all over again if he was going to settle down. Okay. Drunker. Nothing different about the motel parking lot. Not that he noticed. That's what he'd think later, anyway. Two or three cars of no particular account. One of them presumably belonging to the night-manager. So where did that blinding light come from all over again when he stepped out of the car? Whoever it was that called out to him from inside that light.

Now hey there!

Case turned, crouching away from the blow instinctively, but that didn't help, or didn't help enough. Something impossibly heavy crashed into the side of his face. That's it, Case thought, it's a fucking knockout in the opening seconds. Down he went and the boots found him down there, hard to say how many of them, but it felt like a goddamn army of them. Stomping and crashing. Marching over him. The enemy invading. Into the time-honored fetal position he went, our first and last stance vis-à-vis the world, not that it helped much either. He thought at some point that someone would bend down and give him a reason, or a message, or a warning, but no one did. It was a soundless beating except for the muffled grunts Case made when the blows landed.

If he were unconscious it wasn't for long, but then how would he know? He felt the grit biting into his cheek. Saw, close-up, the band of neon pink light reflected in the cold puddle that the lashes of his swollen eye disturbed each time he blinked. Up onto his hands and knees after a time, life goes on, his keys splayed out on the asphalt a few feet away. He crawled over to them. Standing erect seemed out of the question, so did the question of unlocking the motel door, but he was in luck with regard to the door: it was already open.

He crawled on through. Crawled over the shards of broken lamp, the overturned drawers, the tangle of bed sheets and clothes, the slivers of mirrored glass. Dragged his wet and aching carcass into the bathroom, propped it up on the toilet with his forearms and elbows, and puked up a great gout of blood and beer. He was thinking about his life then, the arc of the whole thing up to now, the way you often do at moments like this. Between pukes, he tried to locate the exact moment when it had all gone irretrievably wrong. When that last wrong turn was made and there was no turning back. When he was lost forever. But it was impossible. As futile as yanking at a loose thread. Everything was connected to everything else and it all unraveled no matter how careful he was. He thought maybe if he could have worked it out with that second wife. He really had loved her, there'd been some genuine magic there, even if her neuroses had made it impossible to leave the room for a glass of water without coming back to find her with another man. Or maybe his daughter. If he could only have devoted himself to her. Sacrificed himself, or whatever. His stomach convulsed and Case puked into the toilet again. Oh, who was he kidding? He wiped his mouth, spitting and gasping. Nothing could have been any different. Nothing at all. He stared into the bowl. Shit, there's a tooth.

20.

Burning huts, smoke blackened faces, and the shrieking of the planes low over the trees that a moment later burst into flames like torches. The goop that stuck and melted the flesh off bones. Melted everything. Villages, jungles, entire families. These were the reruns she saw in her sleep. Dreams, that's what other people called them. Nightmares. What she called them were memories, lessons learned, home.

Mei woke up, worked herself up onto her elbows, stared at the window. A blue square in a black wall as her eyes adjusted. She never slept more than twenty minutes at a stretch. The least little thing roused her. A creak of a board. A shift in the wind. The enemy sneaking closer between the trees. It was all the same. There was always an enemy between the trees. Nothing had changed. Nothing ever would. Beside her, the man was sleeping, farting and wheezing, making 'man' noises, old man noises at that. All men 'the man,' more or less, not much difference between them when you came down to it, some a little better than others. But that little bit of difference made all the difference. This one, Leonard Tournier, being one of the better ones.

Out of bed she climbed, quiet as a shadow, not that there was any chance of waking the man without making a point of it. Just that it was her habit to be quiet. Sneaky, Elwood had called it, always getting mad to find her where he didn't expect her, not to find her where he did. You goddamn sneaky gook. Missing the point, as he almost always did. Misinterpreting her, not that she could explain. This was the way you survived in the jungle, by being quieter than other things, by not being where other things saw you first. This was the way you survived everywhere, everywhere being a jungle.

Mei lifted her robe from the rocking chair and eased into it. She slipped out of the bedroom , down the stairs. She might have been a ghost. Maybe she was a ghost.

One day her father walked her out of the village and off through the jungle. He didn't say why. Just told her to follow and didn't look back. That wasn't unusual. He wasn't a man given much to talking. Mei didn't ask questions either. She learned that if she kept quiet and waited she got her answers. She scrambled to catch up. It was a hot day, all the plants were sweating, and not a trace of freshness was left after a morning of drenching rain. They did not go far. Less than a mile it seemed. Close to a neighboring village where sometimes Mei had gone to play. Her father had come to a clearing and that's where he stopped and waited for her. The flies that had been biting her arms and legs the whole time were coming from this place. At first Mei couldn't figure out what all those long white pigs were doing stuck on the poles and smeared all over with blood and filth. Only when she got closer, her father taking her by the hand and leading her out into the clearing, did she see that they were men.

Mei had seen many terrible things. She knew not to ask 'why.' There was no answer to that question. The answer to that question was her father's flat opaque eyes, his taut expressionless face. The look that made Elwood call her a "cold heartless chink bitch." The look that made him hit her because he thought by hitting her it would change. Give her a different look. His hand would have fallen off first.

Don't ever forget. The good guys did this.

When her father did speak, it was important to listen. He was saying something he expected you to remember. Not just today or tomorrow but forever. Mei always remembered what he said that day in the clearing where the men were spitted like pigs.

In the kitchen, Mei opened the refrigerator. Poured a small glass of apricot juice. She looked out the window into the yard. The rain had let up and the clouds moved on a bit to let the moon through. She sipped the juice.

61 Bang

Her father disappeared not long after that day at the clearing. He walked off into the jungle with some other men of the village and did not come back. Then the soldiers came. They were looking for men they thought were hiding in the huts. Looking for weapons. They didn't find what they were looking for and no one in the village knew where it was so they killed everyone but the very old men that had been left behind and some of the women. These they herded together and Mei never saw any of them again. Then they burned the village to the ground. One of those soldiers was Elwood. He found her, hiding, in the roots of a dead tree. She left the jungle with him. Returned with him to this place, this house. It was neither good nor bad. She was alive. Many others were dead. It's what life was now. That was survival.

She was surprised when the doctor told her she was pregnant. Somehow she had simply never believed that it would happen to her. A child. And not just because Elwood was almost always very careful to use protection. Once the doctor convinced her it was true, however, Mei was surprised at how happy she felt. How proud. She thought that maybe she might never have felt happy if this feeling she felt now was happiness. She could not conceive that Elwood would not feel the same. That anyone would not feel the same. But Elwood did not. She thought that maybe she had misunderstood something. Or that he had misunderstood something. But his anger didn't change. He thought she had done it on purpose. As if having a baby was a weapon she had used to destroy him.

He wanted her to get rid of it. Yelled at her, beat her, threatened her. Even dragged her to a doctor who would do it. But no one could get her to sign the paper giving her permission and not even Elwood could get the doctor to do it without her okay. He was beside himself with rage. She thought he might really kill her he was so angry. But Mei had decided that she would die with her baby if it came to that. She would not let the baby die alone. Her mind was made up. Her face did not change expression. And one day, quite suddenly, it was Elwood who changed. He no longer beat or threatened her. He no longer demanded that she end her pregnancy. He even seemed as happy about the baby coming as Mei did. It

61 Bang

seemed almost too good to be true. Maybe, Mei though, Elwood had only needed more time than her to get used to the idea.

The baby came. A little dark-haired, dark-eyed boy. She named him Peter. A good solid American name, Mei thought. She felt very happy, very complete with her baby at her breast. Singing him to sleep. Elwood seemed happy, too. Maybe, she thought, a baby was what they had needed to be happy together. Maybe they should have had one a long time ago.

Then one night Mei could not get up. She heard Peter crying from the next room which was all wrong because Peter seldom cried and Mei was always awake to anticipate his needs. But this night her son was crying and she could not get up. Her body felt waterlogged all over. She couldn't even sit up. Couldn't even raise an arm. When she tried to call out to Elwood, it was like trying to push some immense weight out of her lungs. No sound seemed to come from her mouth. Just little puffs of breath.

The next morning they went to the sheriff's office and reported her baby missing. The window of the room they used a nursery had been jimmied open. Someone had stolen her child, some crazy person, that was the only explanation. But Mei could think of a different one. One that explained the money that Elwood seemed to have all of a sudden when before he was always complaining of having none. The nice things he was buying. Some people in town made a search but nothing came of it. And who would believe Mei? She was just a hysterical mother who had lost her child. Understandable, yes. Believable, no.

When she got pregnant again it was nearly four years later. This time Elwood didn't seem angry about it even in the beginning. This time it was Mei who wanted to go to the doctor and end it. But the doctor wouldn't end it this time either. He thought she should talk to someone, get counseling, and somehow it wasn't surprising to Mei that Elwood thought so too. You steal my baby this time too you bastard is what she shrieked at him. You sell him too you motherfucker. If she lived a thousand years the she would never forget the look on his face. Like an intersection where a lot of cars were about to crash into each other. He raised his hand to hit her.

61 Bang

She didn't even flinch. He did. The look in her own face must not have been so infuriatingly neutral any longer. He must have seen something there at last that could not be misinterpreted. He put his hand back down like it had gotten very heavy. Like it had turned to stone. He turned. Without another word he left and didn't come back until the police found him in an old hunting shack in the backcountry three days later.

As for Mei, she knew what she was going to do all along. That afternoon she sat on the floor of the old nursery upstairs with a short length of branch that had fallen from a birch tree in the yard. She shoved it deep inside herself, stabbed and stabbed it around until both her arms were slick to the elbow. The floor under her, too. Until the job was done. One of Elwood's friends came by looking for Elwood found her. Blood all over. Mei passed out, looking dead, a branch coming out of her. The ambulance, the hospital. She remembered none of it. Elwood came to take her home after a week. By then she had on her expressionless face again. No more babies for Mei, accident or not, not ever again. The doctor said. She and Elwood didn't talk about what happened. Didn't talk about it ever again.

She took another small sip of apricot juice and stared into the yard where he died. She could still see his ghost calling her. Imploring her. Trying to get some reaction from her. Calling her a heartless stone-faced gook. He was a good guy, too. Same as the man who shot him dead on that spot by the tree-line. They were all good guys. In their own minds. That's what made them so dangerous. That's what made life what it was. Her nightmares nothing more than memories. Never forget, her father said. No, never. Her father, also a good guy. The man upstairs, now snoring in her bed, this Tournier who shot her husband decades later. On her missing son's thirtieth birthday. She's with him now. Another small sip of apricot juice. Her stone-face. Some coincidence, huh?

21.

An amazing thing the internet, especially for a Black Widow such as herself, easy to take for granted, and she did, being a child of the age. Peshadonna fresh from the shower in her suite at the Atlanta Hyatt Regency, her smooth café au lait body wrapped in a thick white hotel robe of Egyptian cotton, a towel sculpted atop her head like an Egyptian queen. Lying back on the king-sized bed, minus the king, her elegant spider fingers dancing across the keyboard of her souped-up Sony Vaio. The email was waiting for her, Denny having delivered, as promised, a little something extra in his Xmas stocking, make a mental note.

A sheriff named Tournier made the inquiry. A nationwide law enforcement initiative to link information from police departments around the country all the better to identify and apprehend fugitives made it just as easy for people like her to see who was where and just who knew it. All you needed was someone who could hack into the Federal Law Enforcement system. All you needed was a scrawny little anarcho-nerd like Denny. He worshipped her in her Catwoman incarnation. Whips and handcuffs and down-on-your-knees-punk-bitch did it for him. Had him leaking on the floor through a discard pair of her panties without so much as a touch. More men like that than most men might imagine. Than most women might imagine, too.

She snapped the laptop closed. Called the front desk. A car and driver, eleven p.m. to whenever. Prompt.

Where will you be going?

Wherever.

61 Bang

Yes, ma'am. Anything else?

A bottle of Dom and the cheese platter.

That would be room service.

Right. Call them. Place the order.

Click. Perhsa stared down along the length of her body. Deep in thought of times gone by, some love lost, or chance she'd wish regained. That's what you'd think she was considering if you saw her at that moment. But you'd be wrong. Most everyone was, when trying to decipher Pershadonna Sassoon, what she was thinking, who she was. You thought one thing, and she was always the other. She was like reading Mayan hieroglyphics. Only no one had ever cracked the code. Is there time to call down to the spa and have them send up a girl to do my toenails? That's what Persha was thinking. That, and at the moment, nothing else. Outside the curtained window, it had begun to snow.

Two hours passed.

The car when it arrived was a fully-equipped black Lexus, the man behind the wheel matched it. Persha in black leather pants and trench slipped right inside, at home as camouflage.

Where to, ma'am.

She told him. A place out in the suburbs. Way out.

Yes ma'am.

Off they went, silence for miles, miles of silence, the wipers subtle as a whisper and the light snow drifting down. The snick-snick of new tires on the wet asphalt. She wondered why this sheriff Tournier had called in that inquiry on John Case. A routine traffic stop wouldn't have been enough to run an ID search on a nationwide police fugitive network. Not under ordinary circumstances, not with an ordinary cop. Was this Tournier just a backcountry hard-ass? Or had he had some kind of cop's intuition about Case? Or was it something more than that? Did this local yokel badge in the middle of no place actually know something? No one was supposed to know the name John Case. If anyone ran the name it would come up clean. Just some average Joe with the average Joe background. A speeding ticket or two, no turn signal, failure to yield. Just to make it real. Was it possible that Case had been fingered by someone? That someone had turned? That the information had been tortured out of someone?

Through the quiet streets of one sleeping little burg after another, the houses all in their neat rows, the yards, the gardens. Like a concentration camp, Persha thinks, all planned out, having dreamed of this very world, watching them on TV sitcoms like *Cosby* when she was a little homeless girl with a crack-addicted whore for a mom. One street identical to the next street, a grid of nothing, a labyrinth going nowhere.

Here we are.

The driver turned to see if his silent passenger hadn't drifted off to dreamworld.

M'am?

No chance of that. She was wide awake, staring at the house. Yeah. Thanks. This shouldn't take long.

There are places like this all over the country for people like Pershadonna, not that there are people like Pershadonna, she'd be the first to tell you that. Weapon caches, the assassin's equivalent to a 7-11, open 24/7 for killers on the go. Up the walk to the well-kept split-level, the well-manicured lawn under a dusting of snow, the garden gnome at the bottom stair, the wreath on the door. Ding dong.

Pershadonna. How wonderful to see you again. You're looking splendid. As usual.

Ian is tall and dark. She's used him before. Used him whenever she was in this part of the country on business. His supplier is always fully stocked and his weapons are clean. Virgin. You break their cherry every time. Guaranteed. He keeps odd hours, has strange visitors, and lives alone. He's dark as a Moor, but that English accent fools them every time. Even in a whitebread community like this one. Charming bastard that he is. She follows him down to the basement. And then the basement behind the basement. To a table beneath a bare light bulb that blazes with the yank of a chain.

Two black brushed aluminum briefcases.

Click-click. She lifts the lid on the first.

You were able to get everything.

61 Bang

Do I ever disappoint, love?

Everyone disappoints me eventually. She lifts a Sig Sauer P220 up to the light. It's just a matter of how long it takes.

Well, not yet then. He smiles. Charming, did she mention that? Do you mind me asking? What is it you intend to do with all this hardware? Invade Iraq? Set that bit of mess in order? Good grief, Pershadonna. You've got practically an armory here.

Click-click. She opens briefcase number two. The Ruger P89. The M9. The Kel-Tec P-32 for backup. People didn't understand. Keats was wrong in that poem she once read in the library about the Greek urn. Beauty wasn't truth. Power was beauty. And truth. Both of them in one. She placed the Sig Sauer back in its foam cutout and picked up the Ruger. She handled weapons the way she'd seen priests handle all that paraphernalia behind the altar when she'd sneak into the church to stay warm during the winter. Before they chased her back out into the frozen street. She turned the Ruger in her hand, let the light play on its lines. It wasn't a surrogate penis. She wasn't a woman with a dick when she had a gun in her hands. No, it wasn't that at all. It was more than that. She was some other creature entirely. Not human. More than human. Beyond human. Some kind of figure out of a myth. Some being from outer space, maybe. A god, of some kind, with lightning bolts in her fists, the power of death in her gaze. More than that even.

It's nothing much. Just going a little squirrel hunting.

Those little buggers can be fierce then, can't they?

Rats with upgraded tails.

Quite.

Gay, Ian is. Did she mention that? No way for Persha *not* to know. Being who and how she is. Not a problem, though. Just a different kind of snake to charm, but, in the end, a snake is a snake.

I've wired the payment.

And a little extra too, I see.

Merry Xmas. You've been a very good boy this year.

I try love. I truly do.

Business is concluded. Up the stairs, a briefcase in each hand, out the door, and down the path. No time for tea and crumpets or

whatever. No time for chit-chat. The offer was just pro forma.
There's nothing they could really talk about anyway. Hope to see you
next time you're in town, love. Oh you will. Always a pleasure doing
business with you. The pleasure is mine. Behind her the front door
closes with a hush and the house looks just like all the others once
again. The snow's picked up. Her driver is out of the car and meets
her halfway to help her with the briefcases. Inside the car, both of
them, the driver adjusting the mirror, the heater. Back to the hotel
now, ma'am?

Back to the city. I'll tell you where to go when we get there.

Ninety minutes later, trolling through the downtown streets,
two a.m., she tells him what she has in mind.

You know where the action is around here, I take it?

His eyes appear briefly in the rearview. Then back to the road.
Ma'am?

You know what I mean. A visitor comes to town. Wants to
know where to have a good time at two in the morning. Nothing
complicated. Nothing expensive. You know the place to take him?

Yeah. I know places like that. Looking for anything in
particular?

I'm looking for a girl you see night after night. Maybe she
hasn't been out there all that long. She's just a little too young to be
out on the street. A little too innocent, that's what your gut tells you.
You avoid taking any of the assholes you drive around to meet her.
It's your way of protecting her. Stupid, pointless, but you do it
anyway. You wish there was something more you could do to save
her, but you know you can't. You've seen this all a hundred times
before. It's already hopeless. She's already beyond reach. How does a
kid wind up like that, you ask yourself? The streets are going to eat
her up. Just like the hundred before her. The hundred after. You can
read it like yesterday's headlines. You know a girl like that?

Yeah.

Take me to her.

22.

The grimy buildings, most of them abandoned, or worse. Broken windows. Graffiti over graffiti. Until entire blocks had been transformed into obscene comic strips. Tricked-out cars idling on street corners. Deals worked out of back windows. Bars and nightclubs identifiable only by the buried throb of bass and beat. Garbage. A bodega here and there, each entrance attracting a gang of hooded parkas smoking and drinking 40s like an urban order of gangster monks. More garbage. A light covering of snow over all of it. Like powder on the face of a corpse. Not a cop in sight.

A street running along an abandoned factory. A city storage facility, something like that. Access to the interstate. A place you drive into and drive out of with a minimum of time in between. The archetypal inner-city strip. Buy ten minutes of front seat pleasure and hit the on-ramp back to suburbia. Just passing through.

There she was. As advertised. Sixteen maybe two years from now. Thin beneath a white fake fur coat fit snug above her boyish hips. Not much underneath it. Short leather skirt. Long kid's legs in red fishnets. Face like an Hispanic Madonna. Smoking a cigarette like she was doing it for the movies. Maybe *Basic Instinct 6*. She detaches herself from under the overhang where she's standing with two other girls. Stands at the curb as Persha lets down her tinted window. Beckons her closer. There are snow crystals in the girl's hair.

Get in.

Big dark eyes ringed in makeup looking Pershadonna over. The car. The driver. The whole snazzy setup. Easy money. She slides right in.

61 Bang

First mistake, Pershadonna thinks. They all make it. To the driver, Drive around.

What's your pleasure lady. The girl looking at her mouth in a silver clamshell compact, perfecting her lipstick with the polished nail of her little finger. Giving Persha the tough act. I charge extra if this is a group thing.

Patience child.

She snapped her silver clamshell shut. Fine, but I ain't got all night to be sightseeing. You understand? You're on the clock from now.

Persha reached into her jacket and pulled out a deck of twenty dollar bills. Two inches thick.

The girl did a double-take she tried not to do. She looked up at Persha like a starving animal at the edge of something instinct tells it is a trap. But that can't resist the bait all the same.

What do I have to do for that?

Just ride. Chat a little.

The girl sat the cash block in her lap and let her thumb flip through it. Satisfied. She stuffed it greedily deep into the pocket of her fake fur.

Chat? Shit, it's your money, lady. She stared out the window, saying nothing as the ghost city passed by.

What's your name?

My name? Like the question had never been asked. She snorted dismissively.

Yeah. What do you call yourself.

Angel.

Is that your real name or your working name.

It's just a name.

You got a momma, Angel?

Christ lady. What is this, the fucking Oprah Winfrey show?

The deal is we chat. You talk you get paid. You don't, you get sixty and a drive back to Blowjob corner. Understand?

Yeah. Whatever.

Good. Now once again. Do you have a momma?

Yeah. Rolls her eyes. Course I do.

61 Bang

Is she alive?

Maybe. Who knows. Who cares. I haven't seen much of her since they let her out of the joint. She does a lot of traveling, you know? From one rehab program to one lock-up to one boyfriend to another. A real jet-setter.

How's your daddy treat you?

The girl shrugs. He takes his cut like all the others. Too wasted on his own product to fuck me most of the time. Which I ain't bitching about, you understand. Besides, I ain't exactly one of the new girls anymore. Don't beat me too much. He's alright I guess. I've heard there's a lot worse.

You keep what I gave you. Give him only what he could expect from a normal night's work. You keep the rest of it for yourself. Put it up someplace safe. Don't tell anyone you got it. You hear.

What do you think, I'm some kind of moron or something. She takes out a cigarette, lights it, opens the window a crack to flick the ashes. Her only concession that anyone else really existed in the world. Fuck. You're not a cop are you?

No.

Then what? A Jesus pusher? One of those do-good church ladies?

Do I look like a do-gooder to you?

The girl shot a fierce look up into Persha's face, but lost her nerve, and instinctively sucked her cigarette to cover it. Turned away. Looked back. Trying again. But this time looking not quite at Persha. Off above her head someplace. She sneered. I don't know what you look like. Talking fast now, jittery. Another drag on the cigarette. Why don't you tell me who you are?

I'm someone who's interested in a girl like you.

Oh yeah. Eyeroll. Drag. Dismissive laugh. All of it for show. How's that? I remind you of someone you once knew? Yourself when you were young or some queer thing like that?

No, you don't remind me anything of myself. You're only pretending to be what I was at your age.

A flash of anger in those babydoll Spanish eyes. Passion. Heat. You'll be something special someday, Persha was thinking. If there is

61 Bang

a someday for you, toots. If you don't end up dead in an alley somewhere or in a hospital wasted by some disease. That's not something Pershadonna wanted to consider, it being almost a given.

Do you read?

What kinda a fucking question is that? I'm not a retard.

I didn't ask can you read. I asked do you read.

You mean like books? Oh yeah. I'm on the work-study program here. Goin to Yale. Shit, lady, what planet are you from, anyway?

I'll take that as a no.

Yeah, take it as a no. Besides I get read to all the time.

Oh. Who reads to you?

The cops. They read me my rights practically every night.

This isn't a joke, Angel. I knew a lot of girls like you when I was your age. All of them are now dead.

Is that supposed to scare me?

Does it?

I don't scare too easy.

You should. Listen, girl, our time here is just about done. I'm going to give you something.

The girl patted the pocket where she'd crammed the pack of twenties. You did already.

Something more valuable.

The girl grinned. So now we're finally getting down to business. You want to fuck me?

Not exactly.

Persha reached into the pocket of her leather trenchcoat, pulled out a book. It was a paperback copy of *Bullfinch's Mythology*.

The girl looked down at the book in her hand. You've got to be shitting me right? You're giving me a book?

It's not just any book. It's a book that explains things.

What things?

Everything. Read it. You've got to do something during the downtimes between blowjobs, right? You'll learn something about the world. Something about your role in it.

I already know about the world. And I already know my role.

61 Bang

Resignation, Persha thought, is always death. She heard it in the girl's voice. Behind the bravado. Just a kid. Fourteen. To die at that age, what a waste.

I've put my number inside the cover. If you ever need to talk.
About what.
You'll know if you call.

Persha stopped talking after that; she had nothing else to say. She turned towards the window. The girl sat there for a few minutes, also without speaking. Finally: Is that all? They were coming back around to the spot where they'd picked the girl up some time before. Persha didn't answer. They pulled up to the curb. The snow had fallen off a little. Big slow flakes tumbled in the floodlights at the corner of the building. Everything was quiet. Hushed. Only one of the girls from before was still standing under the overhang, smoking, hugging herself for warmth. Persha didn't look again at the little prostitute. She lifted her hand. Warding her off.

We're done. Go.

The limousine crossed from one side of the city to the other, nearing the hotel, driving through the deserted streets of the city's center, the driver at last breaking the silence in the car.

Does that ever work?
What's that?
Giving them your number?
What do you think?
No.
You're right.
So why do you do it?
I believe in miracles.
You're a regular Mother Teresa. Who knew?
Yeah. But don't tell anyone. I'd have to kill you.

The driver laughed the way you always laugh when people say something like that. He glanced up into the corner of the rearview. Persha was looking right back.

Not laughing. And he knew.

They were at the hotel curb, by the big awning, now white.

Four a.m.

61 Bang

Everything lifeless.

Pershadonna from the back seat: Park the car underground.
Come on up. Suite 534. I'm in the mood for company.

23.

Yes Missus McCutty. Oh. Yes. It's terrible Missus McCutty. Just God awful. I agree. But what can you do? I mean, just look at what they watch on TV nowadays. Those video games they play. Makes even the worst atrocities seem like make-believe. Of course, I'll have a talk with them. I'm sure they were both just wonderful pussies. Well, yes. In the case of Mr. Tinkers still *is.*

This is Tournier, upholding the Law. This is Tournier, keeping the peace. And if you think it's insignificant, think again. This is what keeps the general chaos at bay. People killing each other over a misplaced fence. Or a fender-bender. This is what keeps Hobbes from being right. The war of all against all.

What he felt like saying was that with all the mangy cats crawling over the McCutty place how could the daft old lady possibly miss two or three mangy mousers? For crissakes, she had to be in violation of about half a dozen health codes. If a health inspector ever rode the hell out here they'd condemn the whole goddamn menagerie. Probably condemn the old lady herself. Crazy as a loon, she was. A couple of kids with .22s killed a tabby and knocked the eye out of a calico. Mr. Tinkers. Holy Christ. What he wanted to tell her was that boys will be boys. Because boys would, you know. Be boys. Why, when he was a boy. Best not to get into that right now, wasn't it? Or ever, for that matter.

The man who had just stepped into the doorway of his office, well, how to put it? It's not like Tournier had known him for very long, but he should have recognized him at once. And he didn't. The guy had had a rough night and that was putting it kindly. He hadn't even changed his clothes or washed his face. Maybe he'd just regained consciousness. Maybe that would explain why he was leaning against the door jamb like it was all that was holding him up. The way he launched himself off it when he caught his breath and limped his way to the chair in front of Tournier's desk, crossing the floor like it was the deck of a ship at sea.

I have to get off now Missus McCutty. Tournier watching the man ease himself into the chair like he was being careful lest his ass drop off entirely. A crusty bib of blood on the front of his shirt. Smeared around his mouth. Big purplish knot over his right eye. I promise. Yes. I'll take a drive out to the Baker place this afternoon and have a talk with the boy. And his parents. Really Missus McCutty. I have. I'm sorry. To. A bit of an emergency here. Yes. Yes. Later. Click. Well, Mr. John Case. You certainly look like you woke up on the wrong side of the cliff this morning. What can I do you for?

I'm here. To report a crime.

Sorry chief. He pushed right by me. Insisted on seeing you right now. I told him you were busy. I tried to make him wait, but.

That was Miriam, erstwhile secretary, past and briefly bedmate, contributing factor to divorce number one, sympathetic vagina during the troubles with marriage number two, ready for duty at a moment's notice in case of complications in Tournier's current arrangement, because complications always arise, don't they, nature of the beast. Erstwhile Miriam in the doorway, explaining her failure to keep this disreputable visitor at bay.

It's okay Miriam. He motioned to Case. This has all the signs and significations of something important. Maybe even an emergency. Where's Jackson anyway? That was Jack Jackson, erstwhile part-time deputy, football hero at Gatlin High twenty years ago, how time flies, good man, straight arrow, heir apparent.

He took the radar gun with him. Set up a speed trap on 687.

Hm. Well. I guess that's fine. Let's not bother him for the time being. The legislature needs its pork. If you'd just man the fortifications out there, hold back any more emergencies for the time being, especially Missus McCutty, I'd be much obliged.

Okay sheriff.

61 Bang

And off she went, back to her desk, where she'd sat for the better part of her life since high school, waiting for Leonard Tournier to see the light and marry her, even though she'd been married twice herself in the meantime waiting, married now, happily, whatever that means, happily enough is probably what it means. Whatever that means.

So. Mr. Case. Folding his hands on the desk in front of him. The hands women loved because they were so long and graceful The hands of a poet, they called them, or a concert pianist, even though Tournier had never written a poem or played a note of the piano in his life. You said something about a crime?

I was attacked last night. Outside my motel.

The Paradise, right?

My room was broken into as well. Torn apart.

My. A one-night crime wave. Any idea why anyone would target you for so much mayhem? A man just passing through? Did you piss anyone off lately? I mean, besides me?

I think someone might have followed me back from the Evergreen last night. I was nearly run off the road.

Hm. I wondered where you'd disappeared to. Sure wish you'd taken me up on my offer of a ride home. Bet you do too. You didn't happen to get any kind of description, did you?

No. A white Hummer. That's what nearly ran me off the road on my way back. Didn't get a look at the plates it happened too fast. In the parking lot of the motel I didn't them coming. They came up behind me. They. It felt like more than one.

From the looks of you, it could have been the whole town.

You don't seem too surprised. Why aren't I surprised by that?

Now, Mr. Case, I'll try not to take that the wrong way, although I must admit it's hard to take it any other way. But the fact is, I tried to warn you that this wasn't too good a place to hang your hat.

Is that your idea of law enforcement, sheriff? Telling people to get out of town.

That's an aspect of it, Mr. Case. Yes it is. Proactive policing, I like to call it. Circumventing trouble before it starts. That's three-quarters of the battle. Trouble can't find you if you aren't where

61 Bang

trouble's looking. Do you have any idea why someone might have broken into your room? What they could possibly have been looking for?

A wallet. A watch. Just something of value left behind. Isn't that fucking obvious?

Now, you see, that's just the thing. It's not obvious. Not obvious at all. I guess that's what makes me the professional here. You see…if it was only someone breaking into your room, that would be one thing. You'd be right. But the car running you off the road. The beating. It all adds up to something that's not so simple. It seems to me that you're drawing all too much attention just for some guy passing through.

Yeah. And you warned me, didn't you? You warned me to get out of town. I wonder why that is?

There it is again. Tournier said, raising a finger, as if to put point out the very spot. I'm not sure I like your tone, Mr. Case. Your tone is insinuating something I don't appreciate.

Is that so?

Yes. That's so.

Case stood, but it wasn't an act accomplished with any grace or without a good deal of deliberation, that's for sure. You haven't heard the last of this, sheriff.

Oh? I think I have.

But, of course, Tournier knew he hadn't, not a chance of that, no matter how much both he and Case might wish to hear the last of it.

Crimes like this, like you say, are just opportunistic. Random. That's what Tournier said, not believing a word of it.

No rhyme or reason to them.

Lots of blood between those teeth when Case grinned, that's what Tournier was thinking.

So I take it you don't feel the need to investigate?

I'll investigate alright. Just not sure there's much to investigate. A white Hummer. No plates. Attackers. No faces. A break-in, nothing missing, nothing left behind. Still, I'll look into it, I can assure you of that. But first, I've got a case on the front burner. Cat with its eye shot out. Tournier shook his great head sadly, tsked tsked. Such a sweet puddy too. What's the world coming too, Mr. Case? That's what I ask myself every morning I bend over to put my shoes on. What is this world coming to? Who'd want to shoot the eye out of a cat anyway? And such a fine upstanding cat like Mr. Tinkers?

What more was there to say after that little speech? For either of them. They both just stood there looking at each other for a while. Well, Case standing, Tournier still sitting, fingers steepled under his chin, regarding. But no longer regarding Case. He'd regarded the man long enough. There were other things to start regarding. He'd put off regarding them for too damn long. He was staring at the spot where Case was standing a good ten minutes after Case stopped standing there.

Tournier made fists of his hands, planted them on the desk, and pushed himself up. Not quite as much of a labor as it was for Case to haul his pummeled carcass up, but in the ballpark, dammit. In the ballpark. The years and decades having ganged up on him at last, beaten the crap outta him, warning him to get out of town, too, but he wasn't listening either, was he? Too late to listen. Maybe likewise too late for John Case. Too late to run, imagine that, cornered with no way out, life makes heroes of us all in the end, ha ha. Crossing the room, grabbing his coat from the back of the door, his hat, passing Miriam, going out for a while Miriam be back in an hour or two. Okay chief. A conversation they'd had maybe fifty-seven thousand times over the last forty years. Probably have it a few more times to. If they were lucky. If you called that luck. And you oughta, goddammit, you really oughta, but it wasn't enough. It just went to prove. Luck wasn't enough.

Outside, in the open air, at the top of the concrete stairs in front of the Town Hall, Tournier stood in his shiny sheriff's coat and big Smoky-the-Bear hat, arms crossed, surveying his shabby empire. The sky was the color of a meat locker and the air felt like something coming out of it. No doubt about it now. Snow was falling. It was dusting the grass, frosting it over. Made everything look a little purer, a little prettier. Like putting sugar on something that didn't taste too good to start with and afterwards still tasted like something that

61 Bang

didn't taste too good but with sugar on it. Maybe even tasted worse for the sugar. Intentions were nice but they didn't change anything. Best to take your medicine plain and fast. But who does? Tell me, who really does?

Tournier stood there, arms crossed, watching the world get a little white for a while. Thinking of all the traffic accidents they'd get on the highway if that stuff started sticking to the roads. All these country crackers skating their pick-up trucks into trees. Telephone poles. Ditches. Each other. A regular automotive ice-follies. Well, Tournier thought, descending the stairs, careful-like, just in case of unseen ice, don't need a broken leg now, a hip replacement would just about finish him off, best be getting that haircut I've been putting off, probably won't be much time for it later.

24.

Think, but think carefully. Because this is a complex problem with a lot of variables. There is probably no right answer, an infinite number of wrong ones, and one that'll be just close enough. That's the one he had to try to find, Case thought, sitting on the side of the stripped bed, the mattress gutted down the middle, everything inside pulled out, like an exploratory autopsy. They didn't find anything because there was nothing to find, but that damn sheriff knew something. The question was, what did he know?

Case felt the ice melting in his hair, trickling down the sides of his face, leaking into his mouth somehow, mingled with the blood. A taste of steel. Of razors. He swallowed. He looked around at the ruins of the room.

He hadn't told the desk clerk about the break-in. The mess, the destruction of property. Hadn't seen a trace of him, suspiciously, enough, although it wasn't like Case had been looking. Bastard probably knew about it already. Probably gave the sheriff the goddamn key. He hadn't realized his car had been broken into until he went out this morning to get his gun from the trunk. Someone had found it inside the empty George Foreman Grill box, packed inside the packing foam. When did they break into the car? While he was still inside the Evergreen having that drink with Tournier? Or at their leisure, while he was passed out in the toilet after the beating?

Touched his ribs. Winced. Bruised. Maybe even a fracture or two. Too deep a breath and it felt like a knife in his back. Some mushy sound like wet crackers in his left ear that sounded pretty bad. Time to relocate. Not that there were a lot of options in a town like

61 Bang

this. They didn't build a variety of accommodations in a place that was no one's idea of a destination. A place most travelers passed at sixty-five miles an hour and the few that stopped only long enough to fill up their gas tank, top off their travel mugs, or empty their bladders. It was the Paradise or nothing. But that was okay. Case didn't want to go far, or for long. Across the courtyard would do. He could slip into one of the rooms with a view of this one. Squat there without officially checking in—or out. Keep an eye open for who returned. Because he was sure someone would. Only a day or two more and then he would get going for good. Coming back here was a mistake. Coming here in the first place was a mistake. A day or two more. Then he'd erase the mistake.

The first thing he had to do was get the gun. That was the most important thing. He had to go back up into the hills and dig up the box. Because Case wasn't going to be forgotten in this town. That was for sure. He had personally gone about seeing to that. He'd fucked up things on that score just about as well as you could fuck them up. The sheriff had even questioned him about his walk in the woods. He had to get the gun off that hill. It was his only bargaining chip and this town wasn't a safe place to keep it. Too many arrows pointed in this direction. Too many arrows pointed right at Case. He could feel them painted above his head like he'd been penciled onto a map under the legend: crap here.

He pushed himself up off the bed. Whatever was in his mouth now, something thick and salty and slimy, a clot of blood most likely, he didn't want to swallow. He shuffled through the broken glass, splintered wood, ripped and tangled sheets. The TV had been spared, mounted above the overturned dresser. In fact, it was turned on, had been from when he'd crawled into the room last night, as if whoever had tossed the place decided to catch a rerun of *Barnaby Jones* while they were at it. CNN, the last channel whoever it was had been watching. He grabbed the bathroom door frame, turning so fast he'd lost his balance, his vision momentarily going dark, then rushing back up again, like a movie suddenly turned too loud and too bright.

* * *

61 Bang

Turning this way and that, regarding himself in the mirror, Tournier saw a sixty-seven year old man any which way you looked at it. A face pretty much what you'd expect it to look like after going toe-to-toe sixty-seven years with this bitch of a life. His opponent, undefeated. Not to be defeated either. Some folks got knocked out in the early rounds. Not Tournier. He stood there and took the pounding. Too dumb to fall down. He'd go the distance, no doubt about it. That's the best you could do, too. Some best. He'd go out beaten all to hell. Ideals smashed to smithereens. Dreams atomized. Not a shred of dignity left. Wasn't even a matter of choice either. Just dumb-ass instinct is all it was. He had a solid chin, a good foundation, and the stubbornness of a mule. In other words, he was born to suffer. Tailor-made for it.

The old man's hands fussing at his throat. Old man? Only two grades ahead of Tournier when they were both back in high school. Smoothing the white cape over his shoulders. So what'll it be today? The usual?

Nah. Just a trim, I think. A little off the sides and back. Leave the top alone. Eyeballing the pink flesh under the shiny white silk of his remaining strands. What's left of the top, that is. I ain't asking for miracles.

Neaten it up a bit then.

You got it.

Tournier hunkered down in the chair. The old man's fingers, knotted like an oak with arthritis, rheumatism, whatever the hell, were still a hummingbird blur with those scissors. Probably take him fifteen minutes to tie his own shoe laces if it weren't for the invention of Velcro. But he sure could still make those scissors sing and fly. A touch of grace, that was. You came to appreciate little things like that the older you got. You came to appreciate almost nothing at all the things got to be so small after a while. Tournier tired of staring woodenly at his own poker-face in the mirror. Clicked his eyes to the big front window of the barber shop, the dancing bits of frozen stuff outside the glass.

Some weather we're having, ain't it Vance?

61 Bang

The barber kept his chin tucked, his watery blue eyes fixed on the arch of hair around Tournier's right ear.

Yep. That it is. Sure enough.

Snip-snip. Snip. The white hairs falling soundless on the white cape. Tournier could feel them on his neck. His shoulders. Somehow working their way inside the cape, the tissue paper wrapped tight around his throat. He stared down at the cut hair lying in his lap.

Gonna wreak some havoc before it's done, I'm afraid.

Snip. The barber looked up, stared out the window. Well. He bent back to his task. The head before him. Snip. Snip-snip-snip. Snip. Snip-snip. Let's hope then it don't last for long.

Let's hope.

Propped up in the corner between a bottle of blue sanitizer filled with combs and an ancient tin of talcum, the TV was yak yak yakkity yakking about the ice-storm currently tracking through the south, leaving car wrecks and downed power lines in its wake. Blackouts, stranded travelers, people inexplicably wandering off into the white-out. An atypical weather event becoming more and more typical. A symptom of global warming, a sign of things to come? It was inconclusive, no one knew for certain, scientists disagreed, back to you, Nancy, the blonde at the anchor desk assembling her face in a way that let you know that she was shifting from the serious to the even more serious. The story on the screen. The footage now from New York City. Tournier sat up straight so quickly he very nearly lost an ear.

Pershadonna walking along a corridor of the indoor concourse, a carpeted esophagus adorned with plants and mirrors, watching the faces of those who weren't yet watching her. Heading for the hotel car rental, looking into those tight and closed-up faces, and thinking to herself, well, what are people anyway? Which is it, really? Are they these distant and self-controlled beings in this corridor, not a hint of shared recognition in their composed and neutral features, not needing anything from you, in other words, strangers, so alien they might as well be another life-form, going about the single-minded business of survival.

Or were they like the man she'd left in bed that morning, and like any number of others, men and women, distant and cold as stars, but waiting for contact, invasion, collision? That wrecked expression at the moment of orgasm, that intimate catastrophe, was that the 'real' face of human beings, hidden behind fear and self-protective armoring? Was their fierce and uncompromising self-centeredness, their lethal instinct for survival, nothing more than a realization of how close to annihilation they really were? Not just close to oblivion, but somehow desiring it? Desiring death for the sake of survival itself? Desiring contact with another?

Was the 'real' face of a human being the one she invariably saw the moment she killed one? Even the toughest ones slipped the mask at the very end, showed at least a little of what lay beneath. That same awful vulnerability, that same shattering intimacy, full of panic and desire. Who am I? Where am I going when I leave myself? Am I coming home? Oh God I'd forgotten what it was like. Oh God why did I ever leave? Love me, kill me, love me, kill me. Death or orgasm, if they weren't the same, they were kissing cousins. That was Pershadonna's view. The two great mysteries, solved. But the third? The secret identity of human beings, their true nature? That remained unknown. That was still an x-factor. That was still unsolved. No matter how many she fucked, no matter how many she killed, no matter how many she both killed and fuck. No matter how many she rented a car from.

Up at the counter, filling out the requisite forms, yes to this, no to that, the sliding back and forth of counterfeit documents, the careful eyeballing of her person by the clerk behind the counter all but saying it aloud: what's a black woman like you doing renting a BMW, can you afford it, are you going to steal it, smash it up, are you some drug runner's bitch, some rapper's? Pershadonna with the diamond chip in her nostril, her facial tattoos, her slim and sexy person outfitted in a mustard-yellow pantsuit with French silk leopard-patterned blouse, all of it designer and I'll shoot you where you stand, motherfucker, thank you very much.

61 Bang

Were you able to get the car I requested?

The BMW M6? Yes.

Silverstone Metallic?

Yes, Ms. Sassoon.

HD Radio? Sirius Satellite? CD surround-sound system?

Yes, ma'am. Everything you asked for.

Merino full leather package?

A little hiccup in the atmosphere. A clearing of the throat. The gears turning as he stalls for time, wondering how to tell her. The look of displeasure on Pershadonna's face causing that little wince. What queens had in the heydays of Egypt and Babylonia she had. What made men want to please Cleopatra and Catherine the Great, made them instinctively want to please her, it was hers, too. I'm sorry, ma'am. It seems the Silverstone Metallic isn't available with the Merino leather package. The Stratus Gray, on the other hand, has the Merino leather package optional.

That's bullshit. Who told you that?

Well, our supplier...

...doesn't know what the fuck he's talking about.

I'm sorry ma'am. It was such short notice. I'm sure if we had more time we could get it straightened all out. I'm afraid that I was forced to choose, and you did seem very insistent on the Silverstone Metallic.

I don't have more time.

I'm really very sorry Ms. Sasson. Turning pale and babbling. Then adding, hopefully. I did manage to get you the walnut trim.

But as much as she was genuinely pissed off at the lack of that Merino leather, that wasn't what caused the shadow to cross Pershadonna's sculpted features, to darken her look of mythic sexual command. It was the scene unfolding on the TV screen above them both, muted as a thought bubble in a cartoon, until Persha impatiently waved her hand and had the clerk turn up the sound so they could all hear what the joke was about. Her look blackened visibly by the moment as she watched everything above her become far more complicated, far more dangerous, and far less conducive to a happy ending than it was ten minutes ago.

61 Bang

Is there something wrong, ma'am?
Oh shit.

25.

In this business you had to have a flair for the dramatic, even when there wasn't anything to be dramatic about. People expected it. They were inspired by it. You had to create your own drama, if necessary. That's how things got done. That's what filled the collection plate. You had to have a vision. You had to have pomp, whether you had the circumstance or not. That's how you got God up off His ass, that's how you got Him to work.

In mysterious ways, he provided.

You had to stand out, like a rooster if you wanted to crow in a new dawn, wear the plumage, all shiny and loud.

The rhyming syntax, the hyperbole and bombast, this was the language of the crowd, the music of the masses, this is what got them off their couches and stoops, got them mobilized in hollering mobs. Taking to the frozen streets. You didn't lead the herd by talking in whispers, by walking on tiptoes, by winks and nudges, by editorials and long-winded appeals to reason and logic. It's poetry that moves the hearts of men, gets them to mount those barricades, risk their collective lives. Always did, still does. They could make fun of the suits, the slick pompadour, the jewelry and Dr. Seuss alliteration, but at the end of the day he was the one with the mob at his back, and when he told them to march, by God and all his Archangels, they marched.

He could never be elected president, governor was beyond his reach, probably not even senator or mayor, but that wasn't the point of running. The point was to solidify his base, to be in a position to give his blessing to those who could one day be elected, the ones

61 Bang

who came and went with the seasons, while he remained beside the throne of power, the one who could deliver the mob to the king of his choosing. The point was to legitimize him. To make him familiar enough to seem respectable no matter how outlandish his persona, no matter what scandal had tarnished his attention-seeking past. To get on TV enough times as possible.

They made a mistake if they dismissed him as nothing more than a bellicose buffoon, a ham-handed huckster, a publicity pimp. If they accused him of insincerity and exploitation, if they thought that rising to a position of fame and power standing up for the oppression of his people meant that he didn't believe in what he was doing, they had gravely underestimated. He'd taken a knife in the chest, for one thing, how many others could say that about what they believed? He'd painted a bulls-eye on the back of every flashy suit and he wore it to every street rally, every protest, every boycott, every march.

Content he was to be the man they loved to hate, the butt of their jokes, just so long as they kept those cameras rolling, so long as he appeared on the news at five and eleven, the Sunday morning forums to give the "black perspective." Why he'd become almost tame over the years, a voice of reason, practically a statesman. He'd gone mainstream. Which is what made this very moment so auspicious, one to play to the greatest possible advantage. His righteous anger, his shocked and indignant condemnation was for this very reason all the more powerful. He was a man who'd been holding back for years, hallelujah, who'd toned down his audacious image and combative rhetoric, who tried to play by the rules, live within the system, but now, after this latest provocation, this atrocity of injustice, he could hold back no more, praise the Lord.

This young man who'd just been out for a night on the town, who was having fun in America as was his God-given right, this young man who had a baby at home who depended on him, and a fiancé he planned to marry, with his life and dreams all ahead of him, his promise still to be fulfilled, was gunned down, murdered in a hail of bullets and we ask why?

The Reverend was standing at the scene of the police shooting surrounded by a coterie of solemn bodyguards. Standing in the

61 Bang

dancing snow. The yellow police tape still surrounded the empty
parking place where the bullet-ridden car had been towed away. The
cold turned his words to smoke, as if they were spoken in fire,
burned and vanished in the air. He looked bigger on TV, heavier,
more imposing, his pompadour higher, shinier, everyone told him so,
it was one of the first things they said. In person, on the street, out
from behind the cameras and the pulpit, shopping for ties or having a
sandwich in a deli, everyone remarked on how thoughtful he was,
how soft-spoken, how intent and sincere a listener.

Sixty-one times they shot him. Sixty-one. What does a man do
to deserve being shot sixty-one times? Did we shoot Judas sixty-one
times? Did we shoot Hitler sixty-one times? This wasn't a sinner, this
wasn't a monster, this wasn't a devil…this was a young black man in
the streets of America…this was an innocent young black man in the
city of America shot sixty-one times and we want to know
America…we want to know why…why was this innocent unarmed
black man shot sixty-one times by an officer of the Law?

Surrounding him the victims family, what they could round
together, anyway, the mother sobbing quietly, held by an older man,
next to him, three other women, younger cousins or sisters,
presumably some kind of blood relations, the girlfriend, or fiancé, as
they were calling her, holding a baby, no one was exactly sure who's,
it didn't matter, a tableau of black grief, all-too-familiar, almost
timeless, the crowd not quite so uniformly somber, still variable, but
that was okay, the significance of this event wouldn't become clear,
wouldn't be effective of anything until later, until it was shown on
television. Some of the crowd just there for the party atmosphere,
drinking, goofing around, clowning, mugging for the cameras. Those
cameras rolling, all the major news outlets, CNN, Fox, C-Span, even
the BBC and a couple of news crews from Cuba and China and
communist wherever.

He lifted his bejeweled hand, with great ceremony, reverence,
like a gesture to the Lord, the gun leveled towards the curb, towards
the empty parking space behind the flickering yellow police tape. Not
a real gun, but a Hollywood stunt weapon filled with blanks,

61 Bang

provided by a well-meaning Academy Award-winning actor, but just
as effective for what he had in mind.

He stood there with his arm outstretched, the gun in his
diamond-studded hand and asked the streets, the crowd, God, the
nation, the world, everyone and no one in particular, Does America
know what sixty-one shots sounds like? Sixty-one shots fired by the
Law into the body of an innocent, unarmed black man on the streets
of America? We don't think it does or it would rise up with one voice
in protest with us. We believe in America, the America of the People,
by and for Them, God Bless us All. We are here today to pay tribute
to Jerome James Watkins with a sixty-one shot salute so America can
hear the sound of our grief, our outrage, and our determination when
we say No more, America! No more, America! America, God Help
Us No more!

What happened next was quite amazing, especially in an age of
sound bytes and societal attention deficit. The Reverend had to stop
and reload a few times, but the cameras didn't cut away, the major
news outlets didn't edit it down. They played the sound of every last
one of them until the echo of the last one died away in the wintry
street where the crowd stood at last silent and somber and filled with
a suppressed rage that you could sense even through a TV screen. It
was the greatest speech he'd ever delivered and not a rhyme, not an
alliteration, not a blurred historical reference. It was his Sermon on
the Mount, his Gettysburg Address, the plain-spoken eloquence of
those gunshots, stark and solemn in the winter air. A perfect sermon
for an age that had grown weary of words, practically Zen-like.
Because you really had to wonder, it went on so long. An eternity, it
seemed between the first shot and the last. No matter who you were,
no matter what side you were on, you really had to wonder what
anyone could have possibly done to deserve it.

Sixty-one shots.

Sixty-one bangs.

It was powerful theater, it was powerful ceremony. It could put
you in mind of those pictures of JFK's funeral, not the Camelot
splendor, obviously, but it's complimentary obverse, the simple, spare
richness of the mythic nature of the thing. The cold grey street lined

61 Bang

with poverty-stricken buildings, the flickering yellow police tape, the angry, mournful black faces, the populist minister at their head. It might instigate a riot, mass destruction, bloodshed, but no one with an eye on the ratings and an eye for the dramatic could possibly resist putting it on the air at five, ten, eleven, and six the next morning. Over and over again. It was going to be re-shown for weeks. Oh, to be fair and conscientious, the major networks followed up with a spot of the rattled-looking mayor urging calm and due process, more violence wasn't going to help the situation, he argued, and then an impromptu news conference with the police chief who announced an unexpected break in the case.

A gun had turned up. No, it hadn't just turned up, some spent shells matching, it had been there all along, but they wanted to be sure, they didn't want to come to any hasty conclusions. They still don't. They were working with all diligence and deliberation in accordance with proper police procedure, with the Law, blah blah blah, and, yes, it now seemed beyond doubt that the gun belonged to the alleged perpetrator. He'd been armed, after all. It was too early to say if this was a justified shooting, too early to say anything, that's why he was urging calm, along with the mayor, urging calm until the process played itself out. These things take time. You can't rush to judgment. The truth is worth waiting for. That's what the Law is all about. Calm. Reason. Deliberation. Time. The Truth. Because you see, there's a bit of a problem at the moment. The gun, the gun that belongs to the perpetrator, the alleged perpetrator, Jerome James Watkins, well, for reasons we're still at present unable to disclose, this being an ongoing investigation and all, the exact whereabouts of that weapon, which I assure you is in police custody, is unknown.

Unknown?

Flashbulbs popping and everyone talking at once. Shouting. Demanding clarification. Headline fodder.

We believe it to be mistakenly in the possession of an unauthorized representative currently moving somewhere through the South. We are making every possible effort to locate this person and or persons and reclaim the weapon at this very moment. We have leads. We are attempting contact. We have no further comment at this time. This is an ongoing investigation. We'll make an announcement as soon as we can. Thank you very much.

Pandemonium.

26.

Well, it was obvious at this point, wasn't it? There was no choice anymore. He had to climb that goddamn hill before the earth froze and get his box back. He had to dig it up out of the ground like a homeowner digging up an insurance policy buried in the yard for safekeeping. Because now the house has burned down. And he needs that policy. It's the only thing that's going to get his life back to anything like normal.

Any number of people could have talked, put them on to him. There were a number of people up and down the line and not a single one of them were beyond betrayal. Who was? We like to think we are, or would be, exclude ourselves from the ranks of the skunks and traitors, the finks and squealers, but when our feet are put to the fire, there aren't many who'd even wait for the smell of cooking flesh. Have you got a life, loved ones, eyeballs? You want to keep them for as long as you can. It's human nature. Eddie himself could have talked, when they started pulling his insides out. Who could really blame him? Right from the start they could have known Case had the gun and was making a run for it. But not even Eddie knew the zig-zag path Case was taking, did he?

No matter.

Time to dig. Time to get moving again. Time to find his car keys. They were in the third place he looked: his pocket, where they belonged. Along with the note. Help us God please.

Not today, kid. Sorry. God's got no time. He's busy saving his own ass this morning.

61 Bang

Shoves the note back into his pant's pocket, the small one, where you keep the change. So he doesn't have to see it again by accident, but he doesn't throw it into the trash where he doesn't have to see it again ever. Why? Sorry. No time for why either.

Case stood over the ceramic bowl, hacked it up and spit, something that looked like a small blob of raw meat, a chunk of undigested calf-liver, something like that, maroon, trailing tentacles of phlegm. He stared at it in mute wonder for a moment or two, as if it were something he really ought to keep, as if it might be something he needed, then he shook his head and flushed. Took a piss, squinted, looked closely for a pink tint of rose when he didn't see outright and immediate claret. His right kidney, where he dimly remembered being kicked, repeatedly, felt like it had been used to play a game of racquetball between two guys who hated each other. But it didn't seem to be bleeding, not yet anyway. Shakes it off, tucks himself away. Where there's life, there's hope, he smiled at himself grimly in the mirror, each and every tooth rimmed in blood. Also hopelessness. Where there's life, that is. He looked like a vampire, at dawn, after stake in the heart.

Come on, let's go.

The snow was coming down thicker and heavier when he stepped out of the door, coming down in those big fluffy flakes that usually seem to mean it's going to stop soon, except the sky all around, as far as Case could see, was an unforgiving battleship grey. The U.S.S. Annihilation paused menacingly, issuing its warning salvos, ready to bury them in an all-out bombardment of ice and snow. He was no weather man, except for being wrong as often as one, but that would be his guess. Case wiped the windshield with his sleeve, slid into the car and let the wipers do the rest. Didn't bother with the back window. No need to see what was behind him. He wasn't going back there anyway. Just a lot of trouble. How long does it take the earth to freeze?

Man, he could use a cup of coffee. A cigarette. A new liver. A heart transplant. A kidney or two. A hip replacement. A bionic brain.

A pair of gloves.

61 Bang

Dammit, it was cold. He messed with the car heater, got a whisper of warm air blowing, like bad breath. Who the fuck ever thought it would be this cold in this part of the country?

The roads weren't too bad yet. Not by his standards, anyway. He'd driven through a lot worse. Just some feathery snow cover, patches of black ice shining here and there. He tapped the brake on the curves. What he had to watch out for were the local yokels. They tended to decorate these winter wonderland scenes with spin-outs and head-on collisions. Fortunately there weren't many people on the highway, a couple of tractor trailers barreling through from somewhere else to somewhere else. A few cars slow-poking it along. Headlights on, a funeral for nobody.

In the dark, he knew where he was going, because he wasn't going anywhere in particular. In the light, even grey and dirty as it was, he had more trouble. It all looked, predictably, different. But he found the interstate marker, watched the odometer for seven-tenths of a mile, and pulled off the road, then off the shoulder of the road, around and behind a thin stand of bare trees. They seemed a lot less thin, a lot less bare, seemed to provide a lot more cover in the pitch-black, that's for sure. Case got out of the car, squinted up the hill, somewhere up there, that had been the point, he didn't know exactly where. It was a good plan, he'd thought, at the time. But, like everything else, that was then, this was now. He closed his eyes briefly, tried to conjure up a mental photograph of the spot, saw nothing in particular. Just trees in the darkness. A rock. He got the shovel out of the trunk.

Up the hill he climbed, easier in the light, such as it was, even easier over the snow-covered leaves, using the shovel for purchase and watching the ground for chuckholes and stones and exposed roots. What wasn't easier was all the aches and pains, the contusions and internal damage, the symptoms of battering he was now merrily festooned with. He glanced around at the surroundings, looking again for something that looked familiar, hoping he'd have a sudden flash of déjà vu. I've been here before, done this before, stood on this very spot, etc. But none of it looked familiar. Or, rather, it all looked familiar. It looked like a fucking woods, in other words, a dead

61 Bang

woods in the snow. He stopped on what amounted to a small ridge
left behind by natural erosion, formed by however the rain and thaw
ran off the hill, leaned against the shovel and caught his breath. His
lungs hurt, like they were a couple of canvas bags filled with frozen
wrenches. His leg hurt. His head hurt. What was the point of going
through the whole Sears catalogue of pain. Everything hurt,
goddammit.

He closed his eyes to gather his thoughts, but there weren't any
thoughts to gather, not much of anything to gather, really, except the
question, Where the hell was it? Where did I bury it? When he
opened his eyes again, they were a little heavier, snow clinging to the
lashes. He was staring, unseeing and empty-headed, at the spot for
several seconds before he saw it: a large antlered buck, nearly as grey
as the woods behind it. The animal stared at Case out of a stillness
that could pass for wisdom, only the faintest trace of breath coming
from its black nostrils.

It was off to the right, about twenty yards up the side of the
hill, a patchy quilt of snow and dead leaves, by a rough-barked tree, a
stone neither big nor small, but that reminded Case, idiosyncratically,
of the hump of a dolphin as it arches its spine into the sea.

Motionless, the stag watched for quite some time, as the
creature that was John Case stumbled and tripped, stiff-legged over
stones and fallen tree limbs, three-legged and awkward, using the
shovel to keep from pitching forward onto his face. This wounded,
shambling, desperate creature crashing through the underbrush,
barely able to stay upright, no threat at all. Ten yards away, the stag
gave a small disgusted snort and stepped disdainfully away into the
snow. Case made it the rest of the way up to the rock. The rough-
barked tree. Stood at the spot he suddenly remembered now that he
was staring directly at it. The grave of his hope and his future. He
recognized it alright. Defiled. Torn open. Robbed. Empty. Earth in a
pile. Covered with snow. Someone had been here first.

27.

German engineering, you just can't beat it. No one can make an engine like'em. Take over the highway, the world, whatever. How did they ever lose the war? Both of them? V-8 engine, 325 horsepower, nothing like it, horse-power. Yum. The ball of her slim foot pressing down the accelerator, just so, like the Adam's apple of lover who's been a bad, bad, very bad boy. Lean into it. Just enough to show him you mean business.

Va-room!

Into the curve, around the bend, and off into the straightaway, seventy-eighty-ninety-one hundred in hardly six seconds. The sodium halos above like a white corridor of angels leading the way to heaven. The haze. The snow slanting down. DMX on the surround-sound stereo. Palestrina. 20th Century Fox. Rameau. A compilation disc of her favorite theme music. Get her in the mood. Make her entry. Downshift into fifth, listen to that engine purr, like a big leopard, puts her in mind of that painting, Rousseau, a woman riding above the carnage, a sword in her hand, Apocalypse. Dammit, I really wish they'd had the Merino leather.

Sure the usual thing to do was to come in low-key. Rent a solid and invisible Ford Taurus. Blue, or forest green. Brown, probably. Egads! But can anyone see Pershadonna in a Ford Taurus? She lets out a wild laugh, accelerates past a sand spreader, and fixes onto another straight-away just as Tupac comes thumping out of the speakers. Oh no. Pershadonna is simply not a low-key sort of gal. She could come a-riding into town on an ox-cart and it would still be

61 Bang

Academy Award time. She was just not what you'd call anonymous. She simply wasn't one of those people who went unnoticed. She didn't fly under anyone's radar. Pershadonna with her diamond chip piercing and her black tattoos. Her designer wardrobe. Her bangles and her tiger eyes. Her lethal promise. Her dangerous sex appeal. Pershadonna was born, get this, born to be noticed. Might was well enjoy it, she told herself. Might as well get used to it she told the world. Put it into sixth.

Va-room!

In her line of work, you learned early to expect the unexpected. You learned it fast, too. It was an unforgiving learning curve. You didn't say, I didn't see that coming, in her line of biz. Not many more times than once anyway. And once, was very often, once too many. That the cat had slipped out of the bag, that the missing gun had been made public, that could be the play of any number of players in this drama. Someone losing, most likely, forced to make a bold move. That would point back to the cops, obviously, what with the Revered putting on that little street performance. What nagged at Persha were the who, what, where, and why. The how they knew that John Case was moving through the south. If they were willing to say that much publicly, odds were good they knew even more. No doubt about it. Someone had shown their cards. Or had their cards peeked at without their knowing. Although, given the choice, Persha always suspected the worst of everyone. That way you were never disappointed, almost always right, and, no matter what, you came out the other side alive.

And wasn't that the point?

To stay alive? From the moment we're born?

You bet.

Here comes a steep white curve. Start off slow, squeeze that accelerator beneath your foot, that lover's throat.

Va-room!

Back down the hill he limped, he hobbled. He stumbled. Back down the hill, leaning on the shovel handle, slipping and sliding on wet

61 Bang

rocks and patches of slush. Don't let anyone fool you, going downhill can be harder than going up. Well, it can be. If you're trying to do it with any grace. In any kind of controlled way. Without falling heels over head. Without breaking your neck. Which Case was still trying to do, but why? He thought, that's it, maybe I should just fall once and for all. Tumble down the hill. Let the snow cover me over. Maybe I should just get in the car and run. Because with the gun gone, with no insurance, with the people who were after him closing in on this town and nothing to give the people who were supposed to get him safely out of the country, exactly what the hell do I do now?

The hip throbbing, the ribcage aching, the knee giving out, Case slid sideways a few feet over the slick black leaves. Climbed back up on the shovel handle, paused, gasping for breath with the effort, went on.

Who took it, that's what he wanted to know. Were the Feds here already? In town, gunning for him? They wouldn't let him out alive.

The jaw, the back of the head, something deep inside him, all of it bruised and sore, all of it protesting. The ear full of wet crackers. The blurred right eye. The blood he was alternately swallowing and spitting into the snow. The shovel blade glanced off a stone and down he went, riding along unprotestingly on the seat of his pants, ice-rimmed leaf-rot working its way up his pant legs. He stopped, eventually. Arms on his knees, head in his arms. Laughing. What the hell was the big hurry? Where was he going anyway?

Nowhere.

The sound of the snow ticking against the dead leaves. Melting on the sleeve of his coat. Sticking out his tongue to taste a flake. Doesn't taste like much of anything.

You start out in life wondering what's going to happen, imagine what you'll do, where you'll go, all that you'll accomplish. Things never really turn out how you expect them to. You never think of yourself sitting on your ass in the woods on a patch of wet leaves with a whole bunch of people looking to kill you. You never figure you'll get to the point when you figure this is as good as it's probably going to get.

61 Bang

Climbing up on the shovel handle again. Again. He can't sit there forever. That's the problem.

Going on.

Down through the last of the trees, the snow falling harder, the wet black road just ahead, the Mustang where he parked it, limping out towards it, and there, leaning back against the trunk, casual, ankles-crossed, Tournier, in his big Smoky-the-Bear hat, shiny sheriff's jacket, lighting a cigarette, his cruiser parked just off the road a few feet behind, lights-a-flashing.

How now, Mr. Case. How now. I'm on my third cigarette here. I was beginning to get worried. Thought I might have to come a-lookin for you. Saw your car parked here. Got worried. Like maybe you ran into some trouble.

Drag on the cigarette, squint through the smoke, gesture towards the hills and a smile it was hard to tell how knowing.

Take another little scenic hike did you?

Nature called.

Really? And you brought along a shovel? Well, that was right considerate of you. Keeping our woods neat and tidy like that.

The shovel was to help me get around. I'm a little banged up, as you can see. Any progress, by the way, on who might have gotten me that way?

It's an ongoing investigation, as they say. I can assure you of that.

Ongoing, meaning what exactly.

Meaning, it goes on.

Case leaning against the shovel handle, the snow falling around him, cold, tired aching all over. Scared shitless, frankly. Squinting back at the sheriff, wondering, what does he know, does he know anything at all, if he did know anything, wouldn't this be all over right now, if he didn't, would it be helpful if he did know something? Had he followed him out here the first time without Case knowing, did he have the gun, can he be trusted, can he be trusted to do…what?…the right thing? What's that?

Why don't we cut the bullshit, sheriff?

61 Bang

What bullshit would that be? There's so much of it to choose from.

How about you drop the country cornpone act to start.

But isn't that just exactly what you're expecting? A hillbilly like me. A little bit of Dukes of Hazard. A little Smoky and the Bandit.

Drag. A laugh that turns into a cough covered by a fist. That stare, cool and even, like someone waiting patiently and, one must admit, a little sadly, for an outburst of sudden violence.

Just as much as you were expecting the story of me just passing through.

Did he mention tired? Case was tired. Oh so tired. Exhausted. Expired. Extinguished.

Right you are there, Mr. Case. Well, what do you say we up the ante a bit.

To what?

Let's say you start at the top. The original question. What are you doing here in my town?

It's a long story.

In that case, let's hear it over a sandwich.

28.

The Evergreen had a back room, why not? What didn't? Damp, unfinished, cinderblock walls where it wasn't, and a concrete floor, a basement that wasn't underground, packed with boxes, crates, and such like that. A bulletin board. A filing cabinet. A desk covered with invoices. A storeroom/office for Dale, the owner, who nodded from behind the bar, eyes like a pair of push-pins fixing the scene when Tournier came in, shooting him a meaningful glance, with Case in tow.

Going to be in the office for a spell, Dale. Sandwiches and beer, if you please. Some coffee too. Official business. Anyone comes in here asking, I'm not here, except for Jessica Simpson, or an emergency. Of which the latter would be defined as this goddamn bar being actually on fire.

Will do sheriff.

A wooden table in the center of the room, the rusty parts of something or other in the process of repair being laid out upon it, like the incomplete fossil remains of a baby dragon.

Case said nothing. Folded his hands on the table. Waited.

Tournier unzipping his jacket, hanging it on a coat rack. Lifting off the big hat, hanging it over the coat. Patted down the thin white hair on top. Hitched his pants. Walked across the room and took a seat across the table from Case.

Said nothing for a time. Then a time longer.

Dale came in with the coffee. Sugar. Milk. Set it down. Sandwiches and brew coming up sheriff.

Good Dale, thank you.

61 Bang

They fixed their coffee, drank, and Tournier had a cigarette. Offered one to Case, who took it. They smoked and sipped coffee and Tournier made some remarks about the weather. The latest reports. Intensifying wind. Increased snow. Low visibility. Blizzard conditions.

Looks like, much as I'd like to see you gone, not even I can let you go under these conditions. Looks like you're going to be stuck here for a bit, Mr. Case.

Case said nothing. Wondering what that meant. If he tried to leave, would the sheriff forcibly stop him?

Of course, ain't nothing I can do about it if you decide to risk life and limb on those roads. You being an adult and all.

Smiling over his coffee cup, as if he'd been reading Case's mind.

Still and all, I don't think you want to leave just yet anyway. I said that to myself when I saw you coming down off that hill with a shovel in your hand.

Still smiling, as if he'd read Case's mind a second time.

The coffee felt good, the cigarette, too. Warmed him up inside. Settled him down some. Allowed his mind to begin some rudimentary functioning. Like a lizard heating up on a rock, getting nimble again. The whole time now Case tailoring the story in his mind for when it came time to tell it. That time, coming just about any moment now. He looked across the table at the sheriff, who at some point had started telling him about someone named Mr. Tinkers, a shooting, an eye lost, it took a while before Case remembered this as a follow-up to something Tournier had told him before, something about an old lady, about a cat. Case could hardly wait for that beer to come. He could hardly wait for three beers to come. Four.

Thing is, in three or four years, they probably send those very boys to Iraq or Iran or some damn place like that to shoot real-live human beings. Then they get a chance to put that killer's instinct to some good use on something besides household pets. Sometimes I wonder if that's the real purpose of war. To use up all that young male piss and vinegar. If you leave it here at home, maybe it poisons

61 Bang

the milk. You know what I mean? They end up shooting the eyeballs out of shabby old yard cats. Killing each other in street gangs. Unproductive violence, suchlike. Wouldn't surprise me to find out crime goes down in times of war. All that rambunctious anti-social energy sent someplace else. Shoot the eyeballs out of some mullah's cat, right? As you might guess, Mr. Case, I have what you may fairly call a cynical view of the human species. In all it's multitudinous variety. Occupational hazard, I guess.

Case felt jittery. Unreal. He looked at the sheriff as if he might be a figure from his imagination. If I fall sideways off this chair unconscious, he thought, it wouldn't surprise me a bit.

The beer came. Ditto the sandwiches. Two inches thick and filled turkey and ham, garnered with lettuce and tomato, strips of fried bacon, slathered with mayo. Tournier filled his glass with beer. Case wrapped his hand around the cold green bottle itself and drank off half. He didn't touch the sandwich, nice as it looked, wasn't sure he wouldn't leave a few of his teeth behind in it.

So. Tournier swiping mayo from his lips with a napkin. Storytime. Tell me, Mr. Case. What brings you to town? Regale me. It's a big sandwich. Leave nothing out. Once upon a time. Like that. He motioned with his hand, mouth full, a big wad like a tumor in his cheek. You take it from there. Fill in the rest.

It's hard to tell the truth. Even harder to tell only part of it.

I was paid. To make a delivery.

Hmmph. Tournier nodding enthusiastically around another mouthful, like he'd heard this one already. Like it was a good one, one of his favorites.

I didn't ask any questions. Just said I'd do it. The money is good and all I had to do was drive this package across country. Hand it off. The money is wired into an account. That's it. Clean.

But there's trouble along the way. Tournier said, swallowing, eyes glittering with hopeful anticipation.

Right.

I knew it. Always trouble along the way.

This package has a history. It was originally in the possession of someone else. And they want it back.

61 Bang

Of course. Anything worth having everyone wants. This is getting good. Who are these other people? Good guys? Bad guys?

Case had finished the other half of his beer. Stared at his thumbnail on the bottle. It wasn't just that the thumbnail looked unfamiliar, but the very idea of a thumbnail itself seemed absurd. He scratch at the edge of the soggy label. He looked up. Tournier chewing, tipping the bottle back to moisten a mouthful, putting it down.

That's just the thing.

What's just the thing?

Tournier's own thumbs now, wet, sticking straight up from his fists placed on the table on either side of his empty plate. Leaning forward, as if on tenterhooks with anticipation. He nods at Case's plate, at his sandwich. You gonna eat that?

Case slides the plate halfway across the table.

Be my guest.

So. You were saying? These other guys?

Might be who we'd ordinarily call the good guys. Hell, they might even really be the good guys. But it's not that simple.

Ah.

Fact is, they could be cops.

You don't say.

Technically cops. But they have a sanction. Perfectly legal if it came to backing it up. To covering it up. A sanction to do things. Things you wouldn't ordinarily associate with cops. I'm not sure if you can understand.

Why Mr. Case? Why wouldn't I understand? Because I'm just a down-home hick from the Mississippi sticks? Because I'm not a Yale graduate with an advanced degree in some fancy interdisciplinary rigmarole? You don't think we get TV down here? Why I'll have you know, I've seen *Mystic River*. I've read every John Grisham novel ever published. Robert Ludlum, too. You don't think I can understand moral ambiguity? You think fuzzy ethics is too sophisticated a concept for a big ole dumb country boy like me? You think my education stopped at Gary Cooper in *High Noon*? Why, if I weren't so used to this kind of reversed snobbism, I'd be insulted. What do you take me for, anyway, a cultural Manichean?

Dale came in with more beers, left with the remains of lunch, minus what the sheriff was still working on. At some point. Case drank another quarter of a bottle.

I just meant. He closed his eyes, listened carefully to the pounding of the blood in his head, the sluice and swish, unable to say just what he meant. What did he mean?

I know what you meant.

Tournier lit up a post-lunch cigarette. No offense taken. What you see before you is a slab of a man, a chunk of pink meat gone bad. Shot. Spent. Some old father figure representative of all the ways the world has failed you. Of all the ideals that were disappointed. The world in all it's shortcomings. The Law, in other words, the Law it's own bad self, personified, objectified, a walking talking compromise and contradiction in terms. Ready to have a heart attack and keel over dead.

Case felt like puking again. Was he really hearing this, or was this all some kind of black dream, some kind of bad wiring that presaged what they euphemistically called a "cerebral accident." Had some tiny vein deep in his brain suddenly popped and started spewing a dark curtain of blood? He knew if he opened his eyes it would be all over, like if he opened them he'd see something that irrational and nightmarish that confirmed it, Tournier sitting there with the head of a wise old talking goat, or Jesus, or maybe not sitting there at all, replaced with a seascape or a prison wall or the ceiling above a bed he'd slept in eight years ago, whew, the whole thing some kind of fucked-up dream. He turns to the wife, Hey honey, listen to this…

Thing is, Mr. Case, there ain't no Law. There's a lot written down and all that, concrete buildings, men in black robes, there's a lot of things representing the Law, but there ain't no Law itself. That lady with the scales…well, you throw a little of this on one side, a little of that on the other, you balance things out as best you can, but it's all a little bit like buying a pound of ham. It's all just an approximation and the scale itself, well, who's to say if it's true?

61 Bang

Ambiguity, Mr. Case, or whoever you really are, that's what the Law is, seven types, a hundred and seven thousand types. The Law, the pursuit and administration thereof, makes a relativist of us all. Every Lawman is a postmodernist.

No, he was still in the backroom of the Evergreen. No bilingual Great Dane or hooded Yoda sitting across from him. No flashback to a cottage by the sea. No waking up to the fuzzy dislocated face of ex-wife number two. It was Tournier, grinding out a cigarette, sipping his beer, gazing calmly at Case from a pair of eyes, well, it was just too difficult to say what they looked like, because they seemed to be looking straight right through him into the past.

A philosopher-sheriff? Don't look so surprised. This is the age of hyphenated identity. Everyone living a double-life. Hell, that's passé. They're living a triple-life, four, five, six lives at once. You underestimate me, Mr. Case. I never wanted to be the Law in this crappy little town. I wanted to go up north, attend Dartmouth or Yale, someplace like that, study philosophy. Foucault, Deleuze, nomadology, all that intellectual razzmatazz. I'm like that guy George Bailey in It's a Wonderful Life. Except with a gun. Just couldn't get away for one reason or another. I had to stay behind to take care of things here. Every man must find the hole he's meant to plug to keep the chaos out. So when you tell me that there are men headed here representing the Law but willing to do bad things to achieve their ends, that doesn't cause any great crisis in my world-view. That's not something that will effect in me an Armageddon of conscience.

Was Case really hearing any of this? He looked like a sheriff, walked like a sheriff, dressed and up to now talked like a sheriff, but who was this sitting in front of him now? It was like the channels had gotten screwed up, like everyone had forgotten their lines, like he'd walked into some lost episode of Hee-Haw on crack.

So why don't you tell me. What's in the box? What are these men so anxious to get back that they're willing to propagate all manner of lawlessness and mayhem?

I don't know.

You don't know.

61 Bang

I don't know. I was told it would be better if I didn't know.
That knowing wouldn't help and not knowing might.

You didn't peek?

No.

You're carrying around a box that men up and down the east
coast are killing other men to get back and you're telling me you
didn't look. You've got a veritable Pandora's box there, and you want
me to believe you didn't sneak even one little peek inside? Do you
really expect me to believe that? If this were a game of poker, Mr.
Case, I wouldn't bluff with that face.

Is it really so unusual? So against human nature? You've got a
pain in your chest, your bowels, inside your skull, wherever. Deep.
Echoing. Not debilitating, at least not except for moments at a time,
but there's something about it. It doesn't go away, but that isn't the
whole thing. The placement, the regularity, that's all part of it, but
that's not what makes it what it is. That's not what terrifies him.

Case kept talking, until he began believing the words himself.
Until he convinced himself that he hadn't looked inside the box.

There's a profundity to such a symptom, an eloquence that you
don't have, that isn't part of you, doesn't come from you, doesn't
belong to you. Why doesn't a man with a pain like that go to the
doctor? Why doesn't he get it diagnosed? Why does he keep going
instead, living a normal life as long as he can, as if nothing is any
different? What is he afraid of? I didn't look in the box, Sheriff, for
the same reason. I didn't what to see that what I had might get me
killed.

Tournier lifted his long, pale hands. The cigarette in the corner
of his mouth. He slowly clapped.

Bravo, Mr. Case. Bravo. Totally implausible under the
circumstances, but let's say I allow myself to suspend my disbelief for
the time being. Just to keep the story moving along. What would this
box be worth?

It's incalculable.

Based on?

What they gave me to make sure the men looking for it didn't
find it.

61 Bang

I see. And do you think you could identify these men?

I can't see how it would be that difficult.

No. I don't suppose so. But if they came, I suppose a man could use some help resisting them?

Yes. I suppose so.

Do you think I have the box, Mr. Case?

It crossed my mind.

I don't.

Case shrugged.

Do you believe me?

No.

Well, why should you? But let me ask you one more question. The reason you stopped here in town. Didn't just keep moving on like you should have.

I told you. There was this kid. A little girl.

Right. The ogre no one's seen.

I've seen him. I saw the kid. She asked me for help.

She asked you?

In a manner of speaking?

Tournier put his big hamlike arms on the table and leaned forward. There were stains of rot between his teeth, pouches beneath his eyes where he'd stashed his defeats and disappointments.

In what manner of speaking? Exactly.

He hadn't meant to give it up. Hadn't meant to look at it again. Ever, if he could have helped it. Let it die along with the pants, lost in a rinse cycle somewhere along the line, dug out to wrap a wad of gum. He laid it on the table and watched as Tournier unfolded the grimy paper with his artist's fingers. Watched as he took in the words. A kid scrawling out a prayer with a piece of charcoal on a stray scrap. Giving it to a stranger. Hope, in other words, such as it was. Such as it always is.

Tournier looked up from the note.

Kids say all kinds of things. You ever were a father, Mr. Case? Daddy doesn't buy them a pack of bubble-gum. Suddenly, he's an axe murderer.

It wasn't like that.

61 Bang

Who says?

Case watched Tournier fold the paper and slip it into the pocket of his shirt, the one beneath the badge, button the flap. He supposed he shouldn't have let the sheriff take it, but then, he was glad to be rid of it. Unburdened, somehow. Instead he watched the older man's face, pink and white and stolid across the table. The face of the Law.

If this were a game of poker, Sheriff. You'd lose this hand.

Tournier didn't call him on that.

No, he didn't.

29.

Gin rummy motherfuckers.

You fuck. You caught me with a couple of aces.

Ha ha. You're always caught with a couple of aces.

That's because I always have the third one. What the fuck you throw down that seven for, fuckhead? Didn't you see him scoop up the sevens with that Jack?

I didn't need the Jack.

That's not what I meant.

I need to take a leak.

Get me another Coke on your way back, shithead.

Fuck you. Who do I look like, your aunt Jemima?

That was the boys on the bed ribbing each other, playing that same interminable game of gin rummy they started back in Newark, New Jersey, what was it now, six days and running? How many times had he heard the word "fuck" in all its many and creative linguistic variations? Killing time, which was what this was about at this point, the good ole wait-and-see. He sat in a straight-backed chair by the window, waiting. Seeing. There was a lot of the former, not much of the latter. Staring out the motel window at other motel windows, the curtains drawn on every last one of them, same as the curtain was drawn on the window he was watching from, peering between the edges. The depressing courtyard in the afternoon gloom, the identical vacant units like a strip of film, the same image repeated. The cheerless snow, the trembling bush, the sky the color of nineteen degrees, the view, such as it was.

61 Bang

He noted the failing light, the increasing difficulty seeing the number on the building across the way, which meant they'd soon be sitting here in the dark, four men in a motel room in the middle of nowhere. Take turns sleeping. Catch a cigarette out back. The tedium turning you into a cat, eyes heavy, needing to nap every fifteen minutes it seemed. Stakeouts were all the same whatever you were staking out—the boredom, the universal aroma of men cooped up too close together, farts and bad breath and stale underwear. At least they had a shower, a bed. At least they had running water. At least they didn't have to piss into a jug.

Christ, what a way to make a living. He wouldn't change it for anything in the world. It was what he was born to do. Well, maybe not born to do. Maybe more like what he'd been raised to do. Middle child, the classic sort, trying to negotiate the fragile peace in a house that always felt one dropped fork away from a nuclear event. It was a matter of the tiny subtleties, of shadings and glances, sometimes not what you said, but what you didn't say, where you weren't sitting when someone's angry eyes happened to wheel over to that chair across the table and expect you there. It wasn't something you could explain, it was something you felt, something like art, he supposed, the art of negotiating. That's what Roman had become, a master of shades and subtleties. The Negotiator. You walked into a room and sensed the imbalance. You knew what to put here, put there. You knew what to do to make it right.

The man had switched rooms. Taken one across the courtyard with a view of the room everyone, including the dim-witted motel manager and that shit-kicking sheriff, still thought he was occupying. He was on his own stakeout, watching himself so to speak. Both of them watching the room, waiting to see who comes back to it. It was like a joke, or some kind of mathematical puzzle, a holograph, maybe, the watchers watching the watchers. But only Roman knew that, only he had the whole picture, the panoramic perspective necessary to see it. You had to position yourself properly. That's what it was all about. Positioning.

His father had been right about one thing. Most people were. You just had to extract that one thing they were right about. You could discard the rest. His father had always stressed the importance of finding something you were good at, then becoming the best, becoming indispensable. Make yourself synonymous with that task, like a tool made especially for doing a job, a hammer for hammering nails, etc. That way, he said, when a hole needs to get drilled, if you're a drill, they don't even think about who to find. They find you. Not bad advice from the old man, who was good for nothing, nothing but all the wrong things. Or not good enough might be the more accurate way to state it. Vice, particularly. He was better at punishing it than practicing it, as it turned out. Indicted on multiple counts. Extortion, protection, trafficking. Internal Affairs. Wire-taps. Plea bargains. The whole sordid works. Whispers of relocation. Witness Protection. Mom drinking herself into a tunnel to the center of the earth. Fucking the head of the detail assigned to protect them from whoever while dad was off spilling his guts into a tape recorder. Roman, crouched by a heating vent, heard the grunt and squeak. Mom doing a little negotiating of her own. A boy's life.

They'd been there twelve hours now, long enough to toss the room, search his car, determine he'd in all probability hidden the piece, that this wasn't going to be as easy as he'd hoped, not that it ever was, not that he could ever remember. Establish the basic parameters. They flew out of eastern Tennessee in an old military transport plane piloted by an old mercenary connected to someone connected to someone else, etc. Grizzled old bastard named Tuck, veteran of operations best left unspoken. Speaking of which. Roman also a veteran of more than a few things best left unspoken. Landed in a little valley fifteen miles to the north, incest country, patriot nation, the archetypal Appalachia. A Ford Bronco waiting, fully-fueled, pointing in the right direction. They beat the storm, which the weather service kept predicting would be a real humdinger, an epic in these parts of unprecedented proportions. And here they were, acting on a tip from a highly credible source. Ha. He could imagine.

They knew who Roman was when he joined the force, those kind of histories don't get forgotten. Bad connections were almost as important as good. They tried to discourage him. In subtle ways and not so. They thought he'd be holding a grudge, blamed someone, was

61 Bang

looking for vindication. His old man in the garage thrown backward against the wood-pile under his workbench, the back of his skull and a goodly portion of his brain decorating the pegboard above it, little pieces stuck inside the works of the Black-and-Decker rotary saw hanging there, gumming up the teeth of the thing-a-ma-jab, the hammers, screwdrivers, all these tools someone would patiently clean, too valuable they were to just throw away. They thought Roman would blame the Force for that, a boy and his dad, you know, even if dad was a bad apple, and, of course, everyone knows an apple doesn't roll too far away from the tree.

But Roman surprised them, the kid was just too damn likable, everyone came away saying the same thing, shaking their head, smiling, "the fucking kid is just too damn likable." He put people at their ease, he cleared the air, calmed the atmosphere. You found yourself feeling comfortable, found yourself feeling defused, disarmed, laughing with relief, maybe things weren't as bad as you imagined, maybe someone did understand, maybe this can all be worked out. He talked them off ledges, out of hostage situations, tense stand-offs. He built up a reputation. The Negotiator. Where is he, get him out here, we got a situation. Estranged fathers. Jealous ex-boyfriends. Wannabe terrorists. We got a guy out here, cracked-out, strapped with bombs, armed with an AK-47, and holed up in a classroom full of third graders with a canvas sack full of ammunition. We don't know *what* his point is. Whatever. Get The Negotiator. That's how a reputation gets built, how a legend gets written, how you win friends and influence people in high places.

More times than not, everyone walked off the scene. Exhausted, jittery, emotionally wrung out, like they just took a ten-thousand foot per second drop in a jet airline, but safe, alive. The few times not, the right person got carried out of the building wrapped in a bag, a perfectly placed sniper shot, the money shot.

That's how you get noticed by the right people, how you win favor, how you get plucked from obscurity. You've got to be synonymous with a need. You've got to be a screwdriver when a screw needs to be screwed. That's how you become indispensable. Thanks, dad.

61 Bang

The sheriff was supposed to keep him away until they could finish their search, but he hadn't been able to even do that right. Case showed up while Blake and Harrison were in the room. They might have taken him right then, pulled him off the scene for a little heart-to-heart, when they had unexpected visitors. Someone not in the script. These guys came from outer space, like a UFO. Who these characters in the white Hummer were, he'd sure as Hell would like to know. Not locals, that's for sure. Mexicans, Guatemalans—nope, nothing like that. These were white guys of a height and breadth that bespoke the Nordic heritage. They gave Case a pretty good working over. A few tense moments there wondering if he'd have to intervene just to save the bastard's bacon, at least long enough so he could smoke it himself. His men slipping through a door into the adjoining room when it was clear that Case wouldn't be beaten to death then and there.

Let this thing unfold a little. It was more complicated than it at first looked. Like a surgery, you didn't know exactly what you were up against until you cut the patient open, took a peek inside, started gently moving things around.

Or a bomb. A mass of wires, charges, firing caps, timers. One false move—Ka-Boom! You had to be careful. Sometimes things didn't look like they were connected but they were. Every movement counted. If you didn't consider all the possible repercussions, if you didn't take the long view. Things were connected in the way that average people never suspected.

Like walking into the house when dad was home. In the basement, in the attic, out in the garage. You could sense it. Just the slightest disturbance in the air...

People thought that negotiating was about giving everyone something they wanted. Everyone coming away satisfied. The art of it. The secret of it. You identified what the other person wanted. You gave them some version of it. That was the conventional wisdom. The uninitiated, they held some version of this idea. You had to give a little to get a little, the mark of a good negotiator. They were wrong, of course, that wasn't it at all. That's what you were left to think, talk yourself into when everything was said and done, reason away that remote feeling of dissatisfaction and unease. The truth was. A good negotiator took it all.

That sign across the courtyard was lost now in the gloom, even with some the motel's remaining operational floodlights coming on. The snow picking up, though. That much he could see. The card game breaking up behind him, suspended on account of darkness. The sound of men stretching, groaning, ready to eat because there was nothing else to do. These men, little more than a gang of killers, pack dogs, that he kept in tow, like any good negotiator, a little bark, a little bone.

Well, at least the grub wasn't bad. Better than the greasy waxed paper specials at most stakeouts. Traditional homemade South Asian fare. Who'd expect that in this neck of the woods? Spicy noodles this. Shredded chicken that. Courtesy of the sheriff's woman. Who should be along with dinner presently.

30.

Hard not to think of it, staring down the length of himself, naked under the water, among all that cold tile. His dead body, that is, laid out on the coroner's slab for everyone to see. This is Case taking a hot bath in the dark motel room across the courtyard, sliding down to chin-level, eyes flat across the water like an ancient crocodile, trying to ease the aches and pains of his battered body. The pale chicken-pimpled flesh, odd patches of hair, folds and flabs, the wrinkled genitals floating like a drowned parachutist. What would they make of it, the people who's job it was to cut him open and try to answer some final questions? To make sense of it all? Good luck! The purplish-red bruises, an irregularly-shaped patchwork of pain, that could be the death of him yet. Internal bleeding, anyone? How long does it take a ruptured liver to kill you, anyway? This ain't the body of no kid, either. This is a middle-aged man we're talking about. Some guy who should be standing out on his lawn spraying poison on the crabgrass and dropping the kids off at soccer practice. Sure, honey, I was just going to clean out those rain gutters today and what time is dinner at the Jenkins's anyway? That sort of thing.

You get to a certain point in your life and you start considering what kind of corpse you're going to leave behind. What's going to be written there. Hard not to think these morbid thoughts lying in a bathtub in an abandoned motel unit in the evening gloom.

Case reached out of the water for the bottle on the edge of the tub. Old Faithful. The slug of Jim Beam making up for some of the warmth the water had already lost. Still, he was glad to get his arm back under the surface.

61 Bang

His mind went to rewind. That surreal little tete-a-tete with the sheriff again. Did he have the gun or didn't he? Did he know who Case was or not? It was all coming to a head one way or another, you could feel it building up, like the storm, something in the atmosphere. The cops were no doubt on their way already, but the snow should slow them a bit, give Case some time to think, and they'd still be in a town forty miles away—the site of the 'negotiations,' as Case had specified, if he decided to negotiate at all. He was setting up his options, getting all the offers on the table, and then he'd make a choice. On the phone, the man they put him through to, some guy named Roman, seemed reasonable enough, even enthusiastic, the kind of upbeat can-do tone that tended to make you think he was eager to accommodate you, that you had all the goods.

Of course, that wouldn't last long, that helpful attitude, that eager-to-please pitch. Fact was, his advantage would start diminishing sharply in exact proportion to how much they knew. Familiarity breeds contempt, as always, but in this business it also leads to expendability. When he was empty of useful information, like yesterday's newspaper, he'd be good for nothing but to wrap the trash in. So the idea was to keep them not knowing, knowing as little as possible, for as long as possible, right to the end if possible. Well, that was impossible, but he'd do the best he could.

He was losing his battle with the bathwater. No amount of Jim Beam could hide that. No amount but too much. He'd given up adding hot from the faucet; it hurt like he was being sawed in half to fold himself at the waist to reach the tap. He couldn't help but feel like he was sitting in a cold soup, flavoring it, so to speak, like some chunk of otherwise inedible and leftover meat. Or maybe some kind of pale, hairy tuber yanked out of the ground. His teeth were chattering.

His penis looked like a dead jellyfish.

When was the last time I masturbated?

A few minutes earlier, the water still tepid, it almost seemed possible to drink himself into a state where sliding down into the tub and taking a deep breath wouldn't have been entirely out of the question. Just slide his ass a few more inches along the bottom of the grainy tub and sort of nod off underwater, a few half-hearted splashes in his dreams and that would be that. Not a bad way to go, he'd heard somewhere or other. But now it was just too late to consider it, even speculatively, it was simply out of the question. Life or death, it occurred to Case, often depended on just such seemingly inconsequential chance details as that. A few degrees of water temperature one way or the other. A few minutes here or there. Stopping some place for a pack of Ho Hos.

Case rose out of the bath, not without difficulty, hands slapping the tiled walls. Water falling off him in chunks and splashes. He pictured, for some goddamn reason, Botticelli's Venus. The opposite of that what he must look like. A funny thought. Ha ha. Goddammit, the air made it even colder than it was in the water. Was the heat even operating in this unit? He slapped at his arms, cursed. He groped for a towel, nearly slipped stepping out of the tub. His feet scrambling, a kind of modified hop, the wet floor like a sheet of ice. Regained his balance with a hand on the sink. He yanked another towel off the rack, draped it over his shoulders. Used a face towel to dry his hair, rub some warmth into his head. Too dark to see himself in the mirror: just a dim shape, could be anyone. Don't turn on the light, he had to remind himself. Remember, you're not supposed to be here.

Out into the main room. Turning up the heat if the heat were operating, doing nothing but going through the motions if it weren't. Curtains drawn, no lights, but a spectral glow illuminating the bed, the table, the whole interior landscape. It was the snow outside the windows, whatever snow did to make interiors glow, reflect whatever light there was, starlight, streetlight, maybe it just gave off its own light, who knows?

Case, wrapped in towels, passing under the television mounted near the ceiling. Don't turn on the TV, he told himself. No need to watch, anyway. He'd seen enough. What else is he going to see? A mugshot of his face with the number of a police hotline underneath? If you've seen this man, etc. Traveling through the south. His face. His name. Did they know that much already? Did he even want to know if they knew that much?

61 Bang

On the way to the window that's what he was about, thinking these grim thoughts. On the way to the window to survey the lay of the land. To see what there was to see. A tiny little movement of the curtain edge, undetectable to anyone who happened to be watching his window, not that there would be anyone watching this window. Just one window out of a row of windows. Just a vacant motel room. He looked out the little crack he'd made in the curtains, sat on the chair at the table beneath the window, just sat there and watched. The snow, falling heavier now, white out of the black sky, like something, something incongruous, like the picture out of the biggest television set of all softly coming down, pixels and static, the end of all broadcasts.

He sat and watched, the snow in all its windblown skeins and draperies and variations making it a little less boring, but boring all the same. He sat and watched. His original unit, his car, parked in front, turning into a white mound. He watched and watched. Waiting to see who turned up. Tournier? The hillbilly? The mystery men in the white Hummer? The snow fell harder. No one came for a long time. He took a piss. Came back. Got a glass of water. Came back. Then someone showed up. Rather, they were already there. A gold Jeep Cherokee parked some places down from his car.

A few seconds later a small figure came into view. Bundled up against the storm in parka and boots. Bent over, hard to see in the white cyclones swirling off the parking lot. Looked like a kid, that small. All bundled up. A big hood surrounding a face it was too far and dark and snowy to see. A small, kidlike figure. Carrying a couple of plastic bags with handles. Stopped outside the door of his old room. Looked both ways. Didn't knock. Looked at the ground, like something had fallen. Keys maybe, whatever. Ducked down quickly as if to pick that something up. Stood quickly. Looked both ways again. Hurried off to the gold Jeep Cherokee. Started it up, waited till the wipers cleared the already snow-covered windshield. Headlights on. Pulled out, drove off.

Taillights disappearing into the whiteout.

Gone. Whoever it was.

Having slipped something under the door. A message of some kind. He was sure of it.

31.

Persha hit the brakes, though it went against her every instinct. Though it went against her principles, being the straight ahead, 125 miles-per-hour kind of girl she was, the kind of girl who, theoretically, went through things rather than around them, the kind of girl whose philosophy was never to wait for anything, never follow anyone. Only a split-second earlier she was applying this philosophy to overtake the driver of a Hyundai Santa Fe angling for her lane, muttering to herself where do you think you're going asshole, and why do you think you can cut me off to get there, when she saw the lumber truck planted in front of her, taking shape suddenly in the blowing snow, the trailer canted sideways, the cab jackknifed so that she was able to see the driver faced perpendicular to the correct direction, his eyes popping, a big dark hole in the middle of his face making the shapes oh shit no.

The BMW was beautifully equipped, flawlessly engineered. It had the kind of tires that know what kind of surface they're rolling over. It had a braking system more intelligent than most human beings. It listened better, and acted faster, too. The problem was that the rest of the assholes on the road weren't also driving BMWs.

She was clipped on the left rear fender by a Plymouth Voyager, spun around just in time to see the Hyundai hydroplaning sideways passed her across the slick macadam, and then hit broadside by a GMC Jimmy. Air bags deployed and something thunked against the windshield that left a coconut-sized indentation of sugared glass and a hairy clot of blood. Persha stared at it, for a moment, uncomprehending. Trying to get her bearings. Then a rude blow to the trunk caught her unawares, like she were in a rollercoaster car, and she was moving again, where to?, weel, horns going off all around, the smell of coolant everywhere, a few frames of the film missing, a quick snapshot of the snowed-out sky.

Nothing then, for a while. Presumably unconscious.

Woke up to the sizzle of vital vehicular fluids. A detailed view of tree bark, her headlights accentuating each detail, fascinating, like a painstakingly wrought impasto painting in shades of gray. Really.

Horns still blowing, but fainter.

She reached over the partially deflated airbag. Turned a knob. The CD player leapt to life. Flipped down the lighted vanity mirror. Touched the sore place just above her left eye. The tip of her tongue bit into deeply. The source, and she hoped the only, of the blood she was tasting.

Otherwise, all's well that you can walk away from.

She pushed open the dented door, stepped out into the snow. The interstate was about thirty feet away. As much of it as she could see, in both directions, a chaos of assaulted steel, smoking, flashing with lights and flares, horns bellowing. She staggered forward. Snow. Leaves. Twisted branches. Off to the left, somewhere in the murky weather, she could still hear the shriek of brakes, the abrupt punctuation of slamming chunks of heavy blocks of metal in motion.

Motorists standing around, looking dazed, like they exited their cars onto another planet.

Another fucking disaster, in other words.

He waited until dark, until after dark, until way after dark. Telling himself he was being overly cautious. But still. Then he slipped quickly out the door of the unit, stood against the outside wall, peering into the dancing snow in both directions. Some light spilling out of the office and some illuminated windows of units towards the end of the block. Travelers letting the storm pass over, maybe? He pulled up the collar of his canvas work jacket, thrust his hands in his pockets, and bent his head. Crossed the courtyard quickly. Tried to stay out of the light, but the snow had a way of spotlighting the

61 Bang

scene. Powdery, like lunar dust, it spilled over the tops of his shoes. Two inches? He didn't see anyone. Some television noise spilling out of one of the illuminated rooms.

Around the corner.

Crunch, crunch, crunch.

The cars down the row, already sugared over. No white Hummer.

Nothing that looked like anything he'd seen the hillbilly driving either. The wind woo-hooing through the dead trees.

He walked along the front of the row of units, passed his room, his car.

Didn't see anything out of sorts.

Walked passed the other way.

Ditto.

Stood with his back against the wall. Buzz of sign. Hazy blob of pink and green neon hanging up there in the snow. Otherwise, dark. Reaching behind him for the doorknob, the lock broken. Gives the door a little backward shove and he slips inside the room just like that.

Everything as before: a ransacked mess.

But there it is, on the carpet just over the transom where the hooded figure slid it. In a small envelope, pale blue, like a goddamn thank-you note or party invitation. He worked a thumb under the sealed flap, took out the delicate sheet, unfolded it. Enough light to read the careful, well-turned letters. Lavender ink, for crissakes. A trace of flowery perfume. Not much in the way of a message, anyway. A time, tomorrow, a street corner to be at, a we-need-to-talk, that was about it. A line about how there was great danger. A promise to explain. A warning to tell no one. All of it, despite the pretty handwriting, expressed with the dryness and the verbal stinginess of a telegram.

It was an invitation alright.

No R.S.V.P. included. None necessary, apparently.

Case folded up the note. He just got rid of the one, now he had another. He shoved this one down into his pocket, stared down at his shoes, shaking his head. He lightly stamped his feet, shaking off the snow. Then he peered out the window, checked the coast, it was clear, and slipped out of the room as quickly as he'd slipped in. Hugging the walls, moving in the shadows, such as there were, moving lightly through the snow, avoiding the lights, he headed back to his pirated room, watched every step of the way by the man hidden behind the heavy curtain in the room across the way.

What do you think it means? That was Tantum at his shoulder, slurping hot coffee out of a paper cup, watching Case return to the supposedly empty room across the courtyard, presumably in possession of whatever the sheriff's woman slid underneath the door of the room he was still supposed to be occupying.

Don't know.

Think she's tipping him off?

Why would she?

Tantum shrugged, the kind of shoulders you'd expect on a guy whose specialty wasn't thinking. Just as well. That was Roman's business. And in this business, it wasn't true the more brains the better. Too much independent thinking led to chaos. But the man was on to something; it was the very theory that Roman was running through his mental software. He was taking it a step further, however. That was his job. What if it were Tournier himself who was tipping Case off? A more complex, disturbing, and, therefore, far more interesting problem. Because it just didn't make sense that this woman had any direct connection with Case, did it?

Can't say I can see a reason either. Talking more to himself than the hulking presence hovering behind him. Always talking more to himself than to whosever presence was hovering around him. The two of them watching Case slip into his darkened room. Only because you knew he was there was it possible to see the little tell-tale signs that there was someone behind the curtained windows. Roman flipped a card onto the table. Seven of spades. Resuming his interrupted game of solitaire. The deck having been abandoned by the others, who were mostly sprawled about the room in attitudes of moronic boredom. Why don't you catch a nap or something?

61 Bang

Tantum raised the coffee cup. I been drinking this to stay awake. It's my turn to take watch. You been sitting here for hours.

No problem. I'll let you know when I need a break. Go out back, have a cigarette. Just make sure no one sees you.

Tantum shrugged, retreated.

Roman flipped another card. Four of hearts. He moved the appropriate cards from row five to row two. Flipped over a concealed card. Queen of Clubs. Hm.

Examined the situation, both on the table and outside the window. Wondered if there were an arcane connection, somehow. There always was; at least, it was always valuable to proceed as if there was.

Solitaire was the only card game he could bear to play. The only one that offered a real challenge. He seldom lost in games played against human opponents. Even factoring in the luck of the draw, Roman usually always prevailed. And many of the times he didn't, it didn't matter, or something else mattered more. Sometimes it was just a matter of losing to appear human, something nearly every woman he'd ever been involved with had accused him of not being at one point or another. Men, too, for that matter.

Ace of diamonds.

He thoughtfully regarded the card he'd just exposed. Frowned. Too soon for an ace. In solitaire, you see, there was no bargaining, no bluffing, no feeling out of your opponent's fears, excitements, flaws, hopes, and dreams. There was nothing but the cards, fate, and your own skill against them. Everything else was stripped away. You were playing against yourself, in a sense too. You couldn't bluff yourself, it was like trying to tell yourself a lie. What was he saying? People did that everyday. But it was a matter of faith, of belief, rather than knowledge. You had to stop thinking at some point to believe the lies you told yourself. Stop thinking. Stop looking. You had to believe. And Roman believed in nothing, in no one, and, least of all, himself. Two of spades. This game was lost. You could see it shaping up by the way the cards were lying. Lots of people cleared the table if they saw a loss in solitaire coming at them. Gathered up the cards, shuffled, and started over. Not Roman, not ever. Lost games were his specialty. Lost games of solitaire, wasn't that just about the most effective metaphor of a human life you could imagine?

32.

So there he sat, front seat of his car, staring out the windshield at the appointed hour. Corner of such and such. Left at the intersection and three blocks back from the main drag, not really called Main Street, by the way, but Cornell. Case sat there, smoking cigarettes, occasionally tapping the ash from the two-inch ventilation crack he left in the window. Engine running, heater blowing.

The snow had turned into a kind of wet sleet, streaks of slush that lashed and hissed against the windshield, a form of weather that the weatherman on the radio never seemed to tire of calling "a wintry mix." It's a wintry mix of snow and rain out there, guys, so better be careful. Case must have heard the phrase twenty times already. There were also words like "freak" "deadly" and "disaster" being used. Case heard the words "hazardous" "unprecedented" "victims" "state of emergency." There was a fifty-car pileup somewhere.

Case sat and smoked.

Watched an old masked man walking gingerly to the mailbox on the corner, his boxer on a red lead. Saw someone else further up the road pause in the middle of shoveling a driveway, look up at the sky, as if asking themselves, Why bother? A car trolled by at ten miles an hour.

The shoveling figure, after reflection upon the pitiless sky, gave it up for a lost cause. Trudged back to its garage. A pickup with a plow mounted on the front cruised silently past, the plow raised above the road. The old man and the dog had simply disappeared. His cigarette burned away.

Time, in other words, passed.

61 Bang

Some more of it passed.

Then the gold Jeep Cherokee crunched to a stop about ten yards across the street. Not that there was much gold showing. A block of white. Windows scraped. It sat there, idling, while Case thought things over. Flashed its lights at him, as if he hadn't noticed it, or wasn't certain it was what he was waiting for. Here I am, the headlights flashed. It's me.

Right.

It could be a mistake. A trap. He had no idea who the hell was behind the wheel of that gold Cherokee, what they wanted, or why whoever it was wanted it from him. But Case was being forced to open doors he might not have opened under happier circumstances. He was in a corridor with tigers bearing down on him from the other end. You leap for any exit you can find. Even if, theoretically, there are more tigers at the exit. It's a wintry mix of snow and rain out there, guys, so, better be careful! Case turned off the engine, climbed out of the car. He thrust his hands deep in his pockets. Bent his head, sleet stinging his face. Eyes slitted against the flying pellets of ice. Jogged, sort of, across the street. He peered into the dark semi-circle of glass cleared by the wiper blade of the Cherokee. Made out the small pale face ringed by the fake fur of her parka hood. Small mittened hands on the steering wheel. Both of them. A woman, Asian, fifty maybe.

Huh? was the question Case found himself asking himself. No answer forthcoming.

Case limped around the back of the Jeep. Gave the back seat and cargo area a cursory look, best he could. Didn't see anyone crouched back there with a gun or crowbar. That made the whole thing even more of a mystery. He grabbed the door handle, practically locked in ice. Yanked the door open, slid inside the warm interior, pulled off his stocking cap already crusted over with ice.

I'm here. What's this about.

You want to know child, where is.

An issue, Case thought, not exactly top priority anymore. Ironic, since it was in good part what landed him in his current predicament of abject desperation. Maybe she saw the shades of disappointment crossing over his face, like something large and dolorous over a sea bottom.

Gun too. I know where.

She stared straight ahead over the steering wheel, her hands, in the blue knit mittens, hadn't moved. It was impossible that she'd seen his disappointment: she hadn't shifted her gaze from a spot a foot beyond the windshield. An aperture to some inner world, maybe. Talking before an audience of shades, a past history Case, nor anyone else, could see. A world more real than whatever was going on here. Whatever was going on here. Maybe she just understood that the less she saw the better.

How do you know about the gun?

Is important how? Why? Important I do. Correct?

In a nutshell, that's about it, he thought. Case watched the shadows of ice sliding down the smooth planes of her face. The only expression there. Ageless, somehow, that face, like a statue overgrown in a jungle somewhere, carved from a tropical wood by a tribe long extinct, totemic, not a god, not an immortal, but still something timeless to remember a god by. Suffering, perhaps. Stoic, somehow distinctly female, in an elusive way. If that made sense. If anything did.

Okay lady. You're right. How and why aren't important. Where's the gun?

And child.

Yes, and child.

You get gun. You get child same time. Promise?

Okay.

Not okay. You promise.

Now she turned from the windshield, fixed Case with eyes that…what? It was easy to say her eyes were inscrutable, like little bits of the dark places in the universe, starless, infinite, void, but temptingly void, a place you wanted to tip off the ledge of your own crumbling existence and fall into because something had to be at the bottom, there was no such thing as falling forever, was there? Case wondered if she could tell if he were lying, if she could read some text hidden in his features not even he could decipher, because the

61 Bang

god's honest truth was, Case hadn't the slightest clue what he'd do when the time came to do it. But he said what had to be said and let her take it from there.

Yeah. I promise. Where are they?

She'd found her answer in his face, whatever it was, whatever it really meant. Eyes returned to the windshield, fixed to the past, or wherever.

Same place. Back of the hills, down old lumber road. Factory used to be. I show you this. Drawn on map in glove box. You take.

It's that hillbilly, isn't it. That big guy. Long hair, beard.

Yes, big man. He is what they call survivalist. Dangerous to go back where he is. His camp. Everyone fear. Even Law. What goes on there. Evil. You stop. I believe. Take map. Go.

Case opened the glove compartment. A black automatic lay on top of a folded sheet of notebook paper. A meticulously sketched map in lavender ink. Beside it, an extra clip of ammunition.

You need gun to get gun back. I give you. Not registered. Clean, they say. Correct?

Case held the gun up. Released the clip inside, checked it, shoved it back inside. Pocketed the extra. He glanced back at the woman behind the steering wheel. She could be eight. She could be eighty. It all depended on how you looked at her. Still not a hint of expression, nothing but the shadows of the sliding sheets of sleet like the ghost of geologic plates over millennia, like the ghost of faces washed in tears. Cool, controlled, she could have been a CIA agent contracting a murder. Case reached under his jacket, tucked the gun into his waistband. Damn, he admired this woman, whoever she was.

Correct.

He opened the door. The world sizzling and hissing and white. She muttered something in Chinese or Korean or whatever gobbledygook language she spoke. A blessing, a curse, a threat.

Case looked back. One foot already on the icy curb. Grimacing at the pain in hip, ribs, shoulders, everywhere involved in the ordinarily simple act of removing oneself from the passenger side of a car.

What?

61 Bang

She didn't turn, much as he wished she might, one last time. Her voice not much more expressive than a digitalized fortune cookie.

You have good luck.

He added a little grin to the grimace. It'd be the first time, he told to himself.

To her, he said you too.

He was sure it wasn't what she'd really said.

Hours later, he heard her coming in the back door, small noises, like a mouse. Keys, boots, door, all miniaturized, all in the same order. Annoying sometimes. It got under your skin, someone trying to minimize themselves like that, become invisible, you couldn't help but be suspicious, wonder why. This was one of those times. Tournier was watching the news in a roundabout way, sound turned-down, an overhead shot of a stretch of icy interstate, cars and trucks all which way, like a row of bad teeth, miles of piled-up vehicles, people stranded in the cold, running out of gas. Ambulances, tow trucks, cops from a half-dozen surrounding counties lending aid in the rescue. High winds, sleet, a wintry mix, the newscasters were saying, making it hazardous for helicopters to airlift the injured from the scene. A wintry mix, but if that temperature went down, the jet-stream wavered, the area of low pressure swept through—some such bullshit—if any of that happened, then look out, snow snow snow.

Where you been?

He knew the answer, not the one she'd give, but where she'd been.

Bring lunch. Coffee. To your friends.

She said this without expression or tone, as usual. Just the words. Plain and unadorned, just as they were invented. Signs meant to indicate some simple fact. Yield. School Zone. Curve. Stop. Speed Limit 55. But the way they were chosen. Put together. You couldn't say it was sarcasm or reproach unless you admitted you'd added the tone. A Rohrshach language she was speaking. You were talking, in some ways, to yourself.

61 Bang

They're policemen, Mei. Not friends. Professional courtesy is all. They're here to uphold the Law.

The Law.

She said it flatly. Taking off her mittens, her parka, the floppy velour hat. Even knowing he was hearing his own reproach in her neutered words, his own guilt and disgust, he couldn't help himself.

What the hell is that supposed to mean?

The Law is where? The Law is when? Show me. Men with guns here. Men with guns there. That's all.

She hadn't turned. She was looking at the wall above the clothes pole where she'd just hung her coat, her velour hat. Staring at it in that way of hers, like she'd turned her back on this world, the one the rest of us still lived in, the one Tournier still lived in. More often than not, lately, to his regret. He'd been here two hours waiting, to confront her, and now that she'd come home he found he couldn't do it, not directly, only in this roundabout half-assed way that he knew she'd despise, even if she never said so. He hated to admit it, but he was ashamed of himself, because he despised it, too.

You know it's not that simple. You know better than anyone.

She turned now, turned from the clothes pole, from the wall, from whatever secret world she faced.

I know you are a coward Leonard Tournier. That is what I know.

He was out of the chair, up and out of it before he even knew he was, up and out of it faster than any man of sixty-seven had any natural right to be. He was across the room, too, like reality itself had been spliced, standing before her so immediately it shocked him, his hand raised, ready to do what he'd never done before, and wouldn't do this time either. She was standing beneath him, looking up into his face, half his size, but for the first time she was all there behind her eyes, behind that smooth ageless face. All the pain, all the atrocity, all the betrayal, the burning villages, bayoneted babies, murdered parents, forced marches passed mass graves in the malarial heat…it was suddenly and all-too revelatory, as if the rocks and stones themselves had started to speak. The hatred, the contempt, the cruelty…

61 Bang

Tournier dropped his arm, a useless and absurd thing he was holding up. He said nothing. He turned and walked out through the kitchen. Picked up his big Smoky-the-Bear hat from the table. Settled it on his head. The coat, he hadn't even taken off. He went out the back door. Mei didn't call him back. He didn't expect her to. The past is not something you can redeem, get back, or change. You can't avenge it, it's safe inside the citadel of time. You can't forget it. You can just ignore it, look the other way, talk over it. You can't bury it, it poisons the ground. You can't run away from it, it follows you everywhere, the one and only faithful lover you'll ever know. Best to make peace with it. Love it, if you possibly can. It'll follow you step-for-step right to the grave.

He didn't even slam the door.

33.

A mistake. It was a mistake, he was thinking it when he went into the sporting goods store and bought the foul weather gear, the boots, the gloves, the hunter's parka, many-pocketed, with capacious hood. The deer rifle and extra boxes of ammunition. The buck-knife, with sheathe. The binoculars. The old man behind the counter saying nothing, or very close to it, so little that Case figured he should say something himself. Something patently false about going hunting, just for the form of it, to make each other feel better. But in the end he couldn't manage it either. So they went through the motions, an absurd dumb-show. A mistake, he knew it, when he packed up his things in the car, parking right outside his old unit, not caring who saw him or didn't, and cleared out of Paradise that same afternoon. It was a mistake when, with the map and instructions the woman gave him propped against the steering wheel, he headed out of town in search of the access road to the abandoned logging factory.

From that point, he already knew it, there would be more mistakes. One right after the other. Leading to that last one you can't erase. The bullet in the head, etc.

Stop, he thought.

Stop making mistakes.

Stop right now.

Might as well tell the heart to stop beating, Case thought.

The sleet was slashing down on the diagonal, but the weather was only getting worse, the temperature dropping, and the forecast apocalyptic. How far could he go, anyway, a hundred miles, two, before the weather forced him to stop at the next town, or the next one over? The only alternative was to wait. But for what? The roads weren't going to get any better, as bad as they were now. And the longer he waited the chances were that more people would arrive at the party. So you tell me, he said, addressing exactly no one, what the hell am I supposed to do? What the hell could he do that wouldn't be a mistake?

He went on, the car swishing and sloshing through the icy porridge building up on the road. If he was going to get the gun, it had to be now. The kid, too, whatever that was about.

It was all coming to a head, it was always going to come to a head, it was just a question of where and when.

Here was where.

Now was when.

There was the access road, right where it was supposed to be, almost invisible in the uniformity of the snow, but the woman had calculated to the exact tenth of a mile and Case had been keeping his eye on the odometer. Christ, she could have been Rand McNally. She should have worked for MapQuest. There was a half-hearted attempt to block access, a piece of lumber that had slipped off one post and rose diagonally to lean against the other. Case stopped the Mustang to a slow skid. Climbed out. Walked around the hood and over to the barricade. The side that had fallen down was wrapped in a heavy chain with a locked padlock. Useless, in other words. Case lifted the heavy piece of wood and heaved it out of the way. Then he got back into the car and turned it onto the road that he could just barely still make out because the gravel that covered it still showed through in enough places beneath the slush.

The tires finding the gravel, or trying to. Driving slowly. Up through the naked trees. Exposed boulders. Shuddering bushes, forever nameless. Everything gray, or shifting shades of gray, white and black, like the future, when you come back, after you die. Into chuckholes. Runnels. Little gullies. Trying to avoid anything major. The road wide enough, cut for the trucks that once carried the lumber or whatever back and forth, but the woods had crept back

61 Bang

over the many years, slender trees standing here and there in the path. Case tried to ease the car carefully around them.

The factory, what was left of it, wasn't too far back, but far enough that even the bare woods had long closed up behind him. A big structure, a quarter of it fallen away to expose empty floors, stripped of machinery, walls, insulation, anything of worth, iron beams exposed like the ribcage of some half-eaten behemoth made of concrete and cable. Snow already lining what there was to line. The rest of the carcass a smoked-out ruin, crumbling, lined with blind windows, not a single one of them with a pane of glass.

Case rolled slowly passed it, tires crunching, looking up at the hulking waste, feeling watched, unreasonably so, he told himself. It was the ghost-town aspect of the place, no doubt, who would be sitting there watching, what would they be watching for?

He pulled the car behind a garage, roofless, doorless. If you could rightly call either side of the building the *behind*. He swished the Mustang close to the wall. A spot he figured to be a little less visible than most of the others. The snow should take care of the rest. Turned off the engine. Looked through the rearview at the black-and-white hill behind him. The path went up, rough-hewn, blazed by flicks of orange tape every dozen yards or so, but it helped to know they were there to see them. What drew your eye to them were the posted warnings to keep away. No Trespassing. Private property. Armed response to intruders. Unauthorized vehicles. Keep the Fuck Away, that was the general idea. Case got out of the car, slung the rifle over his shoulder. Pulled the hood over his head. Squinted upwards. From here he traveled on foot.

Oddly, but then again, maybe not, it was only now, climbing another goddamn hill through bad weather, that he began to wonder how the woman knew where the compound was located, knew so specifically, is what he was thinking, as he stood behind the dubious cover of some kind of tree and consulted the meticulous and painstakingly detailed map on the note sheet she'd given him. Two miles east is what Case figured, trying to shield the paper from the patter and batter of the tiny pellets of icy rain falling all over the place. Whistling through the bare branches overhead. He was

61 Bang

traveling parallel, more or less, to the road, every so often a bend of it came into view. Once or twice he may have actually crossed it. Briefly. What he figured is that he was taking a more direct route to the compound, staying out of sight of any surveillance, if any.

He walked on.

Tree trunks, mulch, rocks, frozen pools of muck. He limped and cursed. Brambles, tangled crap underfoot. Patches of thorny stuff he didn't see until he walked into it and was forced to stop and pick it out of the material of his parka. His knee was aching, his lower back, his right foot, like a spike had been driven straight through the instep. The sharp pain exploring his ribcage. He was drenched in sweat under the parka, alternately seized with the shakes. A fever, maybe? Christ, he needed a drink.

He marched on.

Came to a hunter's blind, or what used to be one. Haphazardly slapped together, falling apart the same way. Just where it was supposed to be, according to the map. Had she ever actually been here?

He hobbled his way towards it. Couldn't be more than a few hundred yards to go now. The compound. He had only the dimmest idea of what he was going to do when he got there. He hadn't realized just how dim, how unfocussed, how practically illusory that plan was now that he was only a few hundred yards away from having to implement it.

Improvising, that's what I'm doing, and even Case had to laugh. Improvising.

Beer cans, leaf rot, an empty fifth, an empty red shotgun shell, scat, cigarette butts, the remains of a red-checked flannel shirt. The bleached pages of a bloated porn mag. That's what was in the hunter's blind, the usual. He slid the rifle off his shoulder, unzipped the parka, reached in for the binoculars. He re-zipped the parka and brought the binoculars up to his face. Scanned the horizon, or what you could see of it, a kind of ridge where the trees thinned enough for a view. A line of smoke, perhaps. Just ahead. Hard to tell through the sleet, the built-up clouds, the general gray. He scanned back the other way. The head, magnified out of all proportion, nearly scared

61 Bang

the shit out of him. Forced him a step backward, as if it mattered, it was probably still fifty yards away. The stag.

The same one as last time?

Antlered, poised, staring, so it seemed, right back at him with its large stern eyes.

How the hell should he know if it were the same one?

Case took a few steps out of the blind, still looking through the binoculars, almost as if drawn by the stag's gaze. Hypnotized by...what? Its beauty, its grace. No, he wouldn't say that. Its calm, its poise, its preternatural sense of itself, of its place in this world, which was, of course, completely natural. Case, and his state, being the unnatural ones. Actually, he wouldn't say that either. He wouldn't know what to say. It was a fucking deer, and Case couldn't help but wonder at it standing there like that, because if this hunting blind were being occupied for the intention for which it was built, occupied by actual hunters, Case would have his rifle to his shoulder and that dumbass deer would soon be a head on a den wall.

He stood there in the falling hail staring at the stag through a pair of binoculars. It made no sense, none at all. The heartbeat of fur that punched the chest, the fluff in mid-air, the mist of atomized meat and bone, the long spool of scarlet and stuff unfurling like a banner from the shuddering chest. Case saw the long legs buckle, suddenly too delicate, too vulnerable. The whole construction beginning to shudder and collapse from within. No, it didn't make any sense, until a split-second later, Case heard the gunshot echoing, bouncing off all those naked trees like it was trying to tell each and every one of them a secret Case was the last one to learn.

Just like I was saying, Case thought, turning for cover nowhere in particular, it was a mistake. A shot plunking off a nearby tree, forcing him away from the blind, where he'd left the rifle. Another mistake. Are they like carcinogens, mistakes that is. You can absorb just so many before you achieve a critical mass, before they become fatal. Case reached into the parka, having to unzip it all over again, because trying to reach under it wasn't working, no matter how frantically his hand fumbled around, not so easy in his crouched posture, seeking shelter, if you could call it that, beneath a different bare tree.

Plunk, the shot overhead. Like dropping acorns the sound, until the unmistakable bang.

Zipper down. Reaching inside the parka, he grabbed the gun from his waistband. The automatic the woman had given him. Squeezed off a shot into the great grey surround just to be doing something constructive, just to put in his two-cents worth, so to speak.

No one seemed particularly impressed. A shot zinged off a rock nearby. Because there was more than one, Case figured, no ballistics expert, but judging from the way the bullets were arriving, from a hodge-podge of crisscross directions. Judging as much as you could judge anything, being shot at from this way and that way, hunkered in a frozen woods.

Case made a half-crouched dash for someplace else. Another tree, presumably. One as good as the next, he figured. This one had a rock near it more or less.

Tinkling ice pellets. Like the patter of elf-steps in the mulch. Waiting for the next shot to tell him where not to be.

Not here, this isn't the place to be, that's for sure, the bullet slamming into a nearby log with a rotten thud. As if to remind him, that could be my brain meat.

Let's talk this thing out.

His words hanging there in the silence, the breath too, in the cold air. A suggestion, Case couldn't help realizing, that sounded every bit as desperate as it was.

What do you say?

They didn't say anything for a while. Noises in the foggy woods that could have been sleet or could have been them moving around. Sneaking up behind him for a better shot. The kill-shot. Then someone called out from a position Case wouldn't have imagined possible. He couldn't help but wince, feeling exit wounds opening up in various vital spots on his body.

This is posted private property. You're trespassing.

61 Bang

A bullhorn? They were using a bullhorn? For crissakes, not only was he outgunned, but out-hollered too. No sense pretending he'd accidentally stumbled onto the land. He wasn't going to be sneaking up on them at this point.

I came to get my property back. You've got something of mine.

Silence.

Let's talk this out.

More silence. Case looking all ways, every way, hearing footsteps everywhere, all at once, seeing no one.

Put your gun up.

This voice sounding farther away than expected. Case crouched there, thinking what to do. Too long, apparently. The bullet thumping the tree about three feet above his head.

Put your gun up. I've got you locked. I pull this trigger. Next shot enters you right ear.

Case didn't doubt it. He lowered the automatic, slipped it back inside the parka. Turned his palms out.

Okay. No gun. Okay? We talk this out?

Stand up.

Case stood up. Another mistake? The last one? There was nothing else he could do, not that he could see. This is how they got you in the end. Left you with no more moves. He'd lost enough games of checkers in the joint to know that.

The first one came from behind a tree practically right on top of him. Rifle at his shoulder, head bent, one eye looking through a scope, for crissakes. A second one materialized, crunching out of the fog about fifty yards away, likewise armed, but rifle held at port arms. There'd be another, sitting the jeep on the crest, waiting for them. All three of them armed and outfitted like they were going out on patrol in central Baghdad.

They marched towards the crest, all three of them. Case, still covered by one rifle. The other guy, talking into the transmitter clipped to the epaulet of his military field jacket. Talking to whoever. The guy sitting the jeep, apparently.

The intruder has been neutralized.

61 Bang

Neutralized, Case thought. Really, I wish he'd put that another way.

34.

So there he was bouncing along in the Jeep, back seat, one of them beside him, one of them turned round in the front passenger seat, watching him, the other driving. Three paramilitary nutjobs and Case, and the dead stag tied across the hood, glass-eyed, hemorrhaging from the muzzle, a metaphor of his general situation that he tried not to think about too much. It was a good sign, he'd thought, that they hadn't made him give up his gun. He thought that until they'd walked him to the Jeep and then they did. Took the automatic and his wallet, his "papers" as they put it in their ridiculous pseudo-military jargon, grown men playing GI Joe, but no less dangerous for that, as if this were a foreign country. As if it weren't? The ground under any three hostile strangers with a common agenda was a foreign country.

Coming down on the other side of the ridge, Case saw it, all snug and cozy in the snow, a wretched-looking "farm" with a few structures, one a little more dilapidated than the other, all of it haphazardly ringed with concertina wire and ominously worded red signs on weathered posts. Vehicles scattered around the grounds in various states of repair—or disrepair—it was hard to tell which way they were tending. What looked like the main house omitting a homey plume of smoke from its chimney, like Little House on the Prairie, except with well-armed maniacs. He saw the white Hummer that had nearly run him off the road a couple of nights before. He felt sick to his stomach.

With one guy covering him, the other thoroughly frisked him. He took the buck knife. His watch. His keys and everything in his pockets. This took place in what looked like a tool shed, except there

61 Bang

weren't any tools in it. Bare plank walls. Enough spaces between the planks that the snow had blown inside, lying in long feathery lines on a floor of packed grey earth. A rough-hewn table upon which his possessions lay. They took his belt. They took his shoes.

The guy with the rifle, red-bearded, ear-flapped hunting hat, munched a toothpick as he watched, leaning casually against the long handle of something or other, an antique plow, maybe. They checked his mouth, his ears. What the hell were they looking for? Microphones? Weapons? This was paranoia to a scary degree. This was the capture of Saddam Hussein

Drop yer pants.

What?

We all been speaking English up to now. You heard me.

Isn't this a bit much?

The guy behind Case answered by striking a blow to his kidneys with a riot baton that folded his knees and left him clinging to the edge of the table gasping like a fish out of water. The guy they called Red grinned. Like the others, teeth apparently optional.

Case fumbled with his belt, if just to get the guy in back of him to remove the baton he was pressing down across the back of his neck. Case found himself shivering uncontrollably. They'd already taken his parka. Now his pants were down.

Underwear, jackass. You know the drill.

Snap of rubber glove. Red still grinning.

The gloved man behind him moving closer. Relax, sweetheart. We'll both have an easier time of it.

Case closed his eyes and grit his teeth. What else could you do in this position? Sad to say, Case knew from experience.

It lasted as long as it lasted.

Fun's over. Pull your pants up.

He slapped Case on the rump and called over to Red who was chewing on a toothpick, regarding the scene with a philosophic detachment.

All yours, Partridge. He's clean. In a manner of speaking.

Har har har. Case ground his teeth. A hand up your ass is always good for a laugh, isn't it? Relieves the tension of the moment.

Cheap comedy. At your expense. Case pulled up his pants, not easy to recapture one's dignity in this situation. But you figure something has to be said sooner or later. You have to start somewhere.

I guess this is your idea of Southern hospitality.

He probably should have started later. This wasn't the time for wisecracks, but no one hit him all the same. Instead they made him roll up the sleeves of his shirt and hold his hands out. The third man came forward, that would be Partridge, and examined the inside of Case's forearms and wrists, flicking his middle-finger, thumping around. Red was examining the tip of his toothpick. Out comes the syringe.

What the fuck.

Easy does it.

That was Red throwing away the toothpick and lifting the automatic rifle. Sighting down the barrel. Giving a little shrug with his sited eye on Case's heart. What choice ya got? Better he inject you, than I inject you with this.

Shit, Case thought, shit. Nothing more eloquent than that. The rubber tubing looped around his left bicep, Partridge pulling it tight, tying it off. Thumping the veins again.

At least tell me what it is.

Case watching the man slowly fill the syringe.

Don't worry. Rubber Glove laughs. This is the best part.

All business, Partridge says nothing. Buzz-cut. No chin. Clean-shaven. Probably ex-military, a Timothy McVeigh type. Too serious for his own good. A true believer. Those are the worst kinds.

The needle pricked, nothing more. The drug slid right in. Red lit a cigarette, passed it to Rubber Glove. Lit another one for himself. They all stood around for a few minutes, looking at him, like they were waiting for him to turn into Charlize Theron.

Case hopping from foot to foot, hugging himself. Can I have my parka back? That was the first effect Case felt of whatever drug they'd put into him. He was cold before, now he felt as if the temperature had dropped another twenty degrees. When he asked for his parka, it sounded like a mentally retarded guy on the other side of the room had asked the identical question. Red and Rubber Glove

61 Bang

laughing, smoking, nodding their heads. Moving their mouths, the words sounding like they were coming from the ceiling. Partridge grim as a Marine recruitment poster.

Then they're running across the yard, all three of them, Case in the middle, in loose shirtsleeves, barefoot, holding up his beltless pants with one fist. The sleet. The cold. Everything happening too fast. Another ramshackle building, not a barn, whatever exactly a barn looked like, all the damn structures in the compound looked like barns. Too small for a barn, too big for a latrine, it could have been a chapel, what size is a chapel? They shoved him inside, closed the door, no doubt bolted it, or chained it, or whatever. Case would check later, or not. He was sitting on the floor, holding his knees, teeth chattering. His brain was working, just not quite right. Another dirt floor. High ceiling. The place empty, except for the macabre centerpiece, dangling from its hocks on a chain from a beam. The stag, its throat cut, bleeding out into a large metal basin. A reminder of things to come. Case wasn't surprised, no, he really wasn't, when the dead animal started talking. He closed his eyes, it didn't help, the buck kept right on yakking.

35.

Are you a lawman?

Sometime later, Case opening his eyes, lifting his two-hundred-pound head, and there he was standing there, big as all life, red and smoking in the cold, the hillbilly, in a long leather apron, coring out the rectum of the hanging animal. Yanking the knife down the animal's center line like a tailor unzipping a coat for a customer, pulling apart the halves, exposing the cage packed with lungs, the sack of internal organs, minimal blood. Hillbilly looked more alive than anything Case could ever remember seeing in his entire life, like Zeus or something. He was laughing. He was asking a question. He wanted to know.

Are you a lawman?

Cutting through the pelvic bone with a small handsaw. The diaphragm separates the chest and body cavities and must be cut away. Was he actually saying that even as he did it? Case heard words inside his head. Hillbilly reached inside the chest, rooting around like he was looking for a pair of underwear in a duffel bag and pulled the heart and liver free of the connective tissue. These he put into a separate plastic bag. The intestines, which were already half-falling out of the animal, he scooped out two-fisted and let pile up in the pail, a long sloppy coil of lavender sausage. Case felt mesmerized and nauseated. Loosen the windpipe and gullet by cutting through them as far forward into the neck area as you can reach. Well, are you? He wanted to know. Are you an agent of Zog?

Case tried to retch. Head bowed, nothing came out but spittle. What was in that hypodermic? What did you give me? Hillbilly was slitting the skin around the lower part of the buck's legs, just above the ankles, using the knife to cut it away from the tendons, sticking his balled fist into the resulting pocket and stripping it away from the body. Skinning the damn thing naked. He turned back to Case and winked. Grinning in his big thorny black beard. It's just like a big rabbit. He left the skin on the head, the remainder spectral and blue. The effect more awful, like it was two entirely separate animals, mythological almost, some kind of creature that existed in a never-meant-to-be-seen realm between life and death.

Zog. Zionist Occupation Government.

Had Case even asked?

Are you a lawman?

No. For crissakes. No. Hadn't he answered the question already, hadn't he answered it three or four times? Or was he just answering it inside his head?

Were they just trying to confuse him? I'm not a lawman.

The early European tribes were the true ten lost tribes of Israel. Therefore the white European is the rightful heir to God's covenant.

The head was left intact.

Do you believe in Yahshua?

The head is intact. They leave that for the taxidermist. Don't want to ruin your trophy.

Before Adam and Eve the Bible tells us that the Earth was inhabited by the lesser races, the beasts of the field it calls them, these are your Asians, your Mexicans, your niggers. Eve was seduced by the snake and gave birth to twins. Satan's child was Cain and Adam's son was Abel. The Jews are descendant of Cain. Their goal is to achieve total dominion over the earth, a one-world Order, whose master is Satan.

Even drugged, partially hallucinating, Case wasn't so much amazed that anyone could believe such nonsense in this day and age. What amazed him is that anyone could believe anything at all.

Do you believe in Yahsua?

Case felt like he was trapped in a nightmare, not a metaphoric nightmare, but a literal nightmare, where things happened and you had no control of them, where things happened not outside your

61 Bang

mind, but inside your mind, where you had no control even of your own thoughts, no means of resistance, the skull that separated inside from outside had dissolved away. Even the craziest fears instantly became real. So he had to be careful. What he thought. What he feared. What had they injected into him? Do I believe in what? Who the fuck is Yahsua?

Jesus. Is Jesus your personal savior? Do you believe in His Coming?

I wish he were here right now.

He is.

Funny, unbound as he was, Case hadn't thought of getting up, it hadn't occurred to him to even try. Until now. And he still didn't make the attempt. He felt like a puddle of something on the floor. A heap of empty clothes. He had no shoes. Outside the wind was screaming.

Why'd you bury that gun?

Gun?

You want to be honest with me now. You want to choose sides and you want to choose the winning side. The right side. The End Times are upon us, brother, and that means it's no time to fuck around.

Hillbilly stood there, next to the flayed and gutted buck, knife in hand, gleaming.

It's evidence. In a crime.

It's got to do with that nigger they shot in New York City, don't it?

Case nodded.

Can't hear your head shake, boy.

Did Hillbilly actually say that? It was something Case's father used to say when he was a kid. Only now did it come back to him.

Yeah.

Did it kill anyone?

No.

That gun belonged to the nigger didn't it?

Yeah.

It was on him when he got shot.

61 Bang

Yeah.

It proves he was armed, don't it? Proves the cops had cause.

Yeah.

And the niggers want it to disappear, don't they?

Can you give me back my parka? My shoes. I'm freezing. His skeleton was rattling he was so fucking cold. Parts of him were numb as rubber.

Hillbilly laughed, like it was a joke. Or maybe he was laughing at the situation surrounding the gun. Or maybe Case hadn't said the words aloud, or he didn't get the joke. Maybe he'd said something else entirely. Maybe he'd burst out into baby-talk. There didn't seem to be any rules at all in this living nightmare, which, strictly speaking, is what made it a nightmare.

Case slumped on the floor, the hanging carcass stripped to muscle and nerve, the hillbilly there and then not there, maybe he'd passed out and woke up, it was impossible to say, time seemed to be jumping around, Christ he was freezing, he didn't think it possible for him to be freezing any more than he already was until someone opened the door. Close the door, he wanted to say. He was a prisoner of war, that's what Hillbilly called him. A prisoner of war, he'd said, for the time being. Case clutched himself, shivering. Close. The. Door. It wasn't Hillbilly that had come back, not his paramilitary maniacs. It was the girl, the girl from the convenience store, shabbily dressed under an oversized and oil-stained army field jacket, lank hair, smudged face. She stood above him, looking down, big-eyed. She had what looked like an old horse blanket in her arms. She held it out to him. Case snatched it and wrapped it around his shoulders. It smelled a lot worse than a horse. The girl drew back, laid a plastic jug of water on the floor. She said nothing

Help me.

She said nothing, just stared, looking afraid.

Get me some shoes. A coat.

Nothing, she says nothing.

I'm cold. I'm fucking freezing.

The carcass hangs, turning blue, meat hardening.

If you get me some clothes, I'll get us both out of here.

61 Bang

Her eyes are big and starved in the dirty face, like the eyes of some Dickens pauper. She doesn't believe him. Why should she? He's a guy half-naked on the floor begging for a pair of shoes. How is he going to help her? At this point he's even worse off than she is.

Say something.

She shakes her head no.

Are you afraid to talk? He's not here. It's only us. He's not here, is he? They can't hear you.

She shakes her head no.

What? What is it?

She bends forward. She's wearing rubber boots. Yellow. Four sizes too big.

She opens her mouth, pulling the bottom lip down with a filthy finger. There's no tongue inside. It's been cut out. The wound still looks fresh. There's no tongue inside.

Case thinks, if he only still had the note. He'd hand it back to her. So she could give it to someone. Anyone.

Help Us God, Please.

61 Bang

The Last Will and Testament of
Leonard Jacques Tournier

Is that what they still called these things, it seems impossible they still did. He took a sip from the Flintstone glass of bourbon by his hand, a survivor of some promotional Happy Meal or other, devoured in the distant past, part of another life. Hard to say how we accumulate such things, so much junk, and why some things hang around so long, and others don't. He leaned back in the leather chair, the thing creaking in the empty house. This was his house we're talking about, a place he didn't spend much time in between his time at Mei's and his time at the office, the Evergreen, and anywhere else he could possibly be instead. A big old drafty thing full of old crap and bad memories that he never managed to escape, a tomb full of shabby ghosts where he practically lived his whole life.

Shit, let's get to it.

Another sip of bourbon. He crossed out The Last Will and Testament of Leonard Jacques Tournier. Too dramatic, for one thing. Like something you'd see somebody writing in a movie. Besides, he doubted it made it any more legal or official just to write these words across the top of a piece of paper. What was he going to write next, for crissakes, being of sound mind and body? According to who? Himself? Tournier laughed. Old, drunk, insomniac, haunted by regret and failure, wracked by unaccountable griefs that ambushed him at the most unexpected times, moistening his eyes, goddammit. Stiff in the morning with arthritis, nagged by assorted aches and pains, losing his eyesight, his hearing fading, the hard-on not nearly so hard nor so often, forgetful, but not quite forgetful enough. A deep ache lately in his lower belly, never entirely going away anymore,

61 Bang

probably the prostate gone bad, not quite admitting even to himself that occasional pink tinge at the bottom of the urinal is blood, this was Leonard Jacques Tournier, sixty-seven-years-old and with the mind and body to prove it, not quite so sound, no, not quite. This was the truth and this was a time for truth, if ever there was one. The dark night of the soul is what they called it. The truth being something you tell when you figure there won't be any need to lie to protect your tomorrow.

Tournier crossed out everything he wrote up to now. He started over nice and simple. He started off with what he really wanted to say.

Dear Mei.

If you're reading this, it means I'm dead. If not, stop reading right now, or you might just have to kill me yourself. Ha ha. I'm not planning to die, or get myself killed or anything like that. I'm not suicidal, well, not particularly so, no more than any other old sonofabitch who's finding it increasingly hard to lace his boots up in the morning. Besides, outright suicide is just not something I could ever take to...I've too much of an instinct for survival, I guess. Or maybe it's just as you say, I'm a coward. Fact is, I'm just not in enough pain yet to put myself out of it. But, that said, you get to an age where you're not so sure from moment to moment...

Mei, I love you, let me say that right off, and the sad thing is, I don't know if I ever told you that as directly as I should've. Maybe I muttered it into the pillow a few times afterwards, or only said it in my head awake in the middle of the night or driving along some pitch-black back road by myself someplace. Even now it's too late to tell you, even now when there's still breath in my lungs, but don't ask me why. I don't know myself. No, that's not true. Maybe I do know; it just doesn't do any good to say.

Some things don't. Do any good to say, I mean. Some things are just better left without saying because once you say them everything changes and it's just no good anymore. That's something you always knew. That's something you taught me, Mei.

But I think you knew I loved you. It's just something, in my experience, women tend to know. And one thing I can say for sure is

61 Bang

that I've had enough experience that way, both good and bad. So I guess in the end that's why I never felt I had to say anything. Why I figured it was even better if I didn't. Because I figured it would ruin everything if I did. But one good thing about death is that at least you can't ruin anything anymore. You know right off that things can't get any worse. Yeah, I'm drunk, but there ain't no morning after.

I'm running off at the mouth here, dammit. Let me get to the point.

I always wanted nothing more than to leave this crappy nothing town behind. To make something different out of my life than what I ended up making out of it. It wasn't anybody's fault that I didn't, and maybe I never had it in me to do anyway. That could be the worse thing to happen to a man. To have a dream that he couldn't ever fulfill even if he had the chance. But not to get the chance and forever think, well, if only…maybe that's a blessing, after all.

I killed someone Mei. I'm sorry to spring it on you like this. Without warning. But goddammit, if I don't just come right out and say it, I'll write a whole novel here before I get around to the point of what I'm trying to say. I killed a girl when I was sixteen years old and she was only a year older. I killed her and hid the fact and I might as well have buried myself in this town along with her when I did it.

Tournier laid the neck of the bottle on top of the glass. The bourbon glug-glugged out, Fred and Barney completely submerged, as if they'd driven their foot-pedaled car into a rusty lake and didn't know it yet, still laughing.

He took a long swallow, staring at the words on the page, so many of them already, all going a little blurry, too many to correct or take back, surprised, he was, that he had so much to say, so much of nothing, really, and nothing to do but go forward. Just keep trying to say what he really wanted to say. The truth, whatever that was. Each sentence a brand-new opportunity. Each one a failure. But maybe he could get close enough. Sleet rushed the windows in periodic assaults. Something sounded like it was running through the rain gutters. He put the pen on the paper. He went forward. Started a new sentence. One foot in front of another. Never getting to the destination. Oh well.

61 Bang

Children have a secret world that adults never know about, Mei. They forget themselves how big and strange the world once seemed when they were young. How big and because of that, how small a neighborhood a kid carves out of it for himself. This little neighborhood has its own laws, its own realities. That's just the way it is. It has its own secrets. Maybe it's different for kids nowadays. We like to think it is, anyway. But I'd guess it's not. It's an enchanted time, adolescence, but there are ogres in every enchanted forest. Every kid knows this instinctively. Hell, it's in all the fairy tales.

Another sip of bourbon. Rattling windows. It wasn't the house that was haunted, Tournier considered, but himself haunting the house. Soon it'd be his turn to go out there and join the rest of them, all the rootless ghosts wailing in the cold and stark.

There was a guy who lived round here back then. Probably a guy just like him in every town. His name's not important, who he was, not any more. He's long-dead anyhow. Figure he's got to be by now…he had to be nearly fifty back then. Least he seemed that old when you're at that age when anything over twenty-five seems like fifty. He gave the boys rides and such. Let them hang out at his farm. We'd sit out there smoking and drinking, like teenage boys will, swapping bullshit stories, wrestling, target shooting our .22s and whatnot. Easy-going guy, he was, always unshaved, dressed in the same old flannels and overalls winter and summer, farm practically run into the ground, living in a cloud of alcohol, supplied us sometimes, off-handed like, with smokes and booze, not really that unusual back in the day. He did mostly odd jobs in town. Fixed machinery, patched roofs, that kind of thing. No one knew exactly where he come from. Just showed up one autumn and took possession of the place. People asked a lot less questions back then. He lived alone, as you might imagine. Always did. Never saw any woman with him. Kind of guy he was, you couldn't tell if he didn't want a woman or no woman would have him. Probably just required too much of an effort to overhaul his life to the degree a woman might consider him a suitable mate. That's what it seems to me now, after all these years. Just one of them guys who take the path of least resistance.

61 Bang

He used to pay a couple of the kids for it. A dollar, sometimes a beer and half a dozen cigarettes or an old skin-mag he was done with, all depending. Nowadays, it'd be child abuse, plain and simple. Probably was back then, too. But without anyone calling it that, without any adult to name it, what was it? A hand-job in the front seat of his pick-up parked at the end of an old logging road on a summer afternoon. What was it? Lying on the moldy board floor of a forgotten hunting blind while a middle-aged man lay on top of you, huffing and puffing and muttering with his eyes closed like he was praying in tongues, all red-faced and looking about to croak right then and there of a heart attack. What could you call that exactly? I was one of those guys he picked. Don't know why, or why I went along. Truth was, something seemed wrong about it even at the time, but I couldn't really say what. Maybe the way he acted about it himself, all furtive, making it plain it wasn't something you were to tell anyone. Not that you would, you see. Who would you tell? It was something private, secret, you knew it instinctively, even as a kid, especially as a kid, there were so many things you weren't supposed to do, so many things you weren't supposed to know, the hidden world of sex, that was just one of those things.

Truth was, I didn't do it just for the dollar or the smokes either. That gave it a reason, an excuse, kind of. But there were other reasons, too. Reasons that nobody is really prepared to hear, or wants to hear, nowadays. Or any days, I guess. Another one of those things that's better left unsaid. I was special, Mei. He told me so himself and I did things with him worth more to him than just a dollar or a cigarette. And I can't say that I didn't like it, Mei. I can't say I was just an innocent victim. I just can't. Anyway, that's not really the point of this story. Wouldn't you like me to get to it? Yes, me too. Not that you'd know it by the way I'm doing just about anything but. Let me start off again with what I really want to talk about. Start the sentence over and maybe the paragraphs will follow.

Back to the point.
What is the point?
The killing. That I killed someone.
I killed a girl Mei.

61 Bang

We used to go out. If you could call it going out what we done at sixteen back then. I guess you could, specially when in those days we married at twenty, had babies of our own before we were twenty-one. We used to go out, but not much more than that. Fact is, not long after, I'd fallen in love with the first girl I'd ever fallen in love for, Susannah Chard, and this other girl, well I guess it turns out I only thought I'd loved her, and didn't anymore, the old story, just like it always goes, sixteen or sixty, but she still loved me, loved me, whatever that means at sixteen, or sixty for that matter, and she was going to tell everyone about what I was doing back in the woods with that man. Tell Susannah, particularly. Cause she'd found out. Girls weren't supposed to know about that kind of stuff, but she did. Because someone told her.

Kids world, Mei.

Their own codes and chivalries. Their own society. Secrets and such. Complex as any tribe deep in the jungles. It would take an anthropologist to figure it all out. Decipher that adolescent social hieroglyphic and even then there'd be gaps and omissions. Misinterpretations.

She loved me. She would tell Susannah. She would tell them all, Mei, including the adults. Some of the kids knew, some of them did it themselves, but that didn't matter. It was a thing that by its very nature didn't suffer itself to be spoken. And what I was doing with that old man, well, it went beyond the bounds of even what the other boys who knew would tolerate. It was degenerate. It was faggotry, plain and simple. Peggy would speak it she loved me so much. That's how much she loved me, or thought she did. I see that now, of course, but not back then.

I argued with her. I pleaded. I threatened her

I don't mean to be cynical at this late hour. But love, Mei, consider it. Love. Has any emotion caused so much pain and suffering and evil in this world?

They would have all turned against me like dogs do on one of their own wounded. That's how it works, how it always works. Like a dog with a split belly and a length of intestine dangling out. They'd

61 Bang

have turned on me and torn me to shreds out of the sheer instinct for survival.

It was Maynard who told her. Because I'd made the mistake of confiding in him, my best friend. Maynard who loved Peggy himself. I've long since forgiven him. Half a century is a long time to carry anything, even a grudge. Things change. Life goes on. Bygones be bygones. Stuff happens, other wars, other alliances, and, after all, boys will be boys.

Boys will be boys.

I couldn't have it, Mei. I couldn't have her tell. I grabbed her and didn't even know what. I grabbed her and when I finally let go and realized what I'd done she wasn't moving anymore on her own, that's what I most remember, just flopping around all heavy at the ends of my arms when I picked her up again to shake her awake, a big bulge in the side of her neck like she'd swallow a chicken wing. Terrible the way a body doesn't move anymore when it stops living, stops holding itself up against the gravity always pulling us down. It weighs heavy like dirt, like dirt in a bag. You might never have felt it before, but you know exactly what it is the first time. Never seen a corpse in your life, but you recognize it immediately.

All of this in Leonard's spiky cramped hand, getting worse, spikier and looser as the level of bourbon went down in his Flintstone glass, unraveling, maybe completely indecipherable at this point, although he was trying hard, honest he was, trying his hardest possible to control the pen in his hand, to get it all completely right once and for all. Or maybe not, who knew. Maybe both at the same time. That was more likely, divided against ourselves as we are. He took another drink, turned over the paper, and immediately forgot where he was in the story, but that was okay. It didn't matter. He'd just pick it up wherever. There was no past or present. No order. Not without a future. Without a future, everything just kind of fell apart. Stop feeling sorry for yourself, you old bastard, can the self-pity, if that's what this is.

She's buried out there, on the English property. He wasn't a survivalist, Owen senior, that is, not an anti-government man, not like his son, not exactly anyhow. He ran moonshine back then, burned crosses, and threatened Negroes passing through to make sure they kept passing, nothing out of the ordinary, a segregationist tried and blue, a true American, that's for sure, so the seeds were planted, I guess you could say. My daddy didn't have much liking for the man, not that he was any progressive thinker himself, my daddy, but he thought Owen a particular form of riffraff just the same. But there was a connection there going back to I don't know when and I never knew what, and a favor was owed. He arranged it with old man English to hide the body on his land. Cause I'd gone to daddy not knowing where else to go. He made me bury her myself, crying like a baby the whole time, standing in the grave digging, while he stood there above me with his arms crossed, staring off hard-faced in the moonlight like he couldn't bear to even look at me. We never talked about that night, not once, all the way till the day he died, but it wasn't gone between us, not for one second. I'd become sheriff like he'd been sheriff, that was understood, that didn't need any discussing, that was my fate now, no matter what dreams I'd had before, that was my working off of the sin I'd committed, no question. Owen wasn't nothing but a little child then, six or seven maybe, but old man English passed it on, the debt that the Tourniers owed them, the trump they hold over us, the body buried one hundred paces back the abandoned horse barn.

Maybe if we'd just come clean with it all at the very start things could have been different. Hard to say. Times were different back then. The shame of it, that's one of the big things that was different. People felt shame that couldn't be gotten over with just a confession, with some apologies and excuses. Shame stained you forever, and your family in both directions, ancestors and descendants, it couldn't be borne, a burden both honorable in its way and terrible and dishonorable in the same way. It was an accident, it shouldn't have happened, but it grew into something else with the hiding of it, something bigger and impossible to uproot, like a cancer. This town became my prison, Mei. I could never leave it. I had to watch over things, that girl in the grave holding me here like I was married to her, like I was dead and rotting in the ground with her.

61 Bang

So that's your hero, Mei. The whole ugly secret. I know you loved me just so long as I didn't fail you and I failed you in the end. I don't blame you for that. I don't blame you for anything. Men and women are made different that way, no matter what anyone says. I don't know what all Owen English is doing up at that compound, and most of that is for not wanting to know, for turning a blind eye, and it's cowardice, just as you say, plain and simple, but I swear I don't know if he or old man English had anything to do with the disappearance of your baby. But I'm gonna try to find that out among other things because whatever's going on out there isn't right and I should have put a stop to it a long time ago.

Well, as Porky Pig said, that's all folks. I can't think of anything else to say. I don't figure whatever happens from here on out is going to end too well for yours truly one way or another. But I avoided the inevitable for a long time. I'm ready, Mei, to go out and meet it. Courage comes to different men at different times, I'm convinced of that. It's come to me now, too late for a lot of things, hopefully not too late for certain others. I'd tell you to take care of yourself but you don't need me to tell you that. Of all the people I ever knew, you do that better than anyone. Take this to Sam Bixby in Grangeville. Legal firm of Bixby and Halloday. I leave you any and all of my worldly possessions. Such as they are. Try to remember me fondly. Yours, Leonard.

Tournier leaned back in the creaking chair and stared in disgust at the scrawled pages on the desk. It was all wrong, not what he wanted to say at all. He crumpled up the pages, crushed them tightly in his two fists. There's no time to get it right, but who's he kidding? If he had a hundred more years he still wouldn't be able to get it right. He pulled apart the tight wads of paper and tried to smooth them out with the flats of his palms. Let it stand. He drank what was left in his glass and set it down on the pages for a paperweight. He rubbed his bristled chin and noticed for the first time the wan light filling the room. Well lookit there and whaddya know. Morning already. Cockledoodledo.

61 Bang

January 11th

61 Bang

Lights flashing like Christmas, Tournier came rocking into the compound in his official police SUV, the grounds and buildings shrouded in snow, snow still falling in big cottony puffs, no sign of it letting up. He should have brought Jackson with him, that's what they'll say when this is over. A good man, Jackson, the town is going to need him. Which is why Tournier couldn't bring him along. This was Tournier's battle, his good vs. evil, his old business, plain and simple. His mess to clean up. Let Jackson have a clean slate. Let him fuck up his own world and die in vain trying to make it right again.

No one to greet him, no lookouts, none that he could see. Is this any way to run a survivalist camp meant to defend the white race at the end of the world? Tournier was going to have to have a talk with Owen about that. A real disgrace. Just one man, huddled under the door of an outbuilding, smoking a cigarette. A rifle standing next to him, which he just picked up. A good place to start as any. Tournier slid the SUV to a soft sloppy stop, grabbed the shotgun beside him, opened the door and spit. Here we go. High noon.

Boots in the snow, the slightest crunch. The man in the doorway, grinning, Tournier recognized the face circled in the fur of the hood.

Trouble sheriff?

Could be, Red. It's a possibility.

Can I help ya?

He's smiling, Tournier's smiling, everyone's smiling, everything tight as a wire on a booby-trap.

Maybe. Step aside, Red.

Can't do that sheriff.

Sure you can, Red. First one foot, then the other, a sideways step. It's easy.

61 Bang

Red tosses away the cigarette, hunches up his shoulders, concealing, or not, the rifle coming up a bit, getting a little more serious across his chest. He shrugs.

I got my orders sheriff.

Red, I've known you since you were a baby. Known you since you were shittin in your nappies in your mama's arms.

So?

Red grinning, this trip down memory lane amusing him. Snow falling all around. It's never snowed round here like this before.

So you ain't one goddam bit smarter now than you were then.

Bam. Nothing subtle about the blast of the shotgun on such a cottony muffled morning. No way it's mistaken for anything else. Remarkable, in that sense.

This close, the top half of Red sort of disengages from the bottom half, twisting a bit, connected only by stray ropes of sinew and vein just off-target, a good deal of the rest simply vaporized, no longer really existing anymore, and much of that stuff absolutely essential for Red to even consider living, to go on being Red as we once knew him, internal organs and arteries, stuff like that.

Lots of red and Red all over the door of the building, the snow, etc. Tournier walks over it to find John Case huddled on the floor inside.

Every time I see you, I swear you can't get to lookin any worse. Then, sure as shootin, you pop up again lookin worse than ever and prove me wrong. Get up off the floor, Mr. Case. We've got work to do.

Case, looking up from his folded arms, teeth chattering like he was chopping the words to shreds. Whatever he was saying, unintelligible, even to him. The sight of the sheriff standing there, shotgun in hand, big as day, come to his rescue, basically unreal, another hallucination.

Come on, pull yourself together.

His free hand grabbing Case's upper arm, an old man's grasp, impatient, trembling, sickeningly desperate. Yanking Case to his feet,

61 Bang

which aren't quite under him, not yet, anyway. What the hell happened to your shoes? Never mind. Don't bother explaining.

Fuckin. Freezing.

We get to the car, I've got a spare jacket. How's that sound? Do you think you can make it on your own? I sure as hell can't carry you.

Injected me. With something. Mostly worn off. I think.

Yeah. The conditions in this prison are deplorable. The international community will be appalled. I'm going to let you go now. Think you can stand? It's every man for himself from here on out. Tournier broke open the shotgun, inserted a fresh bright candy-red shell, and snapped the gun shut. I hate to jinx you. He glanced over at the partially skinned and bled out buck. But at least you look a little better than that guy. Case, looking a bit wobbly, was still standing after a fashion. Let's go. Look alive.

Case thinking, This is my chance.

The cold blast of air from the open door slapped some of the remaining cobwebs from Case's drugged skull. A cold even colder than the cold he was already numb to. Tournier peering into the hazy landscape. The yard was a swirling grey broth of blowing snow, the sheriff's car visible within it only as a mad syncopation of muted lights, like some kind of weird Arctic light show. Tournier leading the way into the storm, shotgun held high like a shepherd's staff. Case following, staggeringly.

Mind your step, Mr. Case. Crossing the doorway. There's Red all over the place.

Running, after a fashion, barefoot through the snow, drifted up to his knees in some places, over his knees in others, stepping high, stumbling. Tournier, gun held overhead, goose-stepping through the drifts. Tumbling, practically, into the SUV, pulling the door closed with a hermetic *whup*. The heater blowing, but the warmth still far away. Case sitting there waiting for it, like you'd wait for a train, stunned.

The jacket is too big. A red plaid affair. The hat, too. Fitted for Tournier's big head. Orange, with earflaps stuffed with some kind of fur. He had to look ridiculous. It doesn't feel any better to have them

61 Bang

on, but it will, just give it time. Already he was coming back to himself.

We got to get the gun. And the kid.

Tournier peering through the windshield, not that there's much of anything to peer at on the other side. He nods at nothing. Reaches under his seat and comes up with a holster. Pulls out the substantial revolver inside. Hands it to Case.

Think you can manage it?

Case's fingers hardly any more sensible than the gun. All of it felt alien.

Yeah. Think so.

Tournier, slipped the car into gear, looking at Case, doubtful. But what choice did he have?

Just point it in the right direction. Meaning, at anyone else but me. Get it?

Got it.

Oh, that's good. Consider yourself deputized.

They proceeded slowly across the yard, the main house looming into view like a shipwreck from out of the curtains of blowing snow. Tournier applied the brakes. Overhead lights still going, splashing everything with drama. Not trying to hide their arrival, that's for sure.

Case checked the gun. His hands, the rest of him, starting to feel like something human. Starting to feel, anyway. He checked to make sure all the chambers were loaded, firing pin in place, that the thing was ready to shoot, in other words. Everything seemed to be in order.

Tournier took up the shotgun again. Peered up at the house, at the windows, where nothing whatsoever could be seen. He had the great big Smokey-the-Bear hat setting on his head.

Okay. Here we go.

What's the plan?

The plan, Mr. Case? No plan. We go in there and take what we want. Anyone stands in our way, we shoot them. He smiles. That's how we do things. Winks. It's good to be the Law.

61 Bang

No need to pound on the door, no reason to announce themselves, the obligatory Police! Open Up!, no shooting out of locks, or kicking anything off its hinges. The door was wide open, the welcome wagon out to greet them in the person of a sleepy-looking guy in a military-issue waffle undershirt and grey-and-white camo pants for combat in the snow. Partridge, in other words, tousled and armed.

Police business. Tournier, walking through the dancing snowflakes, affable as a granddad who woke up one morning and decided to kill the entire family. Stand aside, son.

Case could see the uncertainty in the younger man's face, the hand resting on his sidearm, still half-asleep, questioning himself, is this some kind of bad dream? What do I do? Whose orders do I follow? You could see all that flashing across his pale baby face, a perpetual soldier, waiting for instructions, a direction to march off and die.

Is he expecting you? No one told me. You'll have to wait right there. Sir. Don't come any further. Halt.

Looking from Tournier to Case. Out-maneuvered. Fumbling meaningfully with the holster on his sidearm, but meaning nothing.

You got a warrant?

Saying this to Tournier's shoulder as the bigger man pushes right on passed, calling these words half to the sheriff and half up the dilapidated staircase across the room that climbed into the dim ambiguity that was the second floor.

Call a lawyer.

You can't enter here without a warrant.

Tournier now ignoring the man entirely. He's proven him wrong already, after all. Hand to the side of his face, smiling coldly up into that dimness at the top of the stairs. Rise and shine up there, Owen. Put on your bushy tail. We need to have some words.

Case felt jittery, like he should shoot someone just to snap out of it, to make things real again. He took a look around, his revolver up, not quite leveled at Partridge, but, you know, getting there. He took a jumpy look around mainly to distract himself, to keep from pulling the trigger prematurely. Wood stove. Tables. Plates. More beer cans than you'd think possible. An animal's den, that's what

61 Bang

Case was reminded of. Gun magazines. Guns. Porn. Garbage. All that was missing was the pile of bones.

He was coming down the creaking staircase, slowly, in his long yellow-white underwear. Hillbilly, a vast lumbering shape, all black hair and thorns, moving almost gingerly on the rickety stairs, hand on the rail, like a bear on tiptoes.

Sheriff. What brings you out here. In all this weather. So fucking early. No problem, I hope.

Another man, tall, blonde, thin, emerges from a room off to the side, a bathroom, maybe, having just finished a crap and armed with something that looks short and automatic.

Dammit, Case is thinking, five minutes in and here they were already outgunned.

Hillbilly is at the bottom of the stairs now, finally easing himself down off the last step, Tournier facing him, not paying attention to Partridge and this other guy, leaving them for Case to cover, supposedly. His gun sort of wavering around uncertainly. Case saw her, the kid, crouched near the wall about two steps down from the top. Wearing a thin slip, hands over her ears, big eyes, like she was just waiting for the inevitable boom boom boom.

No problems yet, Owen. Tournier with that cock-silly grin still planted smack in the middle of his big country mug. Well, no big ones anyway. It's just that, well, Tournier waving the gun around in general, indicating everything, you know, you're all under arrest. Ha ha.

Hillbilly squaring off casually next to a gun cabinet, a fucking gun cabinet for crissakes, his elbow on it, practically an armory. That's funny Leonard. He points his beard at Case. See you have a friend with you.

Yeah. Imagine my surprise finding him in your barn, half-naked, allegedly injected with an unknown substance, forcibly retained against his will and wishes.

Didn't have an invitation on him, did he? Cause he sure as hell didn't show us one. And as you well know, that's the only way people belong on this here land. That's the Constitution, sheriff. That's the

61 Bang

Law. Now if we'd have known he was a friend of yours Sheriff, we might have been able to make an exception. But the Law is the Law.

Not exactly, Owen. Fact is, the Law is a fluid thing. A very fluid thing. It's being amended and interpreted all the time.

I see he's holding a gun. In my home. Why is that, Sheriff? What authority does he have to do that?

He's had a sudden elevation in the world. Deputized. On the spur of the moment, as it were.

Hillbilly cocks an eyebrow. That so? So this here is an official visit, after all. By the way, you didn't happen to see Red anywhere out there did you? Hate to think he got lost wandering around in the snow. It's awful cold.

Yeah as a matter of fact. We crossed paths. You can find him back by the barn. Better bring a bucket and shovel.

The atmosphere in the room changed. Hard to say exactly how. But Case wondered why they were all still standing there, why the air wasn't already crisscrossed with gunfire. The whole place was painted in gasoline. Only one of them had to light the match. Case was afraid it would be him. Maybe Partridge. Any moment now somebody was going to succeed. Tournier seemed to be trying the hardest of anybody.

Hillbilly showed nothing. Or next to nothing.

The lanky blonde guy with the automatic stopped chewing whatever it was he'd been chewing.

The wood stove hissed.

We come to get the gun, Owen.

Gun?

Owen, the world's splittin' at the seams with ignorance without you pretending not to know what I'm talking about.

That gun was found in the ground. A piece of ground that don't belong to no one, probably belongs to me, if we're going to be technical about it. Who's to say who it belongs to? Might as well belong to me. Finders keepers.

This ain't no child's game Owen. I want the box.

You'd know about children's games, wouldn't ya now, sheriff? Wink.

61 Bang

Case thinking: I shoot Partridge first, try to squeeze off a shot at the blonde guy that came out of the bathroom. Tournier takes care of Hillbilly and whoever else pops out of the woodwork shooting. In other words, he concludes, I'm going to end up getting shot through the throat, I just fucking know it.

You don't have to give him anything, Owen. He ain't got a warrant. That was Partridge, deciding to weigh in with some legal advice.

Slim Jim hitches up his pants, looking straight at Case. He's right Owen. Some kind of accent the blonde guy has, but what? Case can't quite place it, but he's heard it before. Not exactly British. What?

Now now, easy there fellas. Let's all relax here.

Who'd have thought it, Hillbilly is the voice of reason, a whole rack of weapons within arms reach on the wall. In the gun case his big hand sits atop, probably all of them loaded, ready for action.

What's with this gun anyway, sheriff. Why is it so important? Why does it get buried, get you out here in the middle of a blizzard willing to get everyone shot to shit over?

I ain't here to answer questions Owen. I want the gun. Like the figgy pudding, I'm not going anywhere until I get it.

Hillbilly isn't smiling anymore, not even if you called that cold shit-eating thing that's been plastered on his face up to now a smile. He doesn't turn around, no one is taking their eyes off of anyone, but he barks half over his shoulder to the kid still crouched at the top of the stairs. Girl. Get the box under my bed. She stands up like she's been touched with an electric prod and clambers up the stairs on a pair of clickety-clacking pink bedroom slippers. The kind with the puff of pink feathers on the instep. No mistaking how she learned that kind of instant and ominous obedience.

This ain't like you Lenny.

What isn't Owen?

This reckless abandon. What's got into you?

Can't rightly say. Woke up this morning with a bad taste in my mouth. Maybe half a century of bullshit. I just can't stomach another forkful.

61 Bang

The kid was coming down the stairs, careful on the plastic heels, but careful to hurry. Box in hand. Case could see the ribs across the pale chest where the slip or nightie or whatever it was scooped down. Big dark eyes. Hair chopped. She looked like one of those refugees on late night TV. A dollar can buy this kid a year's worth of food and penicillin. Her makeup smeared. Christ, *her makeup*. She couldn't be more than ten. Case felt nauseous, no, he already felt nauseous. He felt more nauseous.

She looks up at Hillbilly who nods towards Tournier. She walks towards him to hand him the metal box. You can feel Death walking around the room, examining everyone's ears, throat, looking into their eyes, squeezing their testicles, making his choice.

This it, Mr. Case?

Case jerks his head around, afraid this is just the opportunity Partridge and Slim Jim have been waiting for. He sees the gun that Tournier has taken out of the box that's still in the kid's hands. The gun that keeps getting people killed without firing a shot.

Yeah. That's it.

The hillbilly taps the gun case with his finger tips. Itching to get a weapon. Put his fist through the glass and lift out anything that'll put a hole in someone.

Happy?

Almost. The kid comes too.

No one is expecting this. A kind of hiccup in time and space. Then a burst of haphazard speech: everyone trying to talk at once. Hillbilly wins that battle, takes the floor. Sheriff you got no right. This kid, she belongs to me.

·Well, we'll just see about that, won't we?

You can't take her from here Leonard. There's no call for it.

I'm protecting a minor.

From what?

Suspicion of abuse. Possible kidnapping.

Whose suspicion?

My own.

You're making a mistake Lenny. A big fucking lethal mistake.

Is that a threat, Owen?

61 Bang

You forgetting the crop we got planted out back in the scrap yard? Cause you acting like a man who doesn't have a skeleton in his closet. Like a man whose whole life isn't a few tractor scoops away from the horrifying secrets of his past.

I ain't forgetting Owen. Now, my deputy here had a pair of boots on the way in. I'd be much obliged if they were returned. I'd hate for him to lose any toes over this.

Case still couldn't believe they hadn't been shot yet. But there he was, stooped over, putting on the boots Slim Jim had tossed him, and nothing happened. There they were, backing out of the door, the metal box with the gun under his arm, and the kid hanging from under Tournier's arm, guns still pointed, but not a shot fired by anyone.

You ain't heard the last of this, you chicken-shit son-of-a-bitch. I promise you that.

Oh I believe that, Owen. I surely do.

I'll have your skin for this Tournier. I'll have your balls in a sack. You're going to be one sorry fuck and on it went, Hillbilly at last losing his cool. Here it comes, Case thought, all that tense civility finally disintegrating and what a relief in a way. Out of the house, snow, walking backwards, trying not to trip or slip. No pratfalls now, please. He reached behind him, opened the door of the SUV and slid inside. That's when he realized, These aren't my boots.

Tournier behind the wheel. The kid deposited safely in the back, kneeling down on the floor as instructed, arms over her head in case of flying glass and ricochets. Now that wasn't so bad, was it? The sheriff still with that cockeyed grin, looking exactly like what he was thinking, I'm fucking enjoying this. The car bouncing through the yard and into the white and swirling snow. Case, his window open, so he can put his arm out and shoot any moment now.

How long do you think before all hell breaks loose?

Tournier squints his right eye, calculating. Oh, I'd say about ten seconds.

He was off by five.

61 Bang

The shot came out of somewhere, but only because it couldn't come out of nowhere, even if that's how it seemed. They hadn't quite cleared the yard, maybe a little less than thirty yards to go. Case wouldn't even have known they were hit, that the shooting had started, if Tournier hadn't made a sound like all the air had been punched out of him. Grunting. Oh shit.

The second shot took out some of the overhead lights in a shower of sparks and red plastic. The third imploded the rear passenger window on Case's side and caused Tournier to lose his temper.

Jesus fucking Christ, already, shoot something, would you?
What? Shoot--

Case screamed over the suddenly screaming transmission, which was trying to haul the SUV out of whatever they'd slid into. An icy declivity, or something.

What?

He still didn't see anything.

Then he did. It was parting the veils of snow, barreling down a corridor of its own making, like *Jaws*, the white Hummer on a path destined to cut them off, a shooter standing in the sun roof, elbows resting on the roof, bent over his rifle, statuesque. Picturesque. Shooting.

Case stuck the gun out the window and squeezed off four or five shots in quick succession, pretty much just in the general direction. The Hummer altered its line of attack, swerving into the blowing snow, the rifleman disappeared, then the Hummer swerved back out of the blowing snow, and the rifleman reappeared, popping back up like a jack in the box.

Fuck it we're stuck. We're stuck. Tournier yelling, yanking around on the gear shaft, like the arm of a slot machine that could be twisted into giving up a jackpot, everything rocking and shaking, the SUV fishtailing like a fish hooked on a line.

The rifleman tucked back down over his rifle, taking aim, when Case started shooting again, and as if it were a consequence, the SUV unstuck itself with a crazed lurch spraying his shots wide, and they were off and racing towards the trees.

61 Bang

Who the fuck are those guys?

They'd reached the edge of the woods, bumping down the makeshift cut road. What you could see of it, anyway, which was hardly anything, just a meandering line of snow-covered rocks and roots without trees standing in it.

Afrikaners.

Afrikaners?

Tournier was sitting in a puddle of his own warmth. His whole seat soggy. Christ, I really thought I'd last longer. I've been playing hero, what, about half an hour?

From South fucking Africa.

South Africa? What the hell are South Africans doing here?

The SUV was fitted with one of those grates to keep drunks and brawlers and assorted arrested hillbillies from reaching into the front seat and strangling the driver bringing them to jail which nixed Case's plan to climb into the back seat with Tournier's shotgun and start blasting out the rear window. Instead, his face pressed to the black grate, he shouted down to the kid still crouched into a tight ball behind the seat.

Are you okay down there?

He forgot about the tongue. The lack of it, that is. Then he remembered. He searched, instead, the frail, trembling little body for bullet holes. Blood. Didn't see anything alarming, nothing but shoulder blades, delicate as a plucked sparrow's, shuddering and flightless.

He couldn't see a damn thing behind them, between the snow falling, the snow they were kicking up, and the iced-over rear window. Visibility zero. Gunshots following them, but not sounding particularly focused. Case leaned out the passenger window. Fired some more awkward shots into the general snow-blind and nothing. His wrist sort of bent back, all he could do to hold onto the damn gun. This would be a good time to be left-handed, he thought. Or double-jointed.

Kill the lights. Kill the fucking overheads!

Tournier was hunched over the steering wheel shouting at him, face screwed up with concentration, that's what it looked like anyway.

61 Bang

Case understood what he meant. Even snow-blinded, they'd be able to see what was left of the roof-lights, glowing against the white-out, like a burning cherry cloud floating through the woods.

Case looked at the dash, uncomprehendingly. Fumbled around with a few likely-looking knobs.

Where? Where's the fucking switch?

Tournier tried to tell him. His own hands clutching the steering wheel, one of them, anyway. Case tried to follow the directions Tournier growled out of his clenched jaw like he was trying to eat a chunk of steak that was fighting back. Case, pulling and turning ineffectually at this and that knob and lever. Goddammit why don't you do it yourself?

I would if I weren't trying to drive and hold my fucking guts in at the same time.

It hadn't really registered. The slickness all over the instrument panel. But now it did. Oh fuck.

Funny, Tournier thought, how you know you're dying. No mistaking it. Even though you never did it before, not once in sixty-seven years. It was like some essential bag deep inside him had been irreparably punctured. All this oily black poison leaking through him. The end of the woods came up unexpectedly, quicker than he would have figured, he almost overshot the damn highway and entered the woods on the other side, everything so fucking white and his mind drifting off to the side, towards shock and dreamland, drifting off like a fat puffy cloud. But he woke up and recognized it, leaned heavily on the wheel, nearly rolling the SUV and ending the story right then and there, but managing to steady the thing out, heading east, heading Mei-ward, before he completely ran out of blood.

Well, Mr. English, that sure didn't go well by any estimation, now did it? This is Roman walking down the stairs, hands deep in the pockets of his black trench coat, like he'd been up and dressed for hours, ready to go, which he had been. Blake coming down behind him, three steps behind, his mismatched shadow, his violent inner man. Roman passed by the hulking hillbilly and over to the coffeemaker,

61 Bang

poured himself a cup of black, while English tried to assemble a response to this latest complication. What the hell is going on here, anyway, Mr. English? Aren't you supposed to be in control of this compound, or what the fuck?

That's funny Mr. Bigshit. I distinctly don't remember seeing you lending a helping hand to the cause. Where were you? Upstairs changing your tampon? Where was your buddy? Helping you?

There's no need for that kind of language, Mr. English. Roman took a sip from the mug. He sat down at the table, crossed his legs at the ankles. The table was carved with insignia, initials, slogans, obscene pictographs, whatnot. It's not constructive and can lead to misunderstandings.

You smarmy bastard. I've got a man down out there. The gun is gone and the kid. I asked you. Where the fuck were you?

A shootout wouldn't have helped the situation. I'm here as an officer of the peace in the loosest acceptable sense of that term. My job here is to prevent a shootout. As far as that's possible.

And that was true. Sort of. It wasn't like it was an eternal truth or anything. But the less violence the better.

The two South Afrikaners had taken off after Tournier and Case in the white Hummer and they'd taken Partridge with them. That left a man named Gant behind and another named Whitelaw upstairs. But Whitelaw wasn't worth talking about, not even worth describing. He was no longer a factor, never was, not in this story, anyway, already cold as lunch meat in his under-heated room, his pillow like a giant sponge under his forever sleeping head, soaking up his red life. Fact was, you couldn't negotiate with an unlimited number of people. You can't make everyone happy. That's the first thing a successful negotiator learns. So you have to clear the table.

Blake?

The gun was in his hand almost simultaneous with the order. A good man, Blake. You didn't have to spell things out to him in triplicate. Sharp. Instincts like a well-trained military police dog. An extension of one's own homicidal paranoia. He shot Gant in the face. The man's features caving in like a cannonball had hit a trampoline, except it didn't bounce back. Another shot somewhere in the body core. Another, like a little flair after a fancy signature.

Hillbilly took a shot from above. That was Harrison up there, standing on the landing, with a perfect view of the scene unfolding below. Forgot about him, didn't you Mr. English? Roman took another sip of coffee. Pretty good stuff, by the way. Folgers? He nodded understandingly when the hillbilly didn't answer. Well, An awful lot is going on.

Truth was, he really did move fast for a big man, nimble too, and the shot that should have disabled him, only gimped him a little, rearranged a tattoo or two. Hillbilly made it to the gun case, smashed both his fists through it, and came up with a Walther, which he didn't bother aiming. Amazingly, Blake caught a round in the windpipe. Just like that. A lucky shot. No other way to explain it. It happens. He was spraying blood like pink soap bubbles. No rainbows in them, of course. In the other fist, English featured a large military pistol of some sort and started running zig-zag for the front door like one of the fucking Three Stooges, guns a-blazing. Harrison shooting from the upstairs landing funneled his shots towards the door just like the professional he was, can't miss right, and dammit he didn't, it looked like English caught two more and still he kept going. Right out the door. Roman watched this action quietly. He was a talker, not a shooter.

Harrison came lumbering down the stairs, a bow-legged gait. Should I go after him?

You think? For the money and the car and the trip to the Bahamas.

Yes?

Ding ding ding. Pack your bags. You're a winner.

Out the door goes Harrison, to no good purpose, Roman suspects, not as good a man as Blake, not even close, poor Blake, who's kneeling on the uneven wood-plank floor, futilely trying to hawk up a bullet, spitting and gakking. He looks up at Roman, now standing over him. It was the look a loyal dog gives its master on the last day of its life, the doctor coming up behind it with the needle to doggy heaven. Roman knew that look well. It caused Blake major

61 Bang

distress, craning his head up like that, stretching his punctured throat. You could tell. The repositioned bullet sawing into the nerves, cutting off the airway, or whatever.

A good man, like he already said. But no more. Roman saw the acknowledgement in the man's quavering eyes, knew what had to come next, what Roman was thinking.

Roman with the gun in his hand now. Not a shooter, but you couldn't talk you way out of everything. Death, the one thing you can't bargain with. One shot, close-range, through the right eye. A little blue-yolked egg. One in a million. Hey, it ain't heaven, but it's better than choking to death.

Fact was, you had to hand it to the old gal. She was taking it like a trooper, like it was just another Tuesday morning. You'd think it wasn't the first time, or even the fiftieth, that she'd come shuffling into the kitchen of a snowy morn to find a gut-shot sheriff, a half-naked child, and a dazed fugitive wearing someone else's boots, all of them on the run from a makeshift militia of neo-Nazi lunatics, arriving home for breakfast. This was the Cambodian or Laotian or southeast Asian-whatever broad that Case had met in the car just the morning before, the one who'd given him the gun and the directions to the English compound, the sheriff's woman, apparently, and to his bedeviled surprise, Mei, by name.

Tournier had driven, one-armed, to the semi-secluded house, having lost their pursuit, no doubt only temporarily, somewhere along the way, probably coming out of the woods. Hanging out of the window and ready to shoot wildly, the hair at the back of his head frozen stiff, Case hadn't seen the white Hummer come out of the trees before the highway slowly bent west and warped out of the line of sight altogether.

They parked in the back of the house. Tournier instructing Case to get the kid inside. Mei meeting him at the door, more or less, the girl bundled in his arms, weighing practically nothing. Filthy, shivering, smelling like a wet lamb. Mei said nothing, or muttered something in her native tongue, which amounted, in Case's ears, to

61 Bang

nothing, and led him upstairs to a bed into which he tumbled his catatonic bundle. He went back downstairs, leaving Mei behind to tend to the kid, whatever tending needed to be done.

Tournier had stayed behind the wheel of the cruiser. He was still there when Case went back to get the metal box, both hands now on his ruptured gut, insisting he just wanted to sit there, leave him alone, he was fine where he was, etc. The sheriff was white as soap, the old-fashioned no-nonsense white kind, not that perfumed green Irish bullshit.

No way. Case tried to make it sound like a self-evident fact. We've got to get you inside. You'll bleed to death out here.

Tournier laughed, sort of. His teeth were fuchsia and his dental plate had come partially unstuck. It wasn't a pretty sight. A little like seeing your grandma with her teeth knocked out after a hockey fight.

Case helped him out. Pulled, yanked, pleaded is more accurate. He caused the man a lot of additional pain, supposedly for his own good. Got him to his feet, or a fair approximation thereof. Case saw his point apropos of staying put. Saw it instantly, and, alas, too late. The seat where Tournier had been sitting was soaked squishy black, like he'd shit out an encyclopedia worth of ink. Case, no doctor, but there's only so much blood a human being can lose before he becomes an ex-human being. Whatever that amount is in quarts or liters, the sheriff looked like he'd already easily lost twice that much. The man leaning against him weighed a thousand pounds, the more he lost, the more he weighed, Case thought, thinking there was a lesson or at least a clever philosophic aphorism in there somewhere, or maybe it just sounded like there was because he was still hallucinating. No matter. Tournier was right. What's the point of this? I should have left him in the fucking car.

Up the three stairs of the back porch. If it were four, Tournier would have had to die in the snow. Through the back door, into the warm kitchen, the tea kettle on the stove screaming like the trumpet on Judgment Day. Mei's interrupted morning cuppa.

Case unloaded the sheriff into a bright yellow chair and turned the gas off. The woman, he presumed, was still upstairs somewhere, taking care of the kid. Tournier motioned him over. No one looks so

61 Bang

hot first thing in the morning under the kitchen light, but what
Tournier looked like, even compared to what he looked like in the
car five minute ago, well, you'd have to dig something out of the
ground and beat it with a shovel for a day or two to get an idea.

Did it seem to you. Tournier was having a hard time talking.
Death, you see, was sitting on his chest, strangling him with both
bony claws. He was having a hard time thinking, also breathing,
living, caring. A lot of spitting, choking, an impossible-to-describe
but absolutely ghastly hacking interfered with what he was trying to
say. He kept trying though. You had to hand him that. You had to
figure it was important, this thing he was trying to say, interrupting
his grim business with the Grim Reaper to say it. That it wasn't. The
gun. Blood was dripping off the chair. You could *hear* it dripping,
hitting the linoleum. Drip-plop. Drip-plop.

Shouldn't we call someone?

Who?

Case was stumped. The fire department. Another cop, if there
was one in this one-cop town. A fucking ambulance. It seemed
obvious. But there was obviously a basic something he wasn't getting.

Not the gun. So much. What set them off.

What do you mean?

The kid. Picture a lot of grimacing interrupting these words.
Like Tournier was trying on a series of rubber Halloween masks,
each one more exaggeratedly horrible than the last. It's all. About.
The kid.

How so?

Some more hacking. Long braided rope of bloody drool,
almost purple black. The infamous "heart's blood?" Rattling around
in the man's broad chest, like a dancing chimp shaking a maraca in
there. The oft-mentioned, "death rattle?"

The SUV. Hide it. They'll come looking eventually. Back in the
yard. Put it. Now.

Are you going to be okay?

Tournier just stared at him, as if it were a question too dumb to
waste one's last breath answer.

By yourself, I mean.

61 Bang

That wasn't much better, but Tournier answered. Perhaps just to keep from being tortured any further.

Go.

Okay.

There was a low wall of stacked firewood, a shed of some kind, stuff under snow-covered blue plastic tarps tucked in a corner of the property and that's where Case maneuvered the SUV, praying he didn't get stuck smack in the middle of the fucking yard, which would be the logical conclusion to how things had been going heretofore. He finally collected the all-important metal box from under the front seat because he'd had his hands full the first two times, tucked it under his arm like a football, and, head-bent, trooped back to the house. The wind had died down, mostly. He looked behind him towards the corner of the yard. The snow had stopped falling. Well, if you didn't examine things too closely, you might not see the shot-up police SUV back there, muted by snow, obscured by this and that, big as life.

Case felt like he was winding down, like he'd done a good life's work, and now he was ready to retire and sit on a rocker somewhere, smiling idiotically at the street and pissing into a bag at his side. He climbed the stairs, barely able to lift his feet in someone else's oversized boots. He felt like he was coming to the end of a marathon, walking through wet concrete. Unfortunately, he hadn't come to the end of anything, there was another thirteen miles to go, but he didn't want to think of that right now. He wanted to make of himself an unnoticed and unconscious pile of something no one was looking for in a corner somewhere.

He stood in the doorway. There was Tournier sitting on the chair, still upright, calmly smoking an unfiltered Camel. Mei had spread the morning papers under his chair. She sat across from him, a cup of tea warming her hands, keeping him quiet company as he bled to death at the kitchen table, no expression on her face at all. Case thought it was probably the saddest fucking scene he'd ever seen in a life consisting of sad fucking scenes.

61 Bang

They'd managed to run plows through from Cullen or Collier, or wherever, some fly-spot town nearby, to clear the breakdown lane for emergency vehicles. The idea was to get the injured, the sickened, the frostbitten, the heart-attacked, the prematurely delivered or those already delivered onto death to a hospital as soon as humanly possible. Pershadonna sat up in the back of the speeding ambulance. Covered in blood. Someone else's liver for all she knew, black and gooey, sliding down her chest. A beautiful suede waistcoat ruined, dammit. In her left hand was Mauser. In her right a Sig Sauer. On the face of the EMT who turned to look at her improbable resurrection, a look like, You gotta be kidding me.

Ma'am, please lay back. You're, umm, seriously injured.

He tactfully ignored the major firepower in each of her fists. A dozen or so miles earlier, still faking serious internal manglement, Perhsa had muttered No needles, no needles…against my religion when this same tech was earnestly bending over her with a bag and a line of who knew what shit she didn't want circulating in her veins. This after he'd spent a good five minutes looking frantically and futilely for the non-existent wound that had produced all that dramatic slip-slop on her torso.

Pull this fucking meat wagon over. Now.

Ma'am, you're in shock. Please. Put the guns down and lay back.

He kept his eyes on Persha, the entire Technicolor splattered spectacle of her, speaking sideways out of his twisted mouth for help, for someone to come with a tranquilizer, as if she might not be able to hear his aside, like this was a production of William the fucking Shakespeare. Irony was, she was the only one who heard him. Everyone else currently pretty busy clamping spitting arteries, stabilizing bones dislodged from sockets or poking splintered from groins, silencing screams of unthinkable pain, the whole lot of them bent over their work in the back of the crowded, see-sawing ambulance like a team of butchers working a bar-be-cue in a Heironymous Bosh painting.

Pershadonna swinging her legs off the gurney, watching her dance steps on the gore-slick deck, these were, after all, her favorite

61 Bang

boots and she wasn't going to find their replacement at the local Wal-Mart. Persha looking all high-cheek-boned and savage chic, Aztec, by way of West Africa, Isis, and Inanna, the Queen of Death. Persha explaining it all again, patiently, like she'd just landed on the Planet Moron. Stop this fucking ambulance. Do it. Now.

Lady, there are injured people on board.

It was something he had to say, stating the stupidly obvious because from where he stood looking at reality, Persha didn't seem capable of realizing the stupidly obvious.

They aren't going to get any better if I have to start putting bullets in them. Stop this fucking ambulance.

Then, again, maybe she did understand . Maybe it was him who didn't understand the stupidly obvious, right?

She motioned towards the driver with the gun, the Sig Sauer, an elegant gesture, all considered.

Tell him. Calmly. Pull over Ned or Billy Bob or whatever the fuck his name is. No explanation. We got a problem back here. That's all you say. Which is true. You do have a problem back here.

So there they all stood thirty seconds later, the three medics and the driver, roadside, everyone covered in someone else's blood, at least so far, everyone wanting to keep it that way, too, and Persha with two guns explaining how things were going to be, no matter how unorthodox and unprecedented it might seem to accepted EMT procedure.

Put your radios and cell phones on the hood of the ambulance, your Blackberries, your Iphones, all the tech, you get the idea.

A chubby woman, her jaw covered with golden down, probably a glandular condition, some poor soul, Saturday Night Dateless, volunteering to clean up broken bodies off the interstate to find a man, no doubt, spoke up.

This is outrageous. This is murder. These people.

She couldn't think of anything more to say, how to finish such a sentence, which was probably a good thing. Persha had just about run out of patience. The woman waved her fat arms around. Then put them down. Persha didn't trust that someone wasn't holding onto a cell phone in a deep or hidden zippered pocket somewhere on

61 Bang

their person, a slim Razr or some new gadget that folded up to the size of a postage stamp but could blab one's presence to anyone anywhere in the world with the punch of a thumb. So she had them pull their pockets out, take off their coats and parkas, their sweaters and hooded sweatshirts and pile them on the hood.

Persha collected the clothes, the radios, etc. They stood there huddled now, arms wrapped around themselves, cold, wind, snow on the ground, everyone but Persha shivering, even with all that adrenaline pumping through their systems.

What the hell are we supposed to do out here without any coats? This was the chubby woman again, not chubby, really, a fat cow, but Persha had been trying to be sisterly, Oprah-like, now she was simply doing her best to refrain from sending a round or two through the perfectly good frosty crisp air that fat bearded blonde bitch was needlessly displacing.

Persha shrugged. How should I know? Apply your training. Pray. Hope the fucking weatherman is right for a change and the sun comes out.

She climbed into the ambulance, put it into gear and onto the rode. Drove even faster than the ambulance driver had driven, bouncing and rocking, turned on all the sirens she could find. The moaning and groaning and weeping coming from the back would've driven her bat crazy otherwise.

Question: you send a trained freelance government agent out the door to finish off a wounded hillbilly, how long do you expect it to take before he comes back, mission accomplished? Ten minutes? Fifteen? Twenty, at most? Roman had waited close to an hour up at the English compound before making his way back to the motel room stakeout at the Paradise. This is what he was trying to explain to an incredulous Tantum, who didn't seem to get the concept, asking, as he was, the same question repeatedly, something that, with minor variations, went like this: "You mean you just left him out there?"

61 Bang

Roman, sitting by the window, staring across the empty snow-swept courtyard at nothing. Case hadn't returned, which actually was no surprise. He'd was probably still with the sheriff, a new and perhaps troubling alliance whose possible implications Roman would have to give some serious and cautious consideration, along with his own changed position vis-a-vis. So he'd lost two men, and wouldn't really mind if it were three if Tantum kept it up, but that wasn't necessarily a bad thing. In this kind of game, a quick exchange of pieces often led to the end-game. Truth was, Roman didn't mind clearing up the board a little. It helped him focus.

Tantum looming over him. I think we should go back up there, both of us, and find him.

Roman nodding emptily, deep in rumination, following the almost endless permutations.

Did you hear me?

The white Hummer on the highway, zipping passed the motel like tape ripped off something.

Going where?

Answer me, you crazy fuck.

Tantum, smelling of coffee, defunct adrenaline, and fecal mucous from his unwashed anal seam…fear, is what it all added up to. The fear of a pawn now that the game no long required pawns.

His cell phone vibrated against his ribs. Roman reached inside his jacket, pulled it out, unfolded it, listened. He stared into the courtyard. He saw twenty-seven different ways this story could end. Okay, now it was thirty-two. He folded the phone closed, slid it back inside his jacket. Outside the window, nothing happened, everything frozen still.

Hmmph. Well what do you know about that.

What. What is it?

Tantum, still hoping for news of his fellow pawn, just some all-but-forgotten hum at the back of Roman's mind. Things had just gotten more interesting. The game had shifted round again. He was thinking out loud.

They want Case to have the gun now. They want him to make his delivery.

61 Bang

Roman was smiling. He wouldn't have known it except that he could see his reflection in the window. He shook his head, approvingly. He had to admit it. He really loved this shit.

He was in the upstairs bathroom, washing his face and hands, shirt hanging open, checking the damages. With a jolt, he realized he wasn't alone in the mirror. Down there, in the lower right hand corner, another face. Too startled, in that instant, too disoriented to grab for a gun. Where was his gun? It's moments like those you understand how you'd react in a true life-or-death moment. Case, in other words, would be fucked.

The kid was standing in the doorway, sentinel-like, one of those haunted-looking kids you wake to see standing by beds in horror films, except without the big bloody butcher knife. One of those kids you see on late-night TV, starving to death in Africa, with flies crawling around its eyes and lips. Or standing, orphaned, in a street reduced to rubble after the tanks passed through. She didn't say a word, just stared, eyes smoked out craters, huge, like some caricaturist's version of a pauper child in a Broadway musical, Oliver Twist, or something like that.

Christ, what the hell did she want?

He wasn't to blame for anything. He was just passing through. He'd come with his own problems; he was going with even more.

What was she looking for, standing there like that, like she were at the edge of an open grave.

The woman had cleaned her up some, put a fresh t-shirt on her, probably the woman's own, she wasn't that big herself, and it hung to the girl's bony ankles. She'd scrubbed the kid's smudged face, her grubby hands and bare feet, removed the traces of chipped polish from the filthy nails, shampooed the lank hair. All cleaned up like that, the kid looked even younger, even frailer.

Goddammit, the whole fucking world was so goddam fucking screwed up.

That was Case's conclusion, after extensive research into the matter, take it or leave it.

61 Bang

She stood there staring at him, looking like she probably hadn't had a regular meal in who knew how long, and you didn't want to think about what she'd been subjected to in that compound, no, you really didn't, Help Us God Please, but what else was there to think about with her standing there like that, staring at you in the midst of all the silence that surrounded her, the silence that condemned you and your cowardice because you didn't dare to break it, you didn't dare to ask...

What do you want kid? Why are you standing there like that?

There were things in his life that Case did not want to remember. Somehow she reminded him of those things, whatever they were.

What are you looking at?

Help Us God Please.

What the hell do you want?

She had taken hold of the bottom of the t-shirt. She'd bent a little at the knees to reach. She didn't say a word. Of course she didn't. She didn't take her great silent eyes from his. Those great dark wounds.

Don't.

She lifted the hem of the t-shirt. Slowly. Like a stage curtain.

Don't.

She straightened her knees as she lifted the t-shirt.

Help Us God Please.

Case didn't want to remember his dreams, didn't dream in the first place. What was the point?

Don't.

There are some things it does no good to see.

What does she want from me, this fucking kid?

The t-shirt was over her skinny thighs now, just a skinny bow-legged little kid with a face older than Case's, older than any face he'd ever seen. The edge of the t-shirt held in her tiny fist above the sunken belly. The eyes pulled, inevitably, towards the lodestar of the navel. Where all eyes cannot help but go. And Case saw it then, and seeing it, understood. He felt everything inside him slowly turn topsy-turvy, his stomach, his intestines. He turned away in spite of himself, braced himself against the sink, and stared at his own face in the mirror, looking, looking, for what? The urge to vomit faded enough to talk. Between the kid's legs, Case saw the remains of the crude operation, the stump and scar tissue, the nest of ridges that looked like melted plastic on a cast away doll. He looked at the kid in the mirror.

They did this?

The kid says nothing. Of course he says nothing. But why is it so difficult for Case to remember the severed tongue? Why is it so difficult? Some things, like dreams, it's best not to remember. Case understood, maybe he always understood, just didn't want to. He understood what Tournier had said about it not being about the gun up at the compound, how it was really about the kid.

Help Us God Please.

Us.

How many? How many others like you are up there?

The kid can't speak. This time Case remembered the severed tongue. He didn't expect an answer. He didn't want an answer. It looked like he was going to get his wish. The kid just stared. Case held his breath. Then the kid's hand slowly rose.

Two fingers.

And Case knew he was going to have to go back, back to the compound, because like it or not, in this time and place, in the middle of this hopeless hell, as insane as it seemed, he'd suddenly been appointed God.

Main Street, Pershadonna strolling down it, looking this way and that. Car shopping. The ambulance she'd left in the parking lot behind a strip mall, sirens off, lights a-flashing. Someone would see it, eventually. Well, you hoped so. It would be awfully bad luck if they didn't. A few shopkeepers shoveling their eight feet of sidewalk. A pedestrian here and there. The road already plowed once. Here comes the plow again.

Turn left, up, what is it, Elm Street, some goddamn name like that. Oak. Pine. Laurel. The kind of towns with streets named after trees. The kind of town with trees. Persha rolls her eyes. Oh Christ, spare me. A parking lot behind the bank and there it is: her car, a Mercedes CLK63, AMG 6.3-liter V-8 engine developed in Affalterbach, Germany, five hundred horsepower, top cruising speed of one hundred eighty six miles-per-hour unmodified, zero to sixty in 4.1 seconds, Nappa leather interior, and all in her color, baby, black.

The man with the keys walking back from the ATM, still counting his money. Oh goody. A rebate, too.

She strolls over, knowing what she wants.

I want your car.

He looks up. Older guy, fifties, good haircut, blue eyes, you know the type. Doctor, lawyer, investment broker, asshole. What difference did it make?

Are you kidding?

Why do people always ask that question? Are there a lot of comedians running around that she doesn't know about? Clowns? Jesters? Is the world really that funny a place?

And the money.

A bemused look on the man's face. Is that the word, 'bemused?' Maybe not. Time for the gun to make its appearance. Whatever you'd call the look on his face now, you wouldn't call it 'bemused.'

Is this a carjacking?

Call it that if it'll help you to understand simple English.

But it's broad daylight. You're not going to shoot me in broad daylight.

Pershadonna pulls the trigger.

You can hear snowshovels scraping from down the block. Behind the concrete retaining wall, the screen of evergreen trees, what the hell are they, yews? They're louder than the muffled shot, those scraping snow shovels. Persha examines the emotions mixing all together on the man's face. She shakes her head slowly. Please, please don't say it.

You shot me.

You are a literal-minded son-of-a-bitch aren't you? Please, don't bleed on my Mercedes.

61 Bang

I can't believe you shot me.

She shoots him again.

I'll make a believer of you yet.

He's on the ground now, in the slush, sloshing around, tending his wounds with a kind of wonder. He's dropped the keys, which Persha retrieves from the bloody ice, the money he's still clutching in one fist, but he gives it up readily to keep the holes in him covered.

That's a good boy. She pats him on the head. Good luck to you.

In the car she slides, fires it up, whoooooom, listen to that engine purr. She didn't think she hit a major artery, the femoral, or whatever it's called. Besides, as he'd pointed out, it was broad daylight. Someone would see him, some good person, maybe the same one who found the ambulance, the world was full of them, wasn't it? Some good person would go to the ATM for money, or he'd crawl far enough into view of one.

Good people, you had to believe in them sometimes. You had to believe they were out there somewhere, willing to help. Well, people with bullets in them did.

Was she a good person?

Hard to say, wasn't it?

There were reasons for the things she did. Pershadonna Sassoon didn't just spring up out of nowhere. She had an origin, a history, formative years. She'd had a hard life, no question about that. You've heard some of it, not all of it, not even necessarily the worst of it, but enough of it to know. She had her reasons, her excuses, her explanations for the things she did, just like anyone else. You'd like to believe she was a good person, a lot of well-meaning people did. Maybe you believe she's a good person, too. Persha herself didn't give it a lot of thought one way or another. She was, she concluded, who she was, whenever she stopped to consider the matter, which was somewhere between half-passed seldom and never.

She reached into her jacket and with one hand opened the CD case, slipped the CD into the player, turned up the volume, track eleven. Tunes, don't travel without'em. The soundtrack is important. You've got to control the soundtrack.

61 Bang

Meep meep. What a nice surprise. It's L7. Shitlist. When I get
mad and I get pissed, I grab a pen and write out a list of all you
assholes that won't be missed. You've made my shit list.
Yeah.
Her life, basically. The meaning of it, too. The time it takes to
cross out every name on that list of shitheads.

He woke from a dream. Case, who never dreamed. He lay there not
knowing where he was he'd been so many places in his life, woken so
many times already, stared at so many ceilings; he knew to just wait
patiently for the feeling of unreality to pass. Or, better put, to just get
more accustomed to it. As for the dream: he remembered enough of
it to know he didn't want to remember the rest.
He sat up.
Imagine falling asleep at a time like this.
Shit.
He was in the master bedroom. The bed Tournier and the
woman shared, no doubt. He'd sat on the edge for only a moment,
only to collect himself, to think, to try to parse out what the hell to
do next. Falling asleep could not possibly have been his conclusion.
Had he really meant to lean back, to pull the covers over himself, for
crissakes? He yanked the bedclothes off and swung his legs over the
side. The sun was coming through the windows like a searchlight. He
heard the tinkle of thaw in the aluminum gutters. What the hell time
was it, anyway?
He grabbed at the electric clock on the night table: 11.04.
The blood pounding behind his eyes as if it couldn't get
through his veins fast enough. He was up and stalking the floor.
Where were his shoes? He pushed back the chintz curtains. Saw
nothing. Nothing was good. Nothing was best of all. What did he
expect to see? Best not to think about that.
Down the stairs. He had to tell the woman to leave, to take the
kid and get out. It wouldn't take them forever to think to come here.
No place in this town would be safe. She had to get the kid away as
far as possible. If the major roadways were passable. Even if they

weren't. She had to try. Another police station in another county, in another state would be even better, far away from contamination with this corruption. Crossing the front room. Into the living room. No sign or sound of a soul. He called out. Hallo? Through the dining room. Hallo? Everything spic'n'span. A very meticulous housekeeper, this woman of Tournier's. They couldn't possibly be upstairs, could they? It hadn't even occurred to him, he'd just assumed. But he would have noticed, anyway, wouldn't he, would have sensed someone up there even if he hadn't looked. That's what you had to think, right? Into the kitchen. Hallo? No one here either. Well, except for Tournier. He's still sitting at the kitchen table, only now he has a white sheet draped over him, like some kind of obsolete piece of furniture set for a move into storage. Dammit, he might still be asleep everything was so unreal. Could they be in the basement? Would the woman have taken the kid to hide down there? He turned and started for the door that looked like it must lead to a basement. You could sense it before you saw it. There was a man standing in the doorway to the dining room. The doorway Case had just come through. The basement doorknob was still in his hand. The door he'd just pulled open. Another man was coming up the basement stairs. Why, it was Slim Jim. Case stood there, flat-footed, empty-handed, except for the doorknob, rather dumbfounded.

Why don't you have a seat, my friend? We have a chat, okay?

That was the man in the dining room doorway. Tall, long dark coat, pale eyes. The gun in his hand trained on Case's ribcage, looking anxious to fire. His distinctive accent. So cultured, so civilized, almost cheerful, even if he were telling you he was going to cut out your eyeballs, so Case imagined.

The South African guys, in other words.

Case was turning over all the cards in his head, looking for an option. All the cards were blank.

Crap.

You did the right thing coming here.

61 Bang

Roman flipped up the Jack of Spades, moved it over to the bottom of row three, examined the layout. The woman didn't give a damn about his approval, didn't need his brownie points. She came back because he was, right now, on the great chessboard of life, the best of a lot of bad options. He could understand that. He didn't hold it against her. Hell, he'd built a life out of weighing exactly those sorts of options. You stand behind the dog with the biggest bite. They understood each other, this Cambodian woman and him, they had a shared foundation, a language in common that spoke histories with a glance. A police department psychiatrist he'd once been obligated to see following a shooting had remarked upon Roman's preternaturally youthful face, a result of his habitual lack of facial expression, the frozen face common to one whose childhood was marked by a fear of being noticed. Tournier's woman, well, she wasn't the sheriff's woman anymore, as it turned out, had to be closing on sixty, but damn if under certain conditions she couldn't probably pass for thirty-five. Under different circumstances, under those certain conditions, he would have liked to have a go at her. But right now he had to go and collect Mr. Case. He had to deliver him from evil and send him on his merry way.

Tantum. See the lady and the kid safely out of town. You understand?

The big man stood up from the bed and nodded. What they'd done to the kid had freaked him out. You could see it in his eyes. Even after all he'd seen. Hard to root out the deeper levels of idealistic humanism. Guys like him, in these circumstances, they needed something to do. And, frankly, Roman was glad to send him off to take out the garbage. Anything, at this point, just to get him out of the way.

Good. He flipped over another card and looked up at the woman. Her face as smooth and unreadable as an old weather-sanded tombstone. Ma'am, good luck to you. And…the boy.

What kind of life could that kid possibly have, that's what Roman was thinking, as he looked, albeit briefly, into yet another pair of impenetrable eyes.

61 Bang

And thanks again for the food these past couple of days. I'll sure be missing those spicy red noodles. It almost made this job worthwhile. Take care.

He looked down at the card he'd just flipped.

Ace of Spades.

He smiled.

Nah, come on now. You gotta be kidding me.

Fact is, you picture all the ways it can end, and because you figure things never go according to plan, you make allowances, allot yourself a fair share of disappointment, a generous extra helping of pain; but still you don't ever picture yourself tied to a kitchen chair beside a dead sheriff draped under a bed sheet with your pants pulled down around your ankles. Oh, and let's not forget the crazy hillbilly, how could you, after the intimacies he's just performed on your most private parts with the kind of sadistic flourish that let you know he was enjoying every goddamn psycho minute of this.

He'd shown up in the meantime, the hillbilly, in the time it took for the South Afrikaners to disarm Case, secure him to the chair with plastic ties, and slap him around a little, all of which you had to figure was pretty much par for the course. This whole nightmare seemed scripted to end with a final confrontation of some sort between Case and that hillbilly from the moment of their first encounter in the convenience store. Damn Ho-Hos.

What are you laughing at? Hillbilly cocked his great shaggy head, like a bemused buffalo. You sure got a good sense of humor for a man about to lose what you're about to lose.

Upstairs you could hear the crash and shatter of lamps being knocked over, drawers being yanked out, chairs and tables being overturned. The South Afrikaners going through the house, looking for the gun and the kid.

Hillbilly had been shot from the looks of it, maybe even a couple of times. Case could see the bloody pads stuck to his meaty body where the thermal vest fell open. If the wounds had any effect on him you'd hardly know it except for a slight hitch in his giddy-up now and then. Where would you have to shoot this monster to bring him down, Case wondered. He grit his teeth as another sickening wave of pain ripped through him. Not that it looked like he was going to get the pleasure. To shoot the hillbilly, that is. Case shuddered so violently the chair rattled and tap-danced on the tile floor.

The hillbilly grinned.

This is an Elastrator. And he held the yellow rubber rings up for Case to see. In his other hand, he held what looked like a pistol-shaped hole puncher. He fit the first yellow ring to the pistol-shaped tool and squeezed the trigger. A pair of metal fingers expanded outwards, like a pliers in reverse, expanding the yellow ring at what was clearly great tension. We use it to castrate livestock.

His face looked like a shovel blade up close, Case noted when the hillbilly bent over him. The way a shovel blade might look when it was about to hit you in the face. Blunt and stupid, just like that. His teeth—and this was a surprise—were fake and he badly needed a bath. But hell, they all needed a bath at this point.

His fingers had been surprisingly deft, Case couldn't help but notice, almost gentle, but then you noticed things like that when another man was monkeying around between your legs. He looked up at Case and his eyes had that dangerous kind of pin-prick light of a man who could only think one thing, but thought it really hard, and usually to your detriment.

What it does is crush the seminal vesicles. Cuts off the blood supply and destroys the veins and whatnot. Hell, I'm no urologist. I don't know what all it does, but I know it makes your fucking balls die is what it does. They swell up, turn black, and fall off. That's what happens eventually. But by that time your nuts are long dead. It only takes a couple of hours to kill'em. And it hurts like a motherfucker in the meantime. Well, that's what I hear, anyway.

Upstairs, mirrors smashing, mattresses being ripped open, chests of drawers toppled. The entire house shook. Where were the woman and the kid, anyway? If they were still in the house it wouldn't be long before they were found. Case doubled over as far as the plastic ties binding him to the chair would allow but there was no

61 Bang

relief. He felt like...well, he felt like someone was slowly and methodically crushing his testicles. Someone who wasn't letting go. Hillbilly pulled out the chair across from Case , sat down, folded his hands on the table.

What we do now is wait for you to tell me where the kid and the gun are. He grinned. Then he cracked his knuckles, put his hands behind his head, and stretched. He yawned. He refolded his hands on the table in front of him. What we do now is wait for your balls to die.

Case wanted to puke.

Oh thank heaven for 7-11, or something like that. Even after a killer ice storm the convenience store was open, ready to take advantage of the inevitable need for de-icer or plastic shovels or a quart of milk. Mei had asked the big man escorting them out of town to stop in order to pick up some food for the boy. Wherever they were going it was going to be a long drive and there was no telling when they'd come across another open store. The big man hadn't spoken much, which was just as well as far as Mei was concerned. There wasn't much to say. But for a man who was supposed to protect them, he sure seemed pretty nervous to Mei.

A loaf of bread, a package of luncheon meat, and some chocolate bars. She tried to get the boy to pick out something he wanted, but he only stood there, staring vacantly up the colorful aisles of packaged foods as if he were watching some sort of incomprehensible parade. He looked like he'd been systematically starved. Mei saw this when she undressed him and washed his pale mutilated body with a wash-cloth as he stood trembling in the bathtub. A little angel made of bones.

Mei looked up. She'd bent down to talk quietly to the boy but now she followed his gaze up the aisle to the big man at the register. She hadn't wanted him along, but she figured him a necessary evil for the time being. Besides, there would have been no talking a man like Roman out of it; Mei, who'd come across enough men like John Roman, knew that right off, no talking men like that out of anything,

61 Bang

not in the short run, anyway. She would bide her time, as always, yield like water and drip away at the rock slowly, or build up like a flood and overwhelm when the time was right. The important thing, for now, was to get away. Far away. Men, like large dangerous animals, could be useful. But you had to be very careful. Very watchful.

Their escort was up front now, at the counter with the enterprising owner, buying cigarettes, that's what he told Mei he'd be doing. And maybe that is what he did, but then he did something else, too, something unexpected that cause the man behind the counter to cry out. Not words, exactly, but perfectly understandable, a plea Mei had heard many times in her life, spoken in a kind of universal language. You could call it a prayer. And, as usual, it was ignored.

The gunshots were somewhat muffled, but still gunshots. Unmistakable. The sounds of things crashing. Chunks of stuff, wet and heavy, slapping the lottery machine and the cigarette case. The heavy fall of a lifeless body. The big man turning from the counter. The gun still smoking in his hand. He was staring down the long aisle of M&Ms, Kit Kat bars, Dots, and Twizzlers. Staring at the end of the aisle where Mei and the boy stood staring back. He leveled the gun.

Bang.

So then, it looks like we're all here. Roman lifted the corner of the bed sheet and peeked underneath. Even Sheriff Tournier. Excellent. He folded his hands and looked around the table, looking pleased. Not long before he'd been led in the door by the Timothy McVeigh look-a-like who'd been standing guard outside. Came strolling in like he'd come a-calling of a Sunday morning, just as calm and friendly as you please, the militia man covering him with his rifle and looking nervous and sheepish, like little more than a kid playing army.

McVeigh shrugged apologetically. I didn't know whether to shoot him or not. He said you'd want to talk to him.

61 Bang

Owen was peeling an apple with a pocketknife. Nothing fancy like removing it all in one strip or anything like that. Just sort of hacking at it. He didn't bother looking up. You got a lot of balls coming in here. Or not much brains.

Case couldn't help but taking that remark about balls personally. But no one cracked any jokes.

What I've got is a deal. A solution to this stalemate that not only makes perfect sense, but that will satisfy all partners involved. He took a look at the situation in Case's lap and winced sympathetically.

Ooh. Now that's gotta hurt.

It hurt alright, hurt enough that he almost wished someone would just put a bullet in his head and get it the fuck over with—a wish, Case realized, that unlike most wishes was all-too likely to come true. Just who was this cocksure bastard, anyway?

This had better be good, Roman. One of the South Afrikaners, not Slim Jim, standing by the fridge, drinking orange juice out of the container. His buddy, still upstairs, pulling the insulation out of the attic walls.

I believe it is Jan. Roman nodded at buzzcut with the rifle. Owen, how about you send Patrick Henry back outside to make sure no one else joins the party. I can only make so many people happy. I'm not Santa Claus, after all.

Hillbilly didn't look too please about any of this. And Case, well, he felt like the new kid in class. Everyone here seemed to know everyone else and he'd missed role call. No one was paying him any attention. He felt left out.

Go on Bobby. And if anyone else drops by to talk. Fuck. Shoot'em.

Yes sir.

Owen set to digging out the apple's core.

Roman waited until Buzz cut took up his post outside. Okay, now what I propose is this.

Case couldn't swear to all the finer details, but he followed the conversation as best he could, his concentration being somewhat compromised under the circumstances. The scene blurring in and out

61 Bang

of focus with the pain. In general, the gist of it seemed to be that Case would deliver the gun as planned without further interference, the South Afrikaners would get the reward money to refund whatever filthy rich perverts had bought the kids, who, in turn, would be turned over to Roman for safekeeping no questions asked, with a little left over for the South Afrikaners time and trouble, and Owen English would get to remain at his compound and await the apocalyptic race war that would reestablish white supremacy or whatever insane bullshit he believed in.

In other words, no helicopter flyovers, no massive loudspeakers blasting 24/7 Barry Manilow, no tear gas, tanks, or snipers. No Ruby Ridge. No Waco. You know we can do it, Owen. You know we have done it. Anytime we want.

Roman sat back, awaiting the reaction. This was the crucial moment in all negotiations. You could almost stick your tongue out and taste the tension in the jellied air.

Maybe he missed it. Could be he was fighting off another wave of nausea or the pain that threatened to swallow him up in what felt like an ever-imminent blackout. But Case hadn't heard what he'd been carefully listening for all along.

What the hell do I get out of all this?

You'd have thought the dishwasher had started talking from the looks he got. This guy Roman, the bastard, whoever the hell he was, but he must have been somebody because here they were—the South Afrikaner and the hillbilly—both listening to him instead of shooting him in the face, a face Case had never seen before in his life and whether it was the last face he'd ever see or not, hoped to never see again, shit, I'm rambling. This Roman, he looked entertained by it all, the son-of-a-bitch.

Mr. Case, I'd say you were getting the best deal of all. You get to keep the family jewels. How can you put a price on that?

Yup, it's all a big fucking joke; still, at the moment, Case couldn't help but admire the logic of the man's point.

So what say you gentlemen? Roman looking around the table, up at the South Afrikaner who'd finished the OJ and thrown the empty container in the sink. Do we have a deal? He looked like he already knew the answer.

Two seconds went by. Three seconds. Case's balls were dying. Ice slid off the roof past the window. Hillbilly's left eye twitched. Faces were blank. Hearts beat. Anyone could see. It was no deal.

Yes, Bang.

In every language. In every calibre. No need for translation. It was unmistakable.

Pershadonna looked up at her reflection in the oxidized mirror. Watched herself cocking her head inquisitively. Trying to get some idea of the situation. She'd stopped at the convenience store before heading into town to buy a box of tampons. The asshole clerk gave her some shit about the restroom being employees only. He changed his mind when she threatened to squat and shed her uterine wall right there in front of the donut case. It was that time of month. Mother Nature didn't a shit what you were up to when she came a-calling. Just another goddam thing you had to deal with if you were a female hired killer that a man never had to think about. Like allowing for your breasts on certain shots. Being a woman could sure be a bitch in some ways.

Bang. Bang. Didn't sount too complicated. One shooter, or others who weren't shooting back for some inexplicable reason. Persha couldn't know for certain but she'd give odds that whatever shit was going down out there it had something to do with the shit she was here for in the first place. So, out comes the gun. She notices the blood on her fingertips. The menstrual flow. The life-giving wound. She dabbed it on her forehead, smeared a line under each eye, down the bridge of her nose. War paint.

Okey doke.

Time to go to work.

Mei crouched down by the frozen food case with a can of dog food in each hand. What else could she do? The boy tucked close to her

61 Bang

side. The two of them waiting to see from which aisle the man would come. Always the same picture, it seemed to Mei. A woman and a child crouching, hiding from the man wanting to hurt them. Why? Why was it this way? Crouching in the tepid water of a rice paddy or at the end of aisle two in a convenience store. What was the difference? Same movie, just a different location. Same nightmare, just a different bogeyman.

She was looking the wrong way when she heard him step on a bag of something cruncy in the potato chip and Cheezit aisle. Like a twig in the forest. That made him give up trying to surprise them and he started running down the aisle. There he was. Mei hurled a can of Alpo and pushed the boy towards the exit. This was their one chance. You had to recognize it cause you weren't getting another. Bang. The glass behind her fell in one piece and shattered on the floor. He'd shot a frozen pizza. Mei hurled the other can of dog food and followed the boy up the aisle.

Tough luck, though.

There was something wrong with the door. Well, not really. It was locked, that's all. He'd locked them inside the store. So you reach out and unlock it, right? No big deal. Well, try doing it with a professional killer walking slowly towards you with his gun leveled on you and the matter-of-fact look of a man making a sandwich.

Still and all, Mei managed to work the lock. There was no time for her to get out the door but the boy could. He'd have a chance. Not much of one crossing the open parking lot, but it was more than none.

She shielded the boy with her body, while she still had control of it, all five-feet-two, ninety-two pounds of it, and threw her shoulder into the door. Time for one last word, the most important word she knew. A whole philosophy in that one word. She pronounced it in absolutely perfect English.

Run!

Her voice was drowned out in the roar of a gun. The boy never heard her last word.

Didn't need to hear it, as it happened.

61 Bang

Because the man's head. Well, everything that you could say made it something you could properly call a 'head,' sort of flew off and splashed all over some cases of A&W root beer stacked against the wall. There was a beautiful copper-colored woman looking between the boxes of Fruit Loops and Lucky Charms in the next aisle. She had a gun in her hand and blood on her face. She said to Mei, Don't be afraid. I'm not here to hurt you. The most unbelievable thing of all was, Mei believed her.

Who shot who first—it was a question that technically had to have an answer, but whatever it might have been was practically irrelevant since everyone seemed to have the same idea at once. And what difference did it make, anyway? The hillbilly leaped back from his chair first, but he'd already been shot, you could see the wound in his thigh like a little mouth spitting blood between its two front teeth. Roman was standing, too, but in a shooter's stance, smoothly phhht-phhting bullets towards the sink where the South Afrikaner was fumbling at his underarm, trying to find his holster. Timothy McVeigh came bursting in the door, rifle against his shoulder, but Roman was preoccupied with English who was ignoring the hole in his groin, as well as the one that got swallowed up into his big belly, to lift his machine pistol.

There were chaotic lines of fire everywhere, bullets whining and zinging all around Case; it was like someone had dropped a big nest of hornets into the middle of the kitchen and then kicked it around like a football to get them good and angry. Kitchen appliances exploded. Shards of Formica kicked up off the counters. The microwave started and then erupted like the Fourth of July.

Roman was a goner, that was Case's opinion. McVeigh had him lined up like an eight-ball sitting on the lip of the corner pocket, but then McVeigh sort of coughed, a puff of smoke coming out of the right side of his chest like a boutonnière, and his errant shot filled the kitchen with a roar of outrage and shook the ceiling, sending chunks of plaster and wood splinters raining down.

61 Bang

That was all for Case, he'd seen enough. He rocked and bounced the chair as if he were having a spastic fit, used the balls of his feet to push, and managed to tip himself over, still bound, chair and all. He'd fallen sideways, his pants around his ankles. From there he had a limited, knee-high view of the action. The hillbilly was gimping forward on a leg stiff and black with blood, his pistol clakedly-clacking like the empty jaws of a novelty store skull. McVeigh's rifle took out a good part of the opposite wall, all those souvenir plates from the Franklin Mint vaporized in an eye-blink, before he went down to his knees, looking at all the priceless pulped organs spilling out of him. The South Afrikaner was crawling out of his own blood on both knees and one hand, the other hand held his gun in a red death's grip. Roman, well, he was nowhere to be seen, but Case could hear his gun from somewhere, from everywhere, it seemed, and the hillbilly had begun screaming some kind of mad war-cry as if he were a Viking berserker in ecstasy, or on Ecstasy. Or both.

That's when the second South Afrikaner, Slim Jim, came bursting into the kitchen, gun out, framed in the doorway, glancing down at Case, as if looking for an explanation. Hello, welcome to Hell. At the same moment, a man in a deputy's uniform entered from the back door with a pump-action shotgun.

Case struggled in the chair, trying to get free and not draw any attention, failing at the first and succeeding at the latter, but for how long? McVeigh was down, splayed, face a wooden mask in a puddle of gore. Case continued to jerk and twist against the plastic ties, hopelessly.

The hillbilly seemed to be caught in a crossfire, a cobweb of gunplay that no one could possibly walk out of, and fell heavily to his knees as if he'd suddenly been struck with the spirit of prayer. The stench and noise. Case could see Roman's black-clad legs scissoring purposefully across the room as he took up another position. Then they were gone. The first South Afrikaner lost his jaw. He was still shooting, though, but no longer shooting at anything. A gun came spinning across the floor. Case stopped struggling to free himself. Stared at the pinwheeling weapon. Frozen. Waiting for it to stop, like he were watching a wheel at a carnival game. Now he was straining his numb, pain-whitened fingers to reach the gun.

Someone turned over the table. Tournier remained sitting there through it all, covered in the sheet, like a man fallen asleep, only without the table in front of him. He looked pretty stupid sitting there like that.

Roman hadn't reappeared. But he's still around, like the invisible man.

A high-pitched zinging sound. The deputy is down, lying on his side, grimacing. Man, they're never gonna get this kitchen cleaned up. Case has his fingertips on the pistol. How many bullets has that goddamn hillbilly swallowed up anyway? He's climbed back to his feet again like James fucking Brown. There's shattered glass all over the place. Believe it or not, I haven't been hit, Case was thinking. Or have I? What happened to the second South Afrikaner? The gun now in his hand, twisting his wrist awkwardly, he could. Just. A pair of legs—the hillbilly's. Can't aim any higher than the ankles. Well it was good enough to bring down Achilles, wasn't it?

So let's recap, shall we? Because a lots been going on and it's easy to lose track of everybody, every bullet, especially when, like Case, you're tied to an overturned kitchen chair with your throbbing balls swollen to the size of purple tangerines. He's done pretty well, I think, all considered, wouldn't you agree? But it's time to get a better perspective, time to take a step back for a little author omniscient, because, frankly, in his current position there are just some things Case is not in any position to see.

Okay, here goes.

First off, McVeigh, as noted, is dead. Never much of a factor, anyway, distinctive only, if at all, because of his likeness to the notorious American 'terrorist,' there's no need to waste anymore time on him.

The South Afrikaner white slavers, dim figures, at best, are also dead. Aside from occasionally taking advantage of their opportunity to provide goods for perverts, they weren't especially perverted themselves (well, not of the pederastic persuasion anyway) except, perhaps, by a blend of chance and temptation and a sort of moral laziness that, let's face it, if given half the chance to act on our worst inclinations, who among us can be absolutely certain we ourselves are above?

They were couriers, basically, mercenaries at worst, as good or bad as the men who paid them, and these were awful men who paid them, which is to say the South Afrikaners had the morality of your average soldier, bureaucrat, company man. Anyway, they're dead, and no one, and I mean no one, is going to miss them. Unfortunately, there are plenty more where they came from, always are, and the untouchable perverts at the pinnacle of the pyramid of power and privilege who hired them in the first place will only hire more.

That's life, that's human nature, you can act locally, but globally, it's all still going straight to hell on a bullet train. Tend your own garden, Voltaire used to say, except nowadays the soil is poisoned everywhere. But enough philosophy, people are still crawling around on the floor with their guts hanging out. Let's get back to it. Okay, where were we?

The deputy. This is Jackson we're talking about now. We heard about him before. A good man to whom Tournier figured to entrust the town's protection after he was gone, to pass on the mantle of the Law, once he, Tournier, cleaned up (some might say cover-up) once and for all in one apocalyptic abuse of police power the festering infection of evil and corruption he'd been trying to manage all these decades. It was Roman who had drawn the good Jackson into this fiasco, calling on the deputy as a representative of the Justice Department to enlist him as emergency back-up in a hostage crisis involving the sheriff, his wife, some abused kids, and a whole bunch of other shit too complicated to explain. Jackson, like a lot of guys who didn't know what they were really getting into, was gung-ho for heroism. Grabbed his weapon and let's do it. When the shooting started, he strode forward from the background bushes, as instructed, sniper-shooting McVeigh as McVeigh was about to shoot Roman, and entered a kitchen that already resembled Ragnarok. Now this good man, which is to say, this naïve and largely gullible boob, was

61 Bang

gasping and wheezing piteously, dragging himself along the blood-slick battlefield of a linoleum floor like a half-crushed lobster, crawling, but from where and to where? There didn't seem to be anywhere really to go, especially not minus a good deal of your chest and all the important goings-on that usually go on there. His face said it all, but you wouldn't want to hear it. Basically, it was a matter of learning way too much a little too late.

Whew, that's all a lot to digest. And by the way, where the hell is Roman?

That black lizard. That slimy bastard.

Case has lost track of him and, frankly, so have we.

We'll get back to him.

It's the hillbilly who occupies our attention now, who takes center-stage as it were, Owen English, would-be savior of the white race, God help us, financing his righteous crusade as the sometime purveyor of castrated mixed breed boys, home-made eunuchs, soon-to-be feminized catamites to the decadent elite of various nations, all those brown and yellow boys who vanish, never to be seen again, and no one really misses them, no one says so much as "boo." There he is, Owen English, his own bad self, a regular Grizzly Adams, no, more like an actual grizzly bear, bleeding, full of holes, shot so many times by now, in so many places, from so many directions, and by so many people, we've honestly lost count. What's more important is that he's still dangerous, maybe even more dangerous than ever, you've got to admire the sheer animal vitality of the man, the sheer will to survive, the sheer balls on the son-of-a-bitch (maybe he really is a suitable candidate to represent the white race for crissakes) well, you don't have to admire it, but you should, you really should even if you don't approve of it, because that's what it takes in the end, when all is said and done, and we're nearing the moment when all will be said and done.

What's more, what's worst, the hillbilly's grinning, yes, he's still grinning, like he's enjoying this, and it's not just a pose he's striking, not just false bravado, he thinks he's going to make it, he really does, he thinks he's indestructible, he thinks he's fated, well, properly speaking, he doesn't really think at all. That, more than anything, is what makes him so dangerous, so good at survival.

It's unclear whether he knows that Case has a gun, that Case is the one who just shot his ankles out from under him, but it wouldn't make any difference, it wouldn't change his concept of what he needed to do next if he did. He'd do the same thing he's doing now. That is work his arm out from where it lay twisted, bent back broken under his shaggy bulk, in order to shoot the trouserless man bound to the kitchen chair, because at this point Hillbilly doesn't care about the mutilated kids, or the hidden gun, or, truth to tell, even the fucking white race. He just wants to kill, to kill everyone, every last living fucking thing.

And it's face-to-face, nose-to-nose, as it were, with that leering, joyfully evil, lust-swollen animal that Case finds himself now, this face fills up his whole world, it is his world, a planet of speechless terror bristling with an impenetrable black forest of hair and pitted with blackheads, the face looming over the bed when he was six, when he was powerless, or bent back over the kitchen sink with the point of a knife at his throat, that snarling face so close you could inspect the contents of the pores, the spectrum of earth tones on individual beard hairs, is that lunch time's tuna fish gunked between his yellow teeth, boogers caught in the wiry nests of nostril hairs, the atomized saliva drifting across your cheeks as his lips work over an incomprehensible language of tendon and gristle…and you had no gun at the time, you had no knife, you had no nothing, but you do now, your hands are still tied, but they hold death, wrist bent back, finger hyper-extended, but you can answer back this time, oh yes you can. It's taken awhile, but you've taught yourself a new language. You've replaced the tongue he took away, the tongue they always take away. Everything isn't yes or no. Sometimes it's neither. Huh? I don't understand. You want to hear what that sounds like? Come a little closer, daddy. Yeah, I got something to say. Bang.

Hard a hearing?

Want to hear it again?

Bang.

61 Bang

Bang.
Bang.

Bent backwards, like the figurehead on the prow of an ancient ship, bent backwards against the natural curve of any possible human spine, looking more like some great hairy half-evolved lizard than anything else, the hillbilly was frozen in a kind of impossible death-yoga pose, made even more impossible by virtue of the lack of even any recognizable remnant of a head. The only thing now emerging from his hulking blood-caped shoulders an obscene something that looked like a half-eaten turkey leg slathered in ketchup with some electrical filaments threaded through it.

Roman, off-stage, clapping. The sound of his clapping, anyway, slowly, mockingly. Good work, Mr. Case. Very good work. Now Roman's on-stage, or rather his left arm is, extended, the gun in it, pointed execution-style. And now all of a sudden we understand where Deputy Jackson is going, or trying to go, so damn desperately, even in his critical condition. Put simply, he's trying to get away from Roman. Desperately. Futilely. Ludicrously. Because it's clear now that Roman double-crossed him, triple-crossed him, hell, crossed and re-crossed him so many goddamn times that if you diagrammed it the page would be full of crosses, like a cemetery, black crosses packed so close the whole page would be black, crossed him out, is what Roman did.

   Would Jackson have survived if, for instance, an ambulance had been immediately summoned, if a helicopter had air-lifted him to the trauma center of the closest top-rate hospital, if he were treated by a team of top-flight emergency medical specialists? With those grievous wounds? Who knows? But surely not with that most recent insult and injury—the single shot that enters the back of his skull and emerges at the bridge of his nose in a wet eruption of meat, bone fragments, and grayish pink mist that, suspended in the air for a moment, glistens with a man's memories, his thoughts, his dreams, his love and hope and fear…all of it now drying on the glass window of a Kenmore oven.

Roman explained: Local cops got caught up in something really ugly. Way out of their league, they were. It all came to a boiling head in this disastrous shoot-out. Among the dead, the sheriff and his loyal deputy. Local rumors abound about Owen English—but, in the end, who really knows what happened? Drugs? Weapons? Money? It's always something like that. No way to call in back up with this storm and all. Everything coming to a flashpoint in this kitchen. Among the dead, you, Mr. Case.

The gun. I know.

The words, you see, not coming easily or volubly to Case anymore, his balls being in a sling as they were. Had you forgotten? About his balls, I mean. Case sure hadn't, it was practically the only thing he could think about, the pain being what it was: the world and all that's in it.

You need. Won't. Ever. Find.

Because Case had pieced together the fact that Roman was a representative in some darkside form or other, of what is euphemistically called "law enforcement."

Oh, I know where it is.

Roman delivered this bad news with distressing good cheer. He had sidled up to the table, carefully staying out of range of any possible, if improbable, one-in-a-million Buffalo Bill-style trick shot Case might pull off. Some ridiculously lucky ricochet off a toaster or electric can-opener. Covering him with the gun in one hand, Roman reached out the other with a magician's cheesy theatrical flair. Case felt sick, sicker, if that was possible. Sickest, then. The sickest you can possibly feel before you finally have the relief of croaking altogether.

Roman's fingers plucked at the sheet and revealed a rapidly rigor-mortising Tournier. The sheriff had been looking pretty ghastly the last time Case had seen him and death and a few stray bullets plunking into his corpse sure hadn't prettied him up any. But that wasn't the most sickening part, sad to say, only the graphic prelude to the really sickening part.

61 Bang

You see, Mr. Case, I recognized the gun that's ended up in your hand. It's the sheriff's gun. Standard police issue, even if I hadn't seen it in his holster over the last couple of days. Which led me to ask myself the question: if the sheriff's gun isn't in his holster, I wonder...maybe if. A clever hiding place, Mr. Case. But, alas, as these things go, not quite clever enough. Not to worry, though. I'll make sure the delivery gets made. But under the new arrangement, I'm afraid you aren't necessary anymore. Your position has been eliminated.

Roman raised his gun, smiled mildly and sincerely, raised his gun like holding out his hand to shake, another deal successfully completed.

Negotiation over.

Shithead. Fuck. Go. Hell.

Inarticulate stuff, even *more* inarticulate stuff is what Case was spitting out, his last words, well, what could you say, Give me Liberty or give me Death?, it wasn't exactly a situation that inspired noble sentiments, but then, outside of books and movies, death wasn't usually a noble situation; then again, not usually quite so ignoble as this.

So Case cursed, nothing in particular, everything in general, Fuck. Shit. Asshole, etc., cursed Roman, death, the world, Roman, people, the ex-wives, God, his mother, his father, Roman, all the women who screwed him over, did I miss anyone, cursing them all, cursing life as a whole package, giving himself the courage to kiss it all goodbye, firing his gun from its crooked angle, hopelessly, it's true, just to make noise before he died, that's all life amounted to really isn't it, just making some noise before you died...

What more can you expect, anyway, but to have your say, to add your voice to the general Babel, your scream to the overall horror show. Can't go on forever, though. You run out of breath, bullets, everything else.

Silence.

61 Bang

Probably none so profound as the one after the roar. After the gunshots. Am I alive? Are you?

Dead silence.

Virgin. Inviolate. But only for about a second or two. Blessed silence. You live for that silence. Holy, it is. Because you think, maybe, that someone was listening, that someone heard. God? Don't laugh. Anyone? Is anyone there? Oh yeah. Someone is there, alright. Too bad, too. The debate is swinging the other way. No one's heard a goddamn thing you've said. You've been talking to yourself. They've only been waiting for you to shut up. Roman, gun in hand. Nodding. Acknowledging. Clearing his throat. He was standing in front of a podium he'd have tapped the microphone. Is this thing working? Can you hear me? Good. Now, he's about to have his say. The last word, as it were.

He stretches his lips, ghoulish like. Smiling, if you can stomach calling it that. And his teeth, all soapy and red, it can't be, can it? His outstretched arm is jumping about, like he's suddenly got the palsy or something. And it's spreading, arm, shoulder, hips, knees; he's doing the jitterbug, a little tap dance of Death. He mouths a bloody word or two, one last proposition, maybe, but it's no deal, this ain't a negotiation, you can't sweet talk your way out of this one, it's all or nothing, and it's nothing, sucker. The gun flips out of his hand, all wet and slippery like a matte black frog. ((We're all little boys in the end, eh? Where's my momma?)). He takes a faltering step forward to catch it and falls flat to the floor on his face. Bang. Like a door slamming shut.

Lucky shot, Case wonders? Tied to the overturned chair in this slaughterhouse. The empty gun hot in his cramped hand. Lucky? Nah, no one is that lucky, him least of all.

Impossible.

It would have to be a fucking miracle. Don't believe it for a second. Because it was neither. Luck nor miracle. Although it's true that many a mistaken man confused her for both. Pershadonna Sassoon, we're talking about. Lady Luck, herself. She stepped carefully across the be-slimed linoleum, avoiding the chunks of stuff, the hemorrhaged blobs, the creeping creepy rivulets. She unholstered the gun as she passed Tournier, examined it a moment, tucked it inside her calf-length leather coat, and stopped, solemn and statuesque, practically iconic above the only living thing in the landscape, aside from herself, of course, a man bound to the chair with a pair of the bluest balls she'd ever seen in all her ball-breaking life.

She bent down, hands on her knees for a closer look. A slow look. From crotch, and, eventually, to his pain-clenched face.

John Case, I presume.

He seemed reluctant to answer one way or the other. She couldn't blame him. She smiled that famous Pershadonna smile, that ghetto Mona Lisa. What's it mean, what's it mean, many a man has asked, and all the answers wrong. She could see him asking it, too, behind his questioning stare, and getting the wrong answer, like all the rest, because there was no right one.

That's really some predicament you've gotten yourself into, isn't it, honey?

The real question, Case figured, was whether she thinks I'm of any use to her. Case waited for the answer. Sometimes, it was all you could do. Because no matter what anyone says, don't let them fool you, not for a fucking second, it's a woman's world, always was, always is, and at least until they improve surgical techniques, always will be.

So, was he of any use to her? The answer, at least for the time being, was a provisional 'yes.' She produced his deliverance from her handbag. With a pair of extra-sharp manicure scissors and a surgeon's flair, she managed to snip through the three rubber bands strangling the base of Case's scrotum. A delicate operation, that was, touch and go. Some sweaty moments, the sweat all Case's.

61 Bang

She helped him stand, pull up his pants, walk, essential stuff like that. She gave him a gun, just in case. Someone might be alive, or half-alive, somewhere in all this bloody mess. They were on the same side, sort of, for now, anyway.

Turned out they found the other two kids in the back of the white Hummer, bound, zipped up inside a pair of canvas surf board covers, half-asphyxiated. The South Afrikaners, apparently, having decided to cut their losses, if necessary, on their way to leave ASAP with at least a partial delivery. That meant it wasn't necessary to return to the compound.

They dropped the kids off with Mei, back at the Paradise Motel, the idea being that she'd do what was best for them, whatever in God's name that could possibly be. Case collected his stuff, which didn't amount to much, and they drove out of Paradise ((ha-ha)) in a hotwired Lexus, Roman's as it happens, a vehicle whose baseless tags were pasted over so much intentional misdirection and bureaucratic bullshit that they were guaranteed not to come up flagged in any police database in America.

So it was zoom-zoom through ever-improving weather conditions, through what remained of Alabama, Mississippi, all the way out of the other side of Louisiana, the alimentary canal of the Deep South. It would be clear sailing and fair winds all the way to L.A., according to Roman, so Persha had gotten the word from the Man in Kali, the dogs had been called off, for whatever reason; they, whoever the fuck 'they' were, this time around, had changed their mind, now they wanted the gun delivered. If you could believe a guy like Roman, that is, not to mention Mr. Muhammed X (((the one and only)), if you could believe any of them, which, of course, you cannot. No you cannot. But even a broken clock tells the correct time twice a day, right? Sometimes even a born liar tells the truth, if only because it's the only way to tell an even bigger whopper.

They crossed the border into Texas, one helluva big state. Of mind, that is. They stopped for a chicken-fried steak, a hot shower, a good night's sleep, and to steal another car just because you never could be too sure of anything.

61 Bang

Persha coming out of the bathroom naked and sleek as a leopardess, as dangerously sexy as one, too. Stalking Case, propped against the pillows, babying his sore groin, she circles the bed, as he watched the bad news from New York. Lifting one smooth round knee onto the mattress, that long lean cinammon flank, to die for. That body, that latte flesh, humid, shower-damp and moist, all the way to the darkly glistening jungle. Her fingertips trace an arabesque along his forearm, decorative and meaningless.

What do you say we check out those balls I saved. See if they still work?

Early indications were, they did.

New York City was burning when Case work up. Windows were exploding under the pressure. The rage. How did they hold it all back until now? Flames pouring out of shop windows, out of cars abandoned in the middle of Park Avenue. On the West Side Parkway. As if their former owners had spontaneously combusted. Smoke belching out of the top of the Chrysler Building. Entire blocks of the upper East Side as if lightning struck. They opened up all the fire hydrants, triumphant arches of water, never-ending ejaculations, a champagne celebration, as if they couldn't decide whether the world should end by fire or flood. Either way, the Fire Department had stopped responding a long time ago.

Here was the future everyone was afraid of, everyone worried about, everyone was waiting for. Hell on earth. A state of emergency, the mayor declared it. The governor, too. Even the president mentioned it, flying back from somewhere or other. Everyone knew what to call it, but no one knew what to do about it. Tanks were on the roll. They showed them on TV. The National Guard had been called up, mobilized, deployed. But where were they? They weren't on the streets. Lexington, Union Square, the Avenue of the Americas. They weren't on 47th Street. No sign of them on 23rd.

They showed a police car, though; it was lying on its roof, like a roach, poisoned, then barbecued just for the hell of it. The streets were filled with people. There were no lack of them. Ever. My goodness, you had to wonder, where did they get all those guns? The rocket launchers. The rockets. There was a Channel 7 news truck shot full of holes. There wasn't a white person anywhere.

There was a traffic jam of dead folks stalled on Columbus Circle. The mayor urged calm. The phrase 'The Rule of Law' was repeated constantly like a prayer. The stores seemed to be doing a brisk business—people were leaving them in droves carrying entire racks of merchandise between them. Stuff was flying off the shelves. But no one was paying for anything. It was like a second Christmas, the Christmas they never had, a Black Christmas, they'd been dreaming of it for years ((ha-ha.)) Massive redistribution of wealth. Everyone was Santa Claus, a do-it-yourself Saint Nick, a sack on your back, a carjacked Cadillac Esplanade, and a Ho ho ho. They'd been dreaming of this day for a long time, judgment day, and now it was here at last. Free at last, free at last, thank God Almighty, it's all free at last!

They shows a homeless guy staggering out of the fur vault of Macy's bundled in three silver fox fur coats with a bottle of Jamieson's in each hand. The toothless smile on his face alone was worth a million bucks. CBS had gone off the air. NBC was broadcasting from an undisclosed location. Matt Lauer might be dead. Black cinders were falling from the sky like ticker tape. There were unconfirmed reports that scattered fighting had broken out between black and Hispanic street gangs. One commentator said the city looked like Baghdad after the second Iraq war. The shock. The awe. Someone else said it looked like Dresden, but no one could remember what that looked like. So they said it looked like New Orleans after Katrina, only worse. City Hall was surrounded by armored personnel carriers. An army helicopter had been brought down on by a surface-to-air missile fired from the Lower East Side: it's ruins lay mangled in Washington Square Park. There were some bodies hanging from a traffic light on Second Avenue. Pink. Naked. During the L.A. riots, the mob had infamously hung a white female mannequin from a lamppost. The camera was unsteady, the image was out of focus, and the haze too thick, thank God, because no one was too sure they were mannequins this time around.

61 Bang

The Chinese were holding Chinatown. The Koreans defending Koreatown. There were rumors that the subway system had been seized in preparation for a coup, but no one knew when, or by who. The question everyone seemed to be asking was, Where was the Reverend? The Reverend could put a stop to this. He had the authority to quell the violence. Where was he? Why didn't he speak? What was he waiting for?

Pershadonna stood before the crappy motel mirror and put her earrings on, first one, then the other, watching the TV reflected in the corner of the glass above her head, the city burning there, as if inside a cartoon thought bubble, floating up from her mind. She had the answers to those questions. She knew what the Reverend was waiting for, what they were all waiting for, the gun, in her sole possession. She saw the whole thing quite clearly now, laid out before her in the looking glass. Yes, she did.

And Case, behind her on the bed, was looking at her look. If his dick had stopped working, as he'd feared, if the hillbilly had succeeded in making him a eunuch, there would have been no reason to spend the night; he'd have been on his way, but on his way to where? Memories of that brown body, the pasties of A-grade coke, the sparkling stardust when he nuzzled the scratchy kitchen pad between her legs…like the trailer of all the hot parts of the hottest porn film you ever saw in your life. These erotic highlights came back to him as he watched her put the finishing touches on, outlining the perfect contours of her mouth with a lipliner pencil. A stirring at his groin. Well, he wasn't dead yet, that much life left, anyway. About six inches worth.

Hands locked behind his head, body stretched out, naked, in the twisted morning-after sheets, hung over, another morning, another motel room, no future. Who needs one? Is this how it is, ad infinitum? Well, certainly not ad infinitum, nothing lasts forever, thank God. More like ad nauseum. She had the gun. She'd take it the rest of the way to California. No one seemed to be after them, no one shooting at them, at least for the time being. The money, Case figured, was forfeited, that much was understood, the moment she found him tied to the chair. She had it all, in other words. Case was lucky to have ever gotten the fuck out of it intact. Lucky to have gotten out of it at all. Even he could see that. So…

What I'm trying to figure out is. He mused out loud. What I don't understand is. Why do you need me?

Pershadonna finished putting her mouth on. She shifted her eyes in the mirror—the man on the bed, always a man on a bed—and set the tube of lipstick on the bureau. She turned, gun in hand.

I don't.

The gun didn't go Bang. It went *Phhhht*.

It went *Phhhht* again, and then again, for good measure. To be sure it was heard. To be absolutely clear. So that there was no possible chance of a misunderstanding. Because it was in the very nature of communication to misunderstand.

Case looked down at the carefully placed grouping of holes. A pulpy throbbing. He made a feeble effort to pull the sheet up. To cover this insufferable intimacy.

He said, Well.

Persha. Baby. This isn't the way. Let's do this thing right. Tell me where you are.

To the left of her nothing. To the right, more nothing. Between the two, the interstate a shimmering grey artery through the desert, which meant there was nothing behind her and nothing in front of her either. She was nowhere, and that was the point. She told him so and he wasn't happy to hear it.

Persha. Please now.

She could see him in is high-backed leather chair. His flawless suit, tailored to make those twenty extra pounds look as grand as they could look. The polished manicure. The understated bling. The partially—only partially—relaxed kink. Former *Time* magazine Man of the Year, Mr. Muhammed X. Courted by every president and presidential hopeful of the last three decades. Voice of his people. Pimp, by another name, in the streets, he'd be nothing but a pimp, and there was nothing but the streets, the world was one big neighborhood. Pimp or prostitute, it's all there was. If you weren't selling it, you were being sold. If by any unthinkable accident of fate, hatred and racism, poverty and injustice should end tomorrow, he'd be wearing a cheap suit and barking used cars off a lot in Bayonne, New Jersey. So let's keep business booming, shall we, let's expand into new markets, open franchises of indignation and outcry, we know there's an untapped market out there somewhere, there's always an appetite for hatred, fear, and resentment, let's be creative, let's reach out to our consumers, baby needs a new pair of shoes, let's do some aggressive advertising, and where there isn't a need, let's create one, this is America, land of opportunity, goddammit.

She'd take a sharp left approaching Houston and made a bee-line for Mexico. With half the Mexican population crossing the border this way, she didn't figure there'd be too much trouble going the other. Always the contrarian, that Pershadonna Sasson. Pulling over before she left cell phone range entirely, fell off the map, the grid, and everything else, before she went incommunicado, no habla Englise senor, Persha stood beside the white Audi TT, the only black thing in miles and miles of white. The mote in the eye. The one imperfection. Irritant-at-large. That's Pershadonna Sasson.

Dammit, Pershadonna. I'm losing my patience.

She looked out over the desert, the badlands, wastelands, salt flats, lunar sea…all that nothing. White, she reflected, can be beautiful. It was the future, after all, the future after the future had come and gone, the future after all futures. White, the color of heaven, of eternity, of nothing whatsoever. The angels always wore white and the prophets always went to the desert because this is where the end began. White, the color of bone, of the most fearsome horseman of all.

Persha waited for him to stop talking. Then she talked.

You'll wire the money into the account as I said. The gun will stay lost, so long as I'm not found. If I even think you're looking, if I so much as have a dream you've sent someone after me, I go public. It'll be all over talk radio by drive-time.

61 Bang

Not a shadow but the one she cast. Not a vulture wheeling in the cloudless sky.

Be reasonable, Persha. We need that gun. If it turns up now, we're back to square one. He'll be a laughing-stock. We'll lose all credibility with the mainstream. It'll set us back twenty years. It's not that I don't trust you, baby. That gun is our insurance policy. You can't keep it safe like we can.

What he didn't say is that it was also their leash, keeping the Reverend to heel, making sure he remembered whose dog he really was, who was the master, but he didn't need to say it. Persha, knowing all about leashes and what it felt like to be at either end of one. A long time ago she decided. She preferred to be the one holding it.

Persha. This is our chance. He puts an end to the conflagration, he's a hero. He owns that city. He's mayor, then senator, and then, it's possible. At last. It's possible. No more lackeys, no more sidekicks, Vice Presidents, Uncle Toms, house niggers. This is bigger than me and you. This is history. This is our people, Persha. Your people. Don't you want to do right by your people?

Persha, standing there, in the middle of all that post-historic blankness, that blinding void, that peopleless afterworld, thought she understood, at last, the point of it all.

People? She said it with genuine astonishment. As if anyone could believe such a preposterous thing anymore. What people? There's no one in this world but me.

She let that sink in for awhile, sink into herself, mainly, into the unquenchable earth. Into the blind and empy heavens. She swished it around mouth, tasting it, and, at last, swallowed it, to see if it would sustain her—across the desert of a lifetime. Yes, she thought, it just might. It would have to.

You've got until three p.m. to make that transfer.

Threats, curses, the usual, the outrage of the impotent. Persha squashed it under a thumb. Disconnected the call.

She'd been named, or misnamed, for Persephone, daughter of Ceres, the earth mother, and she'd been carried off to Hell, where she became the concubine of the King of the Underworld. Her grieving

61 Bang

mother cut a deal and Persephone was allowed to come back among the living for part of the year. There'd be no spring if she didn't. No life on earth. That was the story, the myth. But Persha's mother was dead and Persha wasn't coming back. Ever. The world could go to hell.

She climbed into the white Audi and pressed the accelerator all the way to the floor. There was no stopping her now. Her imagination panned upwards, among the clouds, a reverse telescopic sight, the Sun's scorching eye, showing the endless desert and a very wealthy black girl speeding across those miles and miles of nothing towards the very heart of it all.

Like a bullet.

Bang.

Don't miss these other
exciting titles from

AFTERHUMAN PRESS
...what's next in books

Hardcore Romeo
Mark Nadja

Afterhuman
Michael Cross

The Maniac Manifesto
Nick Caligari

Fake Girls
Matthew Sloan

For more information and free previews of all our books please visit
our website at www.afterhuman-press.com

www.ingramcontent.com/pod-product-compliance
Lightning Source LLC
Chambersburg PA
CBHW050727180626
46814CB00002B/637